An Event to Remember

Also by Steve Farkos

The Filly
Hawk
More Than She Bargained For

An Event to Remember

- A story of an Eventer who with the help of a determined fellow competitor and caring friends overcomes a heart-breaking and life threatening tragedy to rise again into the spotlight of his sport.

Steve Farkos

This book is a work of fiction. Names, places and incidents are products of the author's imagination or are used fictitiously. Any resemblance to actual events or locales or persons is entirely coincidental.

© COPYRIGHT 2012 BY STEVE FARKOS

All rights reserved, including the right to reproduce this book or portions thereof in any form whatsoever. For information, contact Steve Farkos at Winsom Productions 30621 S. Crawford Ave. Beecher, Illinois 60401

ISBN 978-0-9854459-0-4

For information regarding bulk purchases contact
Winsom Productions @ 312-813-7096

**WINSOM
PRODUCTIONS**
30621 S. Crawford Ave.
Beecher, Illinois 60401
312-813-7096

Acknowledgements

Over the past two decades I have been inspired by the real pros of the Olympic sport of Eventing and their ability to comeback from or overcome adversity and injuries time after time. They all have been an inspiration to me as I have ridden and taught others.

It's those people, however, who are in our everyday life that make such an important difference. To my family, especially my wife and daughters, along with my friends and fellow competitors, who have offered so much support, I am forever thankful. Beyond the experiences, memories and my imagination there are others to thank who have made this novel possible. Special thanks to Alice Bennet and Lura Forcum for their professional editing abilities along with their encouragement and belief in this novel. And a great thanks to Molly Siebert for her research, production supervision and handling of the constant changes with which I often challenged her.

A thought for my Event horses, Harmony, Diemo,
Petoskey, Gouldie, Belle and Hawk...

Thanks for all the wonderful experiences and memories these fine horses
afforded me during my competitive years in Eventing. The successes we
achieved are only a small measure of the partnerships we shared.

Chapter 1

STEVEN WILSON IS busy packing up his equipment in the aisle of the show barn. He seems unaware that many of the other riders have already packed and left. Steven's mind is rerunning the events of this special week in Kentucky. It was a long week, pressure packed, emotional and rewarding. Steven had just completed his first ever Rolex. The Rolex is the most prestigious Event in the USA and one of only five Events of this level in the world. Steven had finished in eleventh place almost unheard of for a first timer. He smiled as he envisioned his horse so boldly conquering the cross-country obstacles and laughed out loud as he thought how he must have looked with that huge smile as he completed the best dressage test of his life.

"Hey Steven! Can I give you a hand with that packing?" a passing groom of another rider asked.

"No. But thanks. I'm in no hurry." Steven replied as he was happy with his pace and was enjoying all the time he was using to replay every moment of the past week.

Steven now began to realize that most every rider, their grooms and horses had left. The barn aisle continued to lose all evidence of the previously crowded, busy and emotion soaked atmosphere. He now made a better effort to finish his packing and getting the horses ready for their long drive back north. He finally closed his tack trunk with only the shipping equipment left out now for the last minute safety preparations.

Steven walked down the aisle pulling his tack trunk to put it in the back of his truck. He now was pretty certain that he was the last to be leaving. He didn't have a groom and his friend Peter had to leave earlier. Now he hoped in his mind that the two horses would load well when that time came. Steven really had no doubts as to how Hawk would load. Hawk was his partner and had proven himself in a big way this past week. The two had partnered over the past three years and come a long way in their progress as they had proved today in the ribbon ceremony. On the other hand he didn't know a lot about Stella, the mare he had purchased shortly after arriving in Kentucky. The first evening in town he had arranged to see her after a friend had told him about her. She was cheap, had a sketchy past but proved her boldness and agility when he gave her a test ride over some big fences at the farm where she was being kept. That's all he knew but he was sure the purchase price made her a strong prospect for him to event or to sell with just some more consistent work.

It took only minutes to load the trunk and he walked briskly back to the barn for the final prep to load his horses. Steven was now realizing how much time he had allowed to drift by. It now seemed to take just a few minutes to wrap the legs of the horses. Even Stella acted as if it was something she was very used to. Steven decided to load Hawk first since he was sure that he wouldn't be any trouble and he figured that Hawk would then be an incentive for Stella to load. Even faster than Steven had hoped both of the horses were loaded and seemed quite content. He now made one more trip to where the horses had been stabled to check that he hadn't missed anything. As he walked back to the truck he realized that the only humanity visible anywhere were the two security guards who were talking and smoking just outside the building.

"You finally ready to go young man?" jested the older of the two guards.

"Yep." Answered Steven politely but at the same time a little irritated by the implication that he had been so slow.

Steven got into his truck as soon as he'd checked all the doors on the trailer and rechecked the hitch and running lights. The diesel started up with a puff of smoke and

An Event to Remember ~ 3

Steven allowed it a moment to warm up as he adjusted his mirrors and found the radio station he was looking for. It was actually a bit sad as he started to pull away from the stable area. He just didn't want the experience to end yet. In moments he was at the gate of the Kentucky Horse Park and ready to enter the highway to head home. He paused a moment and looked at the sign at the entrance. Steven had passed the sign for many years as he worked toward the event he had just completed. After a good look and sigh Steven pulled past the sign and onto the road.

The radio was blaring with some of his favorite songs and he sang along, off key but smiling and feeling mighty good. Steven hadn't even thought about the time but as dusk now surrounded him he realized it was later than he thought. It was late April but the days were already longer here in the south. Now the dash lights and truck headlights automatically came on, a sure sign nightfall was eminent and that he had left later than he thought.

After a few hours of driving in rather light traffic he was approaching Interstate 465 south of Indianapolis. Mentally he was foreseeing himself on Interstate 65 which was the longest leg of the journey but an easy drive.

Now on 465 he started what always had seemed to be "the most boring circle made to avoid downtown Indy". It added time to the drive but it did keep one from the stop and go traffic of the downtown area. One of those necessary pain-in-the-ass things, he thought to himself. The radio searched for a new station as the broadcast areas changed. The new station now announced the time and Steven suddenly realized that it was late and he had not eaten anything since early that morning. He had fed the horses in the late afternoon before they left so he knew they were all right but his stomach was now protesting its lack of nourishment. He now began to focus on the exits as they came up looking for a restaurant that looked close and appeared to have a parking lot spacious enough to handle the truck and trailer while keeping it in sight. There it was. A sign announcing "The Broiler Steakhouse", near the exit with a sizable parking lot that seemed to be pretty open. It certainly appeared to be just what he had in mind.

The lack of vehicles in the parking lot could have been the result of poor food he thought but he still turned on his blinker to exit the highway and give it a shot.

As he reached the parking lot entrance he spotted two other horse trailers sitting there. Without a second thought he pulled in and parked. Steven did a fast check of the two horses in back and was satisfied with their calm and maybe tired behavior so he walked to the restaurant.

Walking in he was amazed at the smoky atmosphere of the bar and the very empty looking dining room. The noise in the bar was evidence of the good mood of the people inside. Actually it was a smaller crowd than the noise had first portrayed but nonetheless a happy group of people. Steven had no sooner walked through the old fashioned swinging bar doors to enter the barroom when he was certain he heard his name.

"Hey, Steven. Come and join us. Have a drink and get some food it's all really good."

Steven recognized the woman speaking to him as Ellen Roth, one of the four-star competitors who had been eliminated on the cross-country course. She was all smiles now and sitting there with two young women who she had brought as grooms. There were another four people also sitting at the round table where she sat. Another large table of people in a celebratory mood flanked them. A younger man sitting at Ellen's table swung a chair from a nearby table and instructed members of the table to make room. Motioning to Steven to sit he introduced himself. "Steven, have a seat here. You're a celebrity in my eyes. My name is Patrick and I am a big fan of yours. I just want to tell you I thought you did an awesome job this weekend." As Steven began to sit he realized other members at the table were congratulating him and teasing Patrick for his excited greeting.

An Event to Remember ~ 5

Ellen introduced Mary and Sue as the two grooms she had with her. Then with a laugh in her voice she continued. "Patrick competed at the intermediate level earlier this week and has watched you for the last two years. We could hardly contain him as they announced your placing today." Steven looked sheepish and a bit embarrassed as Ellen continued. Patrick brought his mother, Betty, his girlfriend, Amanda, and friend Alex." Steven nodded to each as they were introduced and listened as a woman at the other table introduced the people at the other table.

"I thought you all had left much earlier than I had. I'm sure I was probably the last to pull out. I'm surprised that you aren't farther along. How far do you have to go? Where are you both from?" Steven inquired. Ellen explained that she was from upstate New York and that Patrick was from Minnesota. Both had made arrangements for the horses and themselves to spend the night just north of Lafayette where a private barn could handle the horses for a night or more.

"We only have about an hour and a half to travel and I guess that's why we have been sitting here so casually burning time. How far are you planning on going tonight?" Ellen asked. Steven sipped on the beer that someone had brought him and then answered. "I probably have about another four hours ahead of me. Fortunately, I live closer than either of the two of you." Patrick then piped in, "You should stay overnight with us. It really is late and then of course you could give us your take on your good weekend finish." Steven shook his head as a negative answer but politely took time to answer the questions being asked by people from both tables.

Ellen looked at her watch and announced in a surprised voice that it was now 10:30 and they were to have been to the overnight barn by 11. Patrick's mother, Betty, then offered to go outside to contact the barn and let them know they were still coming but would be late.

Everyone now started to pack up and split up the bill as Steven finished his steak that had grown cold. It was a good meal he thought as he finished, just sorry that I didn't eat it while it was still warm. "What do I owe?" he asked. Patrick then answered with a big smile that he had taken care of the bill. Steven just said thanks and then pushed away from the table. They all walked out to the parking lot and the riders quickly checked on the horses. All the animals seemed quiet and so they all said their good-byes, after exchanging cell phone numbers, and got in the trucks. Steven started out of the parking lot first while the others seemed to be making some final adjustments to things in their rigs.

It didn't seem long before Steven made the turn north on Interstate 65. He was surprised at how light the traffic was a bit amazed that he hadn't seen the others anywhere behind him so far. Steven put the cruise control on and settled in at sixty-five miles an hour figuring that should get him home by about three in the morning. He wasn't really in any hurry, as he didn't want the experience to end. He kept trying to recall both Ellen and Patrick's performance during the Event, but who was he kidding he hadn't paid much attention to anyone else. He was focused on his partner, Hawk and looking ahead to the next challenge that they would be facing. Even now he could remember almost every footprint of the weekend and whether it was good or bad.

As he drove along he would often check his rearview mirror to see any signs of Ellen and her group. Looking at the gauge on the dash he now started to plan a fuel stop in Lafayette before everything would be closed for the night. Steven guessed that he was probably about a half hour out yet from the south end of Lafayette. He checked his rearview mirror again and this time he was pretty sure he was seeing a truck and trailer catching up to him. He assumed it probably was the group and now found himself checking the mirror more often to check their progress.

His cell phone began to signal that he had a message. His hand fumbled around the consul as he searched for his phone and kept his eyes on the road. He picked up the phone and prepared to open it. It showed that the incoming message had been sent by Ellen's phone and again he checked the mirror again to see them only a few miles back.

Steven was not a fan of texting, let alone while driving. Normally he wouldn't even read one if it was from family but he somehow felt required to view this one. He now tried to thumb his security code to open the message but miss-dialed it. He now looked down at it to be sure he was redialing it correctly. As he looked up he lost the phone as he yanked the steering wheel in an attempt to swerve as far to the right as possible. The headlights of an out-of-control semi blinded him as it came racing across the median. His instincts demanded that he speed up and not brake. The guardrail splintered as the huge International Semi blasted through it and at him. As it had traveled through the median the trailer had tipped and the cargo had dumped out the back end allowing the cab to gain speed as if shot from a canon.

Chapter 2

THE IMPACT OF the collision momentarily knocked Steven out. His truck had spun completely around as the semi had ripped the truck bed and trailer from the cab, where Steven was now trapped. The semi itself was well over a football field's length away from Steven's truck, another indication of its speed at impact.

As he started to come to Steven tried to open his door, but the pain was more than he could endure. His arm had been broken and his driver side door was punched in. The window was broken and had blood all over the shattered area as his head freely bled and was now obstructing his vision. There was a loud pounding on the passenger side as Ellen, Betty and one of the grooms worked to get a door open. Betty realized that the door locks were still engaged and talked to Steven to see if he could possibly release the locks. Slowly Steven's right hand fumbled over the console and touched on the window switch instead of the lock switch by accident. "That's good Steven push on that one some more" Betty yelled hoping he would move it enough for them to unlock the door. "No. No. Push it the other way, you're closing it now." Steven now slumped over as this simple task well demonstrated the state he was in. Then the window started to move again and it became obvious that Steven wasn't about to give up.

Betty stood on the running board and reached through the window barely reaching the lock and convincing it to open. The women now opened the two passenger side doors and crawled in to better assess the situation. Mary reached around the headrest and put some pressure on

Steven's head wound with a tee shirt she had quickly pulled from his duffle bag that was in the back seat. Ellen was now in the back seat also reaching through the bucket seats and trying to undo his seatbelt. "Hang in there, big guy." Ellen said in a soft voice. "What happened?" Steven asked in a whispering voice. Betty then told him that the semi driver had either fallen asleep or had a heart attack. The semi had come across the median at a high speed and grazed the truck and hit the horse trailer. Steven flinched as he heard the news about the trailer. His voice strengthened as he asked, "How are the horses? How's Hawk? He's all right isn't he?" The questions exhausted him as he slumped forward and Mary lost a hold of him. As they righted him again Ellen delivered as much of the news that she could based on what they had seen as they skidded to a stop behind the wreckage. "It appeared that the semi grazed your truck but it hit hard enough to rip the truck bed off, dislodging the goose neck. The trailer is about forty feet or more back from here and on its side. Patrick and the others are seeing what they can do." With that news Steven collapsed and Betty was suddenly concerned that he had passed away.

The ambulances were arriving and sirens could be heard both near and far. Overhead a chopper sounded as if it were approaching but it wasn't obvious whether it was a news vehicle or an air ambulance. Suddenly they realized that the truck was being surrounded by EMTs and firemen. Ellen and Betty were being asked to come out of the truck as the EMTs started to check Steven's vitals. The radio headsets they all wore squawked and barked commands back and forth. The fireman close to Steven now called for someone to bring the jaws of life.

A fireman came running with the equipment as the paramedics applied a wrap around Steven's head. The fireman now stood outside Steven's window and addressed the paramedic. "Is this one still with us? He's looking pretty bad." The paramedic responded that he was sure they could save this one but inquired about any other victims. "The only other one we've seen so far was the truck driver and he's gone. Not sure yet if he died in the crash or before. Now step away while I get this door off this truck."

Ellen had walked around the truck to be near to the driver side. She wanted to be close enough to overhear any discussion about Steven as they worked to pull him out.

The ripping noise of the jaws on the metal was a spine tingling sound. Betty joined Ellen as she continued to watch. Betty had stopped a moment to view the scene behind the truck. "Ellen, I'm worried about those horses. The entire front of the trailer is smashed in and ripped up. There's even part of the pickup bed from the truck still attached." Ellen looked to her with a terrified face as she asked, "Have you seen or heard of any signs of horses back there?" Betty just moved her head in a negative manner that was enough to send the message she didn't care to speak.

At that moment the two firemen working on the truck door stopped and made a super strength effort to move the part of the door they had been cutting. "Good enough. Let's get this guy out of there." the one said to the other. While the two firemen worked to free and dislodge Steven from the driver's seat another pair of paramedics were coming now with a stretcher. Betty grabbed Ellen's arm and turned her attention to the rear. Patrick was now walking toward them. Patrick and the other grooms had been working to help with the horses. Ellen assumed bad news as he approached with a concerned look on his face. "Did you all get the horses out ok?" Patrick waited until he was closer and then started telling what they had been working on. He told them that the trailer had not only flipped but had also been pushed back against the guardrail behind it. We had to get equipment to shift its position and we had to do it slowly. He didn't know which horse it was but one of the firemen had seen through the side window, which was now topside, that a horse was standing upright and motionless. Patrick thought that the horse was probably in shock or injured even though he was standing. "God I hope its Steven's Hawk horse he competed at the Rolex," Ellen said. Patrick wasn't sure of anything but asked Ellen to join him to maybe help with the horses. If they were ok he thought they could offer to reload them on his and her trailer to get them to the barn in Lafayette they were going to.

Ellen agreed to go and check out the situation as the firemen were very slowly working to get Steven out as they assessed his injuries. Steven seemed very limp and lifeless but they had put him on an IV already and Ellen was sure they were probably doping him with morphine to control the pain he had to be in.

As Patrick and Ellen approached the trailer he looked to her to see her reaction. Ellen's eyes were welling up with tears already it was certain she was beginning to expect the worst. This was Ellen's first focused look at the trailer scene and it was overwhelming to anyone, let alone horse lovers. The front of the trailer in the tack area was completely crumpled and shredded. The gooseneck portion was all but ripped off with and only a small portion of the truck bed now remained with it. The area on the side that wasn't crumpled seemed in reasonable condition but then it hit Ellen. "Jesus! Patrick that semi had to hit the tack area and then pushed down the side. It had to have hit Steven's horse, Hawk. I remember he was in the front because I looked in at the horses in the parking lot before we left the bar." Tears were now obvious on Ellen's face as she quickened her pace to the wreck.

Four men stood at the rear of the trailer discussing the next move and stalling for the arrival of Patrick and Ellen, who they hoped might help with ideas and the actual handling of the animals. "Where do we stand with the situation?" Patrick inquired in the final steps of their approach to the waiting firemen. The firemen let them know that they were waiting for his return but they were sure at least one horse was standing inside. "What's the plan

12 ~ *Steve Farkos*

then?" Patrick asked. The taller fireman then started to explain how they would open the trailer when everyone was in place and ready. The fireman's concern with the plan was how they would handle the horse. "I don't want that horse charging out and into the dark or across the median into oncoming traffic." Ellen now jumped in and pleaded that they start and insisted she would handle the horse. She felt strongly that time was now becoming an enemy to the situation.

The firemen started to take their places as they had discussed in their plans for opening the trailer. One young fireman was now on top of the capsized trailer and was carefully letting out some of the rope he had taken up top with him. Another guy was now tying one end of the rope to the latch of the door that was now positioned on the top. Two others were positioned on either side of the capsized vehicle ready to handle the doors. The whole area was now being lit by huge lights, which had been brought in, assembled and turned on. The noise of all the generators running almost prevented normal speech levels. Yelling seemed the only way to converse. The lights were incredibly bright and made the disastrous scene even more chilling.

The plan was to drop the one door down creating a ramp while the other door would be hoisted up with the rope from the guy positioned topside. The big question was what the standing horse would do, if anything. Patrick and Ellen agreed they couldn't have a plan until they could see the horse. They were concerned now that the bright lights outside might make it impossible to see much as the darkness inside the trailer would be even a bigger issue now. Too much time was passing and not knowing the condition of the horses it was time to act and not plan.

On the signal of the lead fireman the top door was raised and then the other one was dropped. The two men on either side needed to assist the one up top as he started to slip and lose his footing as the door rose higher but its resistance grew greater. Ellen and Patrick came forward and peered into the trailer. The standing horse whinnied but made no effort to come forward. The horse was standing with its feet literally through what once had been the side windows. Ellen started in now with the hopes of putting a lead rope around the horse neck. The horse no longer had a halter on since it probably broke and freed the horse during the crash. Ellen talked to the horse softly as she approached her. The mare waited her arrival with almost no motion. Patrick realized by the animal's size that the standing horse wasn't the big guy that Steven had competed. The standing one must be the mare Steven had just purchased. "Ellen, you're doing great. The mare seems quiet and looks like she's standing on all four legs evenly. Can you see or hear any signs of the big horse?" Patrick asked. Ellen didn't respond as she felt only one thing at a time could be accomplished. She wasn't hearing any other sounds besides the mare breathing that actually seemed very relaxed for all she had just experienced. Ellen was ready to try and convince the mare to step forward and hopefully out. "Ellen there's a vet here now so if you can get her out he'll be able to give her a good inspection." Patrick called out to her. Ellen now slowly urged the mare forward. The mare began to tremble as she slowly lifted one foot then another out of the broken windows as she began to more forward.

The mare was now at the doorway and took one step onto the open door that now acted as a short ramp. The horse then put the brakes on and snorted loudly. She sensed the angle and unsteadiness of the makeshift ramp and was in question about the brightness outside of the trailer. "Patrick I think we can get her to jump out. Get a halter and lunge line to me." Patrick turned and ran off at a sprint to his trailer. In minutes he returned and passed the items to Ellen. Ellen continued to speak to the mare as she put the halter on and then attached the lunge line. Ellen now took the loose end of the lunge line and tossed it out to Patrick. Patrick picked up the loose end and motioned for everyone to step away and give enough room for the mare. "Patrick, gently take the slack out of the line and start to put some tension on it. I'm going to encourage her to jump out." Ellen then instructed Patrick to increase the contact as she gave the mare a loud slap of her hand and urged her forward with an assertive voice. The mare stretched her neck forward but made no effort to move. "Come on girl, go for it." With that the mare sprung forward in a jump and landed on the ground with a buck and a few canter strides. Patrick settled her and slowly drew her in and now had her standing. In minutes the vet was checking her out.

Ellen now exited the trailer and asked the firemen to try to move some of the rubble inside. She hadn't heard any life sounds from the big horse. He was probably under some of the wreckage which had been created by the stall dividers that had been torn down and kicked about by the mare as she righted herself. Betty now appeared at the back of the trailer as Ellen exited. "They finally got Steven out of the truck. It appears that he's busted up quite a bit. He has a broken arm, several broken ribs, a compound fracture on his leg and that head injury we saw bleeding. After they made the first effort to pull him out I heard them say he was unconscious. They have him on a gurney now and are loading him into the ambulance." Betty told Ellen as the sirens of the ambulance and police escort sounded loudly as they pulled away. "Any idea where they will be taking him?" Ellen asked. Betty told her that she had gotten the information and would share it when things settled a bit.

Ellen and Betty watched as the firemen removed some of the debris from the back of the trailer. Now Ellen approached the back of the trailer where a fireman stood like a solitary sentry. The lone fireman then told her that they were now waiting for the vet to finish with the mare and then they would send him in to inspect the animal inside. Ellen asked for the fireman's flashlight and his permission to let her go in now to check the horse that still remained in the trailer.

An Event to Remember ~ 15

The fireman didn't hesitate and handed the flashlight to Ellen. Ellen pushed the switch forward and turned the light on as she began to enter the dark box-like tunnel. It took a second as she came from the brilliant light being generated outside to the soft restricted light that the flashlight now offered inside. Ellen carefully moved forward. It seemed so much bigger now that the other debris had been removed. The side of the trailer that lay on the ground offered uneven ground from the rippled aluminum with shattered glass and metal pieces for the footpath. The light now caught the frame of the horse that she had just admired so much the day before. Hawk laid still and his contorted position was the first to speak of his death. His neck was bent backwards against his torso and his hind-quarters were twisted toward his shoulders which the crash had done to force fit him into the space allowed. A large piece of aluminum had been snapped and broken by the impact and now stuck up through the shoulder of the great animal. Hawk's body lay in pools of blood and Ellen could no longer deal with the enormous emotional pain that now overcame her. She stepped forward another step and then collapsed on the giant horse and began to sob. She now imagined the torture that this would still be for Steven and with no closure to help cope with it. Ellen then felt the hand of a friend on her shoulder. "Come on Ellen we need to get out of here. You can help me load that mare in my trailer and we can go get all of the horses bedded down." Patrick suggested. On her other side one of the firemen had begun to lift her up to help her out.

Chapter 3

ELLEN CAME OUT from the trailer and the bright spotlights showed the dirt, blood and tears that were now a part of her experience. "Are you all right Ellen? Patrick asked. "I'm sure I can get someone else to help me with the mare." Betty now rejoined them and offered Ellen the hot coffee she was carrying. Betty insisted that she take it once she had a full view of the young woman. "Where did you get hot coffee out here? Patrick asked. Betty explained that there was a truck that came to help out and he had coffee, water and sandwiches for all the men out here working. Betty's voice prompted Ellen's thought once again to more important topics. "Betty did you say that you had the information of where they were taking Steven. Has anybody heard anything about the truck driver? I know they said he was dead but weren't sure why." No one had heard any more about the driver but Betty had seen him being taken away in the coroner's truck.

Ellen went to where the vet was taking one last look at the mare. Both of Ellen's friends who had groomed for her last week had stayed with the vet and gave whatever help they could. Mary came running up to Ellen as soon as she saw her. "Ellen what have you been doing. Whose blood is that on you? Are you OK?" Ellen gave them a fast update of what she knew and explained that Steven's Rolex horse had not made it. Then Ellen seemed visibly shaken as she stated a lack of knowledge as to Steven's condition. She felt somehow she might have let Steven down even though she knew down deep there was nothing else she could have done. She had made the choice to help with the horses only because she knew she had to be doing something.

Betty saw the mare with the vet again and asked if he had found anything else when he inspected her the second time.

An Event to Remember ~ 17

The vet then spoke up and gave them a fast report. "Outwardly the mare has multiple scrapes that have shaved her down to the skin. There was also a cut on her hip that required a few stitches but nothing to worry about."

"So are you saying that other than a few scrapes and bruises that she came out of it clean? That's amazing." Ellen said shocked after seeing Hawk. The vet then continued saying that he knew she had suffered some real shock and was also betting that the mare would need some chiropractic attention but he also felt that shouldn't happen for maybe another week or so. Ellen was still shocked at what seemed to be a miracle. The vet then suggested that they get her loaded while he was still there and get her to the barn where Patrick and her horses were headed. "I don't want her going any farther than she has to. I'd really like to see her in the next couple of days to feel sure we haven't overlooked anything. If she is close long enough I can do the chiropractic work also," the vet offered in a compassionate tone.

It took some patience and coaxing but after about fifteen minutes or so the mare bravely stepped into the trailer. Patrick's horse whinnied and greeted her and maybe that was what it took to convince her that this trailer ride would end better. Patrick slowly moved out with his truck and trailer and was then escorted by two state police cars. They had to travel along the shoulder until they traveled past Steven's truck and the debris that the fireman had tossed aside. Once past the debris they turned unto the proper lane and then resumed highway speed with their escort. The police escort stayed with them until they reached the exit for the barn where they had been expected for hours.

Ellen asked her friends to stay with her truck and she went back up to where Steven's truck was sitting. The firemen were continuing the cleanup efforts as she walked up. "Excuse me." Ellen said as she approached the one closest to the unusual looking pile of wreckage. "I'd like to get some of his personal items to take to the hospital." But the fireman she was addressing answered with a gruff sounding no. Just then the fire chief came walking up and OK'd her request as long as she was willing to sign for the items. Ellen then went to the open driver side where they pulled Steven out. With a flashlight that the chief had offered her she scanned the floor, consul area and under the seats. Before long her search had produced Steven's wallet, his blood spattered watch and the ribbon he had won at the Rolex. She found a large manila envelope and opened it to check its contents. Ellen's heart suddenly seemed like it had lodged in her throat and her sad eyes again filled with tears. The envelope contained a photo, which was slightly bent now, of Steven and Hawk jumping into the water complex as they approached the famous duck jump. They were a stunning partnership that the night had now taken away. She regained her composure and grabbed a duffle bag from the back seat. After signing for all of the stuff she was now responsible for she slowly walked back to her truck.

As she approached her truck, she saw her friends waiting for her but talking to a few of the younger firemen who had been working on the semi wreckage and making sure that all the flammable liquids were contained and safe. Mary was the first to spot her and now came up to her offering her help with the stuff she was carrying. "Is that Steven's ribbon from the Rolex? It was smart of you to recover that because I'll bet it would have been ruined as Steven's truck sat in some junkyard till someone claimed it. Are you going to try to get it to him somehow?" Mary asked as they started making their way back to Ellen's truck. Mary then added, "We fed your horse and got some water from one of the fire trucks. He seems to be fine for all the time he's had to stand on the trailer. He's a good one. Oh! He did perk up and answered a whinny as Patrick left with the other horses."

The young women said their thanks to the firemen and asked a state trooper standing nearby if he could get a squad car to lead them out safely. He agreed and in minutes the squad was there and ready to lead them. The officer made sure that they had gotten all the information from the girls, as they were the eyewitnesses to the accident. Once they were sure they had what they needed, the trooper sent the squad rolling ahead of them on the narrow shoulder to safely avoid all the debris still scattered from the wreckage.

The first thing they had to pass was the semi and trailer that had been scattered and stopped as it twisted into the ravine on the far side of the road. It may as well been a missile for all the damage it had caused. Mary injected still another thought as she wondered out loud if the truck driver was married and had a family. They all realized that none of them had seen the driver and had no idea of his age or look. Now they were approaching the twisted and capsized trailer where a crew was working to pull Hawk's body out so they could load the trailer on a flatbed semi to haul it away. Ellen began to cry as she saw the winch begin to expose the body of the great horse as it emerged from the trailer. "What will they do with Hawk's body?" Mary asked. Through her tears Ellen answered her telling her that she was sure a renderer would just come and take it away. Mary now joined in with Ellen as they cried. Sue then spoke up from the back seat, "It's almost unfair that a magnificent animal has such a cruel death and then not even a fitting burial. I only wish there was something we could have done even though we all just met."

Riding on the shoulder with the trailer was a bit scary and very slow. No sooner had they felt the pain of Hawk's final demise than they found themselves passing the truck that had absorbed a lot of the initial contact. The semi had only grazed the truck cab before it tore apart the bed of the truck and trailer. The driver door had been removed to get Steven out and it was even more obvious how the semi had collapsed the entire driver's compartment. Steven's truck had lost half its bed and most of the backend. "Do you think he'll live?" Mary asked. "I really liked him and he seemed so down to earth and a real gentleman. Do we know if he had family? I wonder if they had been notified." Ellen then answered her. "I read last summer an article about him and his efforts to get to the Rolex. He doesn't have family anymore as they were killed in a plane crash when he was twenty years old. I believe it took his mother, father and sister away from him. The article said he lived with and helped his ailing grandmother, but she had passed away just before the article was written. All too sad for me," Ellen told the rest. They slowly passed the last of the wreckage and swung unto the smooth surface of the highway.

It took only an hour to reach the barn that they should have been at hours ago. It was 4:45 am as Ellen pulled the trailer up the driveway toward the barn. Both Sue and Mary had fallen asleep and now began to wake. Ellen spotted Patrick's trailer and pulled near to it. His trailer was unhooked and she didn't see his truck anywhere. She felt that made sense since they all needed some rest and she assumed they had gone on to the hotel. As she was putting her truck into park she saw Patrick walking out from the barn. "I thought that I should wait and see if you needed any help. Mom, Amanda and Alex went on to the hotel to try to get some sleep. As soon as we finish we can go and get some too. Any trouble getting here?" Ellen told him that the trip to the barn was uneventful. She was in favor of getting some sleep as her eyelids seemed to double in weight. Ellen's horse unloaded quietly and seemed more than ready to have a place to lie down. Patrick had readied the stall and the barn owner had gone to the house to sleep after hearing all that had happened. Patrick walked down the aisle and opened the stall door. Sue and Mary removed his shipping boots and changed out his halter to the one he normally had for shows. Patrick had put a sign on the stall door and pointed it out to Ellen. The sign boldly said 'Cheap Trick', her horse's name, with feeding instructions for the morning.

An Event to Remember ~ 21

"The barn owner said she would feed our horses in the morning to let us all get a bit more sleep." Mary brought a bag of pre-mixed grain for Trick's morning feed. Sue brought hay for him now and some for in the morning. Sue tossed the hay for now into the stall for Trick but he waited to start eating it. He had surveyed his surroundings and now dropped down to enjoy a fun roll in the clean shavings in his stall. He rolled from side to side multiple times and then sprang to his feet and shook hard enough that he looked like he would fall over. "Trick is a happy camper now. I think he's been waiting for that roll," Patrick said with a smile.

The horses were safe and they had parked the trailer so Patrick joined them and they headed off to the hotel. The hotel was within fifteen minutes and Sue was convinced she could already smell the fresh sheets on the bed. It was now 7:00 o'clock and they bid Patrick good night and went in their room to get some sleep. Sue and Mary shared a bed as they felt Ellen needed extra comfort after her tough day. It was about 12:45 when Ellen woke to a knock on the door and the other two didn't even stir as Ellen rose to see who was there.

It was Patrick and he hoped to get everyone together for a lunch where they could plan out the timing for the rest of their trip. "It will probably take a good half hour for us to be ready." Ellen explained, as she looked over to the two still in a deep sleep. Patrick agreed and made plans to meet them across the street at the little waffle house diner he had spotted when they arrived last night.

Ellen, Mary and Sue walked into the diner and saw Patrick and his entourage looking pretty awake as they drank coffee and chatted. The three young ladies on the other hand looked like they just woke and were in definite need of some strong joe.

They discussed the events of the night. All had been touched by what they had witnessed especially Ellen. After hearing Patrick's plan to leave yet that afternoon Ellen

22 ~ *Steve Farkos*

announced that they wouldn't be leaving until possibly Thursday. Sue and Mary looked at her very surprised because they hadn't heard any discussion about this. Ellen then let them all know that she would talk to the barn owner to make plans with him to keep Steve's mare, Stella, for a while. She would then also let the vet know where the mare was so he could do a follow up exam and schedule his chiropractic session with her. Ellen then let them know that she would be going to the hospital to check on Steven, if it was possible to see him. Mary and Sue were surprised as they hadn't heard any of this before and they had concerns about getting back to home and for Sue's work.

After they had lunch and relaxed a bit Patrick went off to repack his vehicle and organize things for the rest of his trip home. Ellen asked Mary to hand walk Stella and asked Sue to walk 'Trick while she went to talk to the barn manager. She was able to get the barn manager to agree to the two horses staying for a few more days and the manager offered it at no cost based on the circumstances. Mary had given the hospital information to Ellen and she now tried on several occasions to reach Steven or the doctors for an update.

Frustrated by her inability to reach anyone Ellen was now determined to go there and get some answers. She met with Mary and Sue and gave them the option of going with her on her information quest. Mary decided to go with and Sue felt more sleep seemed like a good idea. "I'll stay behind, catch a nap and check on the two horses later. I'll wait till you return and then we can grab dinner and you can fill me in on any news you may get," Sue said. So Ellen told Mary to get ready and they would leave in a few minutes.

Ellen and Mary headed to the hospital and according to the GPS they should arrive within a half hour. It was pretty accurate as they pulled in to the hospital parking lot about twenty minutes after leaving. "Not often you can beat the GPS. Guess that was some good driving on your part," Mary teased. The parking lot seemed pretty empty and they

An Event to Remember ~ 23

found a spot really close to the hospital entrance. Ellen marched up to the front desk as if she had been there a hundred times. The older lady behind the desk asked how she could be of help. Ellen politely asked if they could get visitor passes for Steven Wilson who would have been admitted last night. The lady behind the desk rustled through a stack of papers in front of her. Now it seemed like she was repeating her search yet had said nothing so far. "Miss, I'm not seeing any Steven Wilson being admitted. Are you sure they brought him here?" the woman behind the desk asked. Ellen and Mary were taken aback. Ellen then asked if there were any other hospitals nearby they might have been taken him to. The woman behind the desk basically assured them that they were the biggest and most modern hospital in town. Things just weren't making sense. Then the woman behind the desk seeing Ellen's frustration asked the two young women to hold on a minute as she checked the emergency room staff for any possible information. She picked up the phone and dialed the emergency room desk. "Can you tell me if between last night and this morning if you have any records in your area about seeing or treating a Steven Wilson? Ah huh. Ah huh I see. Thank you so much." The receptionist ended her conversation with the emergency room. She then hung up and scribbled something on a notepad and then looked at a laminated sheet for additional information.

"Here you go young lady. He never actually was here but the ambulance was in communication with the doctors in Emergency. After assessing his status it was decided to take him to Indianapolis to Indy General as he would have a better chance there. Here's the hospital information you'll want." The receptionist had handed a sheet from the notepad to Ellen. The sheet contained the phone number and address of the hospital they had taken him to. Ellen thanked the receptionist and headed to the main door. As they walked she handed Mary the sheet and asked her to read the phone number as she dialed it on her cell phone.

By the time they had reached Ellen's truck she had confirmed Steven had been taken there and that he was now listed as an ICU patient. Ellen no sooner was in the truck and she had it started and headed out of the parking lot. As they came to the main road Ellen had put her right turn signal on. "We came from the other direction coming here." Mary stated. Ellen told her she was aware but she was going to Indianapolis now. "That's almost an hour from here. Should we be going now?" Mary asked. With that Ellen completed the turn and drove north to catch interstate 65. There was no stopping Ellen as she was bound and determined to find out exactly how Steven was.

"I'm a bit surprised at your intensity to track down Steven. After all, none of us really knew him. I'm sure we can try again tomorrow. We could even start home and stop at the hospital. With the three of us you could go up and check on him and we could take turns checking on the horses," Mary suggested. Ellen made no effort to slow down but instead made her reasons clear to Mary. She explained to Mary that even though they had never met she had followed his career for the past year or so. Ellen actually admitted that she had made a video for the sake of studying his dressage and stadium jumping. "Are you telling me that you're a Steven Wilson groupie?" Mary jested. "No. But I am impressed at what he has accomplished. He was mentioned at a clinic I had done with Wolford. He told us that he would be a good one to watch.... And so I have and I've seen a lot I liked. Meeting him at that bar and grill seemed to open up his personality and I was impressed.
He interacts the same as he rides I think, quiet, accurate and effective." Ellen said as her rebuttal to Mary. "Wow! You got all that from that short introduction meeting at the bar?" Mary teased. Ellen didn't respond but continued north to Indianapolis.

Mary's cell phone rang. It was Sue. Sue wanted to get an idea when they might be back and about what time they might get dinner. Mary told her to go have dinner, as they hadn't even reached their destination yet. Sue questioned where they might be, as she couldn't imagine why they wouldn't be in Lafayette yet. Mary brought her up to speed as to what was happening and then ended the conversation by admitting she had no clue as to how soon they would return.

Ellen pulled off at the next exit and pulled into a gas station. As she began to pump fuel she suggested that Mary run in and pick up a couple of coffees. In minutes they were ready to go again. Ellen guessed that it was about another half hour till they would reach the outskirts of Indy. "Once we get closer to the 465 bypass we'll resort to the GPS and let it guide us from that point." After another twenty-five minutes had passed they saw the sign for the bypass. Mary plugged in the address of the hospital that she had looked up on her iPhone. "Seriously what did we ever do without all our fancy technology?" Mary said in wonderment. It took almost another eighteen minutes longer in traffic but they now reached the entrance to the hospital parking lot.

It appeared to be a very new hospital as they reached the front entrance. The entrance opened into a large reception area. The initial area seemed to have everything you might need to be well prepared for a visit. There was a florist, a card shop, a huge candy store, a gift shop and computerized directory of the whole hospital. It was a very impressive area and right in the center of it all, there was a beautiful information desk manned by four well dressed, middle-aged women. Two of the women appeared to be the phone operators and both seemed very busy.

Ellen marched up to the information desk with Mary trailing a step or two behind. One of the receptionist offered Ellen assistance as she reached the desk. "Can I help you?" asked the kind voice behind the desk. "Yes," Ellen said. "We're here to see Steven Wilson, a patient I believe that was admitted last night." The receptionist looked up the name and then let Ellen know that Steven was in the system. "Steven is in ICU and hospital policy will only allow family to see him." The receptionist explained. "I'm his sister," Ellen said as if she were. Mary almost swallowed the gum that she had purchased at the gas station. Then Ellen continued, "This is our cousin Mary who I dragged along with me." The receptionist didn't have any reason to doubt Ellen and she then made out two visitor passes and told them they would need to check in at the desk once they got to the ICU department.

The receptionist then pointed down a hallway and to where the ladies could find the elevator that would take them to the fourth floor where ICU was located. With that information and visitor passes the two marched down the hall to the elevator. Once they found themselves alone on the elevator Mary turned to Ellen and said. "You never cease to amaze me. You handled that as if you had rehearsed it for a week. I'm impressed, girl. " Ellen just laughed. The doors opened and they exited the elevator. A sign directed them to go right. As they walked down the hall they could see a set of double doors that read ICU department. The hall seemed very quiet as they walked along yet they could see nurses working in some of the rooms and patients in other rooms just resting quietly.

Ellen and Mary opened the doors to the ICU department and were instantly greeted by a nurse sitting there at a desk. "Can I help you ladies?" the nurse asked. But before they could answer the nurse made sure they had passes for the area. After she saw the passes the nurse asked whom they had come to see. Ellen told her and the nurse went on her computer to look him up. Mr. Wilson is in the 'R' suite. "Go to the end of the hall and you will see a glass doorway to your left. Wait there and a nurse will buzz you in once they are ready to let you in," the nurse told them. Ellen and Mary reach the glass door destination but waited there a while until one of the nurses inside spotted them and could stop what they were doing and buzz them in. The two were amazed as they looked into the room. The room seemed to be arranged in a horseshoe configuration. They could see

An Event to Remember ~ 27

hundreds of LED lights doing read outs everywhere. There were six beds in this particular complex that they could see. IV bags in multiples were hung near every bed and plastic tubing seemed to be hanging everywhere. There was a crash cart near the desk in the center. Ellen had pointed it out recognizing it from some of the medical shows she often watched on television. Four nurses were working in the room and none had noticed them yet. A sign on the door asked them to wait patiently and not to knock on the door, so the two quietly awaited their acknowledgement.

Finally a nurse came over and opened the door. The nurse apologized to them but explained that they were really busy today. Then she asked Ellen whom they wished to see. Ellen told her that they had come to see Steven Wilson. Mary started to realize how eerily silent this room was that now had twelve people in it. The nurse now walked them over to a bed that held a small sign at the end of the bed, 'Suite R'. Mary gasped as she saw who was supposed to be Steven in the bed where they stood. The handsome young man they had shared a drink with last night was unrecognizable in that bed.

Steven's head was wrapped in gauze from his hairline to the tip of his nose. His left arm was in a cast from his shoulder down to his wrist. He had two IVs in his right arm and oxygen tube wrapped about his head. His left leg was elevated, cast, with a metal looking halo thing around his thigh area. His foot hung loose out of the end of the cast and looked like a black and blue blown up cartoon foot. Mary looked to Ellen and saw a tear run down her face. "What's his condition internally?" Ellen inquired. The nurse with them picked up his chart and flipped through a couple of pages. "What you can't see I would say is the fact he has some pressure on his brain from the bleeding he had in his skull. He also has three broken ribs on his left side one of which punctured his lung. Obviously a broken arm and compound breaks in two areas of his leg," The nurse explained. "Is he in a coma?" Ellen asked. The nurse explained that he was in a drug- induced coma and also was being given strong doses of morphine. He would be kept this way until he was out of the woods. Ellen and Mary were shocked at what they had just heard. "Do you feel he will fully recover?" Mary asked. The nurse answered affirmative and said the doctors seemed pretty confident that he could turn all this around considering his age and physical condition. "How long will he be in this induced state?" Ellen asked. "Hopefully just a couple days at most," the nurse told her and then she let the two know their time was up and she needed to get back to her duties.

The two women left and rode down the elevator without any words being spoken. They were about half way out to the truck and Mary asked Ellen if she was all right. Mary admitted she was blown away by what she had just seen. She had expected it and admitted that she thought she might faint when they first saw him. "He'll be back and be as strong and great as ever," Ellen said in a very convincing tone. Mary realized that Ellen's mind was going at warp speed about what she had seen and she decided to leave any other questions or thoughts till later. It was time now to get back to the hotel, Sue and the horses.

The trip back to the Lafayette hotel was quiet as Mary fell asleep shortly after they had left the hospital parking lot. Ellen allowed her mind to relax and found a radio station with some good country music and sang along in a muffled level as to not wake Mary. They had been on the road for about forty-five minute when Mary's phone rang. Mary woke and had that look initially of where-am-I.

Her sleepy state made her slow to answer the phone and it stopped ringing before she could answer. Now a bit more alert Mary checked her caller ID and hit the call back button to get Sue. Ellen listened as Mary gave short answers from her end of the conversation. Mary looked to Ellen and asked how much longer till they would be at the hotel. "I would guess we're about a half hour out yet. Ask Sue if she was able to check the horses out. And see if she has eaten.

We need to get a real meal somewhere. I'm starving," Ellen said. Mary passed on the conversation to Sue and then ended the call. Mary then let Ellen know that Sue had taken a cab out to the barn and checked on the horses. Sue had told her that Steven's mare seemed pretty stiff so she had taken her for a walk and hand grazing after inspecting her everywhere. She had also given her two grams of the anti-inflammatory drug known as bute to ease any pain and swelling. Mary then added that Trick was as good as ever and seemed attached to Stella as he called to her several times while Sue walked the mare.

Ellen and Mary arrived at the hotel and Sue was at the door of their room to greet them. After reviewing their day and realizing Sue hadn't eaten, they decided to clean up, put some nice clothes on, and go to a little Italian restaurant downtown.

While they sipped their wine and enjoyed some appetizers, Ellen and Mary shared stories of their daylong trip. They were all enjoying the downtime when Ellen threw them another surprise. "Let's get a good night sleep and in the morning we'll head back home. I'm going to call the barn when we get back to the hotel and make arrangements for them to keep the mare and watch over her for the next couple of days. I'm hoping to get someone to hand walk her." Ellen said. "I thought you wanted to stay another couple days?" Sue asked. Ellen then explained that after seeing Steven she had a different plan. "I want to get Trick home and have Mary take over supervising the barn. "Sue you can get back to your job and helping Mary when you can. After I check things at home I plan on coming back down here to see how I can help out. Remember Steven doesn't have any family and who knows if there is anyone else to help. And I feel obligated for some reason to be the one to break the news about his horse, Hawk." Ellen explained. Both Sue and Mary were surprised.

That night the women prepared to leave in the morning. Ellen was successful in making arrangements with the barn and also called the vet to make sure he could make it out tomorrow afternoon to check on the mare. Everything seemed ready and they went to bed knowing that morning was going to arrive faster than they may have wanted. It was apparent that Mary and Sue had fallen asleep but Ellen's mind wasn't ready to give into the pillow yet. She lay there replaying her efforts at the Rolex and the little she had seen of Steven on cross-country. Visions of Hawk in the trailer and Steven in the ICU haunted her as she now hoped for sleep. She questioned herself about coming back to help Steven. But no matter how she looked at it there was no doubt in her mind that she wanted to be there for whatever help she could be.

Chapter 4

MORNING AGAIN SEEMED to come quickly. Ellen wondered if she had really had much real sleep. The three packed up their stuff from the room and Sue and Mary finished packing the truck while Ellen settled the bill. They made a fast stop at the little diner across the street and had a good breakfast and plenty of coffee. Next they were on the way back to the stable to hook up the trailer and prepare Trick for the long trip back to up-state New York.

Once they arrived at the stable they all went about the duties that would be needed. Few words ever needed to be spoken as the three of them had so many times done the drill before. Sue checked on the mare and gave her a short walk to see how she was moving today. Mary pulled Trick out and brushed him up and then put his shipping wraps on.

Ellen first went to the manager's office and settled up payment wise and paid forward another month's board to keep the mare. She also gave complete information for them to reach her and let them know that the vet would be out in a few days to check on her and would be coming another time to adjust her. "I'll leave this envelope for the vet. There's a check made out to him but he'll just have to write in the amount. Please be sure that you get a receipt and put it in the envelope for my return," Ellen continued.

Ellen then went outside and hooked up the trailer. Sue helped to check the lights and brake signals. Then Sue put

Trick's brushes, buckets and leftover grain in the trailer tack room and then locked it. Ellen had opened the back of the trailer and Mary walked him in and hooked him to the trailer tie. They worked together like a well-oiled machine. Everything was ready to go as the three took their places in the truck and then headed out.

They hadn't traveled very far when Mary asked where they would be stopping overnight. "I'm not planning on stopping. I want to make it in one trip," Ellen announced to their surprise. Sue reminded Ellen that it was about an eighteen-hour trip from where they were. "We'll trade off on the driving and make several short stops for food, fuel and rest for Trick in the back." was Ellen's answer. The ladies had no more to say since they realized that Ellen's mind was made up and they weren't about to change it.

The trip was going smoothly and after a couple hours of talking and reading Mary fell asleep which then gave Ellen her choice as to who would be the next driver. After Ellen had driven about four hours they pulled in for fuel, coffee and an opportunity to switch drivers. They sat for about a half hour and gave the horse a rest while they took care of any personal needs. They then started off and switched off twice more and made a dinner stop for both the horse and themselves.

It was nearly 2 a.m. when they arrived at Ellen's stable. It had taken about as long as they thought in hours but they hadn't considered the time change. They had left close to 8 a.m. and the trip had gone smoothly and quicker than it seemed like it had.

"Sue, please hand walk Trick while Mary and I take any necessary equipment off tonight. After we unhook the trailer and make sure his stall is ready please give him some probiotics and a lot of hay. I'm not going to grain him tonight after that trip. Let's also hang an extra bucket of water for him too. Then we'll all get home and the two of you can sleep in tomorrow. Actually Mary if you can just stay tonight and we can go over things in the morning." Sue

An Event to Remember ~ 33

put Trick in and then returned to say good-bye. She planned on going to her job in the morning but hoped to call about noon to find out what Ellen's plans were. Ellen thanked her and also said she would give her something in the next day or so for all her extra help.

After Sue left, Mary and Ellen took their suitcases in and made a dash for the showers. After good hot showers they both had a small glass of wine and then went to bed. Mary was still sound asleep in the other bedroom when Ellen got up. The barn help had come and were busy feeding and turning horses out. Ellen went out in her robe and tall muck boots to bring her help up to date with all that was going on and thanking them for their extra efforts. She implied that they were all due for a bonus but had to realize she would need more help for a while.

Ellen went back in and sat at her office desk and dug through her purse to find the number for the hospital. She dialed up the hospital and once connected asked to be transferred to the ICU unit. The operator put her through right away but then she sat there listening to the phone ring over and over. She figured that the nurses must be doing morning duties and just couldn't get to the phone. Ellen waited about forty-five minutes and then called the hospital back. This time she got through and the nurse on the other end politely asked how she could help. "I'm calling to inquire how Steven Wilson is doing. I was in to see him two days ago." The nurse was silent as she was obviously looking up the information she had. The first words that she then spoke were, "He's gone." Ellen gasped loudly and the nurses instantly realized her choice of words had been taken wrong. "No. No I meant he was moved out of our department. He had stabilized enough to go to the neurology department and we needed the bed for a more critical patient. Mr. Wilson made a huge change overnight and they brought him out of the drug induced coma. Maybe your visit made a difference," the nurse said and then added, "He's strong and his good physical condition will make a difference but he has a ways to go and there will be some tough times yet. Although he is conscious now he's still dopey as he is still on a morphine drip and some oxycotin."

Ellen was pretty happy to hear the news but also realized that the nurse was still cautioning her to not expect him to get up and dance quite yet. Actually she was pleased at how much information the nurse had offered. Ellen guessed that maybe she was thinking that she was his sister after the false introduction she had left them with. At any rate, she was happy to have gotten all the information she had.

Ellen put on a pot of coffee and then went on the Internet to find information on Steven's stable. She was pretty sure that the stable was called, Steven Wilson's Training Center. It came up right away and she was able to get the address and the phone numbers she had hoped to get. She was ready to make a call to the stable when Mary walked in. "Good morning, sleepy" Ellen teased. "I can't believe I slept so long. I probably would still be sleeping if I hadn't smelled the coffee. But I'll admit that outfit of yours is enough to make me go back and sleep through such a scary dream," Mary offered with a laugh and a wink. Ellen realized that she was sitting in the kitchen with her robe, which now was   dirty from the outside, her tall muck boots and the hairdo from a rough night and a windy morning. Both of them laughed out loud as they realized the morning looks they were sporting.

Ellen then excused herself without having any of the coffee that was filling the room with a great 'good morning' aroma. In about twenty minutes Ellen returned to the kitchen where Mary sat enjoying a cup of coffee and a bagel. "I'm going to run to the bank. Is there anything I can get you?" Mary looked at her friend who was now standing there nicely turned out and so different from how she had looked when she had left the room. Ellen's dark, almost black, hair normally up in a ponytail or a twist, now flowed softly unto her shoulders. She was a very striking woman

An Event to Remember ~ 35

but most people always saw her in riding pants and a helmet. Mary complimented her look and added that she didn't need anything.

As she drove to the bank in town she tried calling the number for Steven's stable that she had copied down. Just as she reached the bank someone answered her call. The voice on the other end was hard to understand because of the soft-spoken Hispanic accent. She attempted to explain who she was but the voice on the other end stumbled along trying to understand what she was saying in her fast mode of talking. Then a new voice came on the phone. It was the voice of a younger man who spoke very clearly. He introduced himself as Jake, Steven's barn manager and apologized for Juan, a young worker, who had answered the phone originally.

Ellen explained who she was and the nature of her call. Jake told her he had not heard anything from Steven after he had finished the victory gallop. Steven had called him and gleefully reported how great Hawk had performed and told him he would be back soon. Ellen hesitated and then began to relate the story of the accident. She told him about Steven's condition and how there was some improvement but it would be some time before he would be ready for home. As she described the condition of the truck and trailer Jake broke his silence. "Oh my God, how is Hawk?" Ellen lied about the extent of the damages that she had witnessed and instead just said that Hawk's condition demanded that he be put down. Jake began to cry. "Mr. Steve and I broke that horse and he was to be a champion. We knew how great he would be." Jake now was sobbing on the phone. Ellen waited a moment and then told Jake she would be coming to see him on her way to see Steven. Both now feeling the emotions of the phone call, said good-bye and then ended the call.

Ellen withdrew two thousand dollars from her account and drove back to her farm. She met with Mary and let her know that she was going back to Lafayette and also to

Steven's training stable. She gave Mary a thousand dollars and let her know that in her absence she was to take care of the farm. "Oversee the help and give Trick some light workouts. Give our two barn helpers a bonus of $100 for taking extra care of things while we were gone. Use the money for groceries, and emergencies while I am gone. You all will still get your normal paychecks. Any cash left on my return will be yours," Ellen said with a smile.

Ellen then explained that she was going to pack some clothes and things and then planned on driving into Ohio yet today and then would go to St. Charles, Illinois to meet with Steven's people before she went on to Lafayette. She then told Mary of her conversation with Jake and how he had reacted to Hawk's death. "I didn't give him the gory details just the fact that he needed to be put down."

Ellen left and started her journey. Mary had no problem staying behind but she was puzzled as to why Ellen seemed to be so drawn to be involved in Steven's recovery. Whatever the reason she would stand by her as she was her best friend and had been there countless times for her. If it hadn't been for Ellen, Mary thought she might not have even been alive now. Ellen had taken her in when Mary needed help breaking bad habits and pulling her life back together. Because of Ellen she had a life and a purpose. Mary would do anything she could to help Ellen, whether she understood the reasons or not.

After an uneventful drive Ellen pulled into a small motel near Columbus, Ohio. It was just a small place off the main highway, just a place to sleep. By six o'clock the next morning Ellen was back on the road, now headed to Illinois to meet Jake and see Steven's place. She sang along with the radio even though the first hour or so the radio stations constantly changed as she passed through the rural areas of Ohio and Indiana. Once she could pick up the Chicagoland stations her station choices multiplied and offered more than just country. Using her GPS she was able to find Steven's place in the countryside of St. Charles. As she

An Event to Remember ~ 37

made the final approach to the driveway she slowed down to get the best look of the place before she turned in. Now as she drove up the drive she felt a chill, as she knew that Jake would want more detail about the accident, Steven and Hawk.

As she pulled up the driveway she was very impressed by the white vinyl fencing as it wound its way up toward the barn area. Along the drive were sections of well-kept landscape areas with a mix of shrubs and beautiful flowers. She felt as if she was entering a fancy show grounds or a maybe a national park or something. It was truly beautiful. Now as the barn came into full view she was even more impressed. The facade of the barn was done up in brick and stone while the rest of the long building was the traditional steel siding. The entire area around and in front of the barn was landscaped to perfection. It was as if the place was owned and run by a landscaper and not an international rider. Ellen was impressed, a lot, and couldn't help but wonder how such a place came to be.

Ellen would find out later that Steven's father had bankrolled the start of the complex but the unfortunate deaths of his parents and sister had since paid for some of both its beauty and expansion. Since their deaths he had added addition acres and all new white vinyl fencing. The outside arenas were upgraded and the entire area was all dressed in the best of landscaping. Steven had scheduled a very impressive lineup of clinics to be run by some of the most sought after international experts. His hope was to become the hub of the United States Event training. On the additional acres he now had people creating cross–country obstacles and bringing in young maturing trees of size and other landscaping to develop an almost instant outdoor complex that offered a full range of challenges.

Ellen was very impressed as she pulled into a parking space in front of the barn. As she started to get out of her truck a young man approached her from the barn. It was

38 ~ *Steve Farkos*

Jake and he had been expecting her and whatever news she could give him about his boss.

"Hi. I'm Ellen and I'll bet you are Jake." Jake nodded affirmatively and then spoke. "Welcome to the farm. I am pleased to meet you. I can give you a little tour. I will get you anything you might need to drink, eat or a place to rest. My wife and I have prepared a room for you tonight if you'd like to go there first. We most of all want to know more, as much as you know, about Mr. Steve, my friend." Jake spoke quickly with a Hispanic accent but in good control of the language. Ellen thought it was a good testimony of how Steven treated people seeing that Jake was so eager to show off the place where he worked and yet couldn't contain his concern about his boss.

Jake took Ellen into the stall area first. "I can't believe the size of these stalls. They're huge," Ellen said. Jake told her that each stall was twelve by sixteen. The foaling stall at the end was twenty by sixteen but to date it hadn't been used. Outside all of the south side stalls, six in all, there were Dutch doors and small individual run outs sixteen feet by forty feet. Ellen couldn't believe what she was seeing. These features were nicer than any she had ever seen. All the stalls were oak. The aisles were concrete with a brick patterned look and covered gutters along the fronts of the stalls so that the aisles could easily be washed down. Ellen just kept shaking her head in amazement as they moved along and Jake told her about the heating in the aisle floor for the winter.

"This is the viewing room but it's not finished yet. Mr. Steve is doing much of the work and is very fussy," Jake stated. Ellen thought that it was cute that he had called him Mr. Steve and wondered if he always addressed him that way. Across from the large looking unfinished viewing room was a state of the art grooming and wash rack that butted up to an impeccably set up tack room. Then Jake walked Ellen into the arena. He turned on the lights that showed off the beautiful chandelier-like fixtures that were throughout the large arena. The footing was the same stuff that the Kentucky Horse Park had installed for the World Equestrian Games. The sidewalls were beautifully stained wood on the lower half and conventional metal siding uppers interrupted on the entire short end and midway on the long sides by mirrors. It was like a dream Ellen thought as she slowly looked around to take it all in.

The barn tour was finished so Jake suggested they go up to the house so that she could get settled in. Jake then suggested they could sit and eat some dinner and learn more about each other. "Please don't go through any effort making dinner. I felt we could just go into town and grab something simple," Ellen suggested. Jake laughed a little and then explained that his wife, Sophie, was the housekeeper and cook. "She has been looking forward to meeting you and she has probably been cooking all day. Come in and I'll show you the room that she has ready for you."

As they entered the colonial style house Ellen was again blown away by its size and the furnishings that she saw. Every accent as they passed through the foyer was perfect and a great statement of the decorator's taste. "Who did the decorating in the house?" she asked as she peered around the corner to take in another room and its furnishings. "Mr. Steve and my wife Sophie have done it together," Jake proudly answered her. Ellen was very impressed and smiled a little as she thought Steven could have probably been a hell of a designer and decorator. 'Wow!' she thought. Maybe Steven was gay, something not uncommon for some high-level riders it seemed. But it wasn't his sexuality that had brought her this far to help. It was his persona and what he had accomplished.

They approached the kitchen area where Jake planned to introduce his wife Sophie to Ellen an alluring aroma was filling the air. "It smells absolutely wonderful. What are we having for dinner? Suddenly I'm feeling very hungry," Ellen said smiling and realizing that she hadn't eaten anything since before she left that morning.

As Jake began to introduce the two, Sophie turned around to offer Ellen her hand after she wiped it on the apron she wore. They shook hands and Ellen looked carefully at her. Sophie seemed like a perfectly matched partner for Jake. She was hard working, absolutely adorable looking and it was obvious in a minute that they were very happy as a couple. Jake leaned over and gave her a kiss and a playful pat on her backside right after he had introduced her.

Ellen decided to go to the room they had showed her for the night in order to try and clean up a little. Sophie appeared a second later to bring her some extra towels that she had meant to put into her washroom earlier. Ellen felt like a queen and wasn't sure that she even deserved all the attention. She graciously thanked Sophie for all she was doing and took time to compliment her on her great taste in decorating. "I'm so impressed by the decorating that has been done. The entire place inside and out is gorgeous," Ellen said with a true appreciation in her voice. Sophie was thankful and let her know that she would have dinner on the table in a very short time.

The three sat down to the feast that had been prepared. There was a salad with fruit and nuts included premixed with a homemade dressing that was out of this world. Dinner consisted of roast beef, sea bass, with side dishes of potatoes, mushrooms, onions and peppers all grilled and seasoned to perfection. Then to top it all off was a wide selection of homemade sweets arranged in the middle of the table as if set up for a banquet. Jake asked Ellen for her choice of either a Merlot or Pinot Noir wine for dinner. Ellen was fast to choose the Pinot Noir since she was focused on the delicious looking sea bass.

Sophie passed the dishes about the table until they all had filled their plates. As the serving plates settled Jake offered a toast. "To our newest friend and someone who has helped Mr. Steve in his time of need. Also to the health and speedy return of Mr. Steve. We pray that he will be

An Event to Remember ~ 41

home again soon." As they all began to eat Jake couldn't wait any longer. He needed to know more about the accident, Steven's condition and the details of Hawk's death.

Ellen had hardly even tasted her first bite of the epicurean delight that now sat before her but realized that Jake and Sophie needed to hear what she knew of the accident, Mr. Steve and Hawk.

Ellen first explained how they had had passing conversations as competitors at the Rolex. How she and Patrick had watched with their grooms and friends as Steven completed his stadium round and secured a spot in the ribbons. She smiled as she told them Steven had tipped his hat as he passed the crowds in the victory gallop and she and others were certain they saw tears of joy in his expression.

"We had all left the Rolex grounds at different times," she told them but her group and Patrick's group decided to stop at a small bar and grill for dinner. While they ate some locals had come in who had been at the Rolex as spectators. Talking about the exciting weekend allowed time to slip away and we suddenly realized we had been there much longer than we planned. As we contemplated actually leaving the front door opened and in walked Steven. He said he had pulled off the highway to get some food and pulled in at this spot when he saw our two horse trailers.

"Steven left the bar before us and pulled out of the parking lot ahead of Patrick and myself. We didn't even see him get on the highway as Patrick and I got caught by a couple of traffic lights before getting on the highway."

"Take and eat some of your food before it is all too cold," Sophie instructed. Ellen took a few bites and then continued telling them the story. "As we caught up to Steven on the highway I text him to let him know we were not far behind him. It was then that we saw headlights coming across the grassy median and then hitting Steven's truck and trailer." Sophie gasped out loud and then made the sign of the cross on herself and then seemed to slip into a silent prayer. Jake just had a look of shock on his face as he asked, "Was the car going very fast did you think?" Ellen looked at him almost reluctant to answer his question. "It wasn't a car it was a semi-truck and trailer." Sophie now cried aloud and Jake buried his face in his hands as he mumbled words in Spanish.

Ellen gave them a minute and took a big swallow of the wine she had been hugging as she was recalling and telling them of the accident. She explained that the truck driver was pronounced dead shortly after the accident had happened. "Myself, Patrick's mother and my groom, Mary, rushed to Steven's truck since we were the first on the scene. Steven was pinned into the driver seat and had suffered several broken bones and was bleeding as we got to him. Patrick and others checked on the semi driver and began to check on the horse trailer that flipped over and taken a part of the truck bed with it. Steven was conscious at first but was bleeding from his head a lot. Once the firemen and paramedics arrived they made us move so they could stabilize Steven and cut away his door to free him." Jake and Sophie couldn't believe their ears. Then Jake asked about the horse trailer and Hawk.

Ellen took another bite of her food and another gulp of her wine and started again. "We went back to help unload the horses. We knew one was standing but didn't know what the status of either of them was." Jake interrupted, "You say two horses? Mr. Steve had only taken Hawk with him. Whose was the other horse?" he asked. Ellen then had to explain that Steven had bought a mare that he was bringing back here. Jake was surprised to hear that. He was even more surprised to hear that the mare was the horse that survived the crash and was being stabled near the accident area to be checked over and relaxed. Then Ellen added, with as little detail as possible, how she found Hawk and that he didn't make it. Both Jake and Sophie started to cry then causing tears to come to Ellen's eyes also. Sophie surprisingly was the next to speak. "Mr. Steve loved that horse. They were perfect for one another. He had raised him from a colt. They were like good partners." Jake just nodded affirmatively at each of her statements.

Sophie took Ellen's plate to the kitchen and warmed up her food. They gave her a few minutes to sample her food and then asked questions about the mare and Steven. Ellen told them she had seen Steven at the hospital and assured them he would have to be there a while and that she was going back now to check his condition and hopefully come up with a plan to help with his care. She then told them that she had paid for the mare to be boarded and vet checked. She would either eventually bring her to them or her place once they felt she was good to travel a long distance.

Jake and Sophie expressed their appreciation for all of her help and agreed that they would do whatever was needed. Ellen had explained her lie about being his sister and told them once the hospital was accepting more visitors for him she could let them know so they could see him. Sophie came around the table and gave Ellen a big hug and thanked her. Jake began to clear the table and Sophie asked if she could warm Ellen's dinner again. Ellen declined on the second warm up but then asked for a large piece of the cake from the middle of the table and raised her empty wine glass to get a refill.

Ellen sat tired at the table slowly eating her cake and sipping her wine. Jake and Sophie worked together to clean the kitchen and the table. With the two of them the task went quickly. Jake then excused himself saying that he had to bring in the horses for the night and check their water. "Can I come with you?" Ellen asked. "I never even looked at the other horse when we toured the barn." Jake explained that the four were out back in the far paddock and she probably didn't know they were out there. Two others, mares, were in the individual runs outside their stalls. "Those two will be in and we only need shut the outside doors."

Ellen went out with Jake and they made fast work of bringing in the horses. They were well behaved and each of them walked two in at a time. As she put them into their respective stalls she could see that like everything else here they were quality. Jake pointed to each of them and then gave them a name, breed, age and the training they were in. All but one mare, the one with the three white socks, and the black gelding belonged to Steven.

Once the horses were bedded for the night Jake and Ellen returned to the house. The events and driving of the past few days were now taking a toll on Ellen. Sophie could see that she was fading quickly. "Ellen you should go to sleep. We can talk over breakfast in the morning again. Did you have time in mind that you hoped to leave?" Ellen thought about ten o'clock would allow her time to see the mare before she went back to the hospital.

Minutes after she had changed and her head fell to the pillow she was sound asleep.

Although she slept well she woke earlier than normal to sounds in the main part of the house. It was only 5:45 a. m. but she was used to sleeping until about 6:30. She got up and showered and repacked her stuff. By the time she came out the kitchen she was wide awake and couldn't wait for a cup of the coffee she smelled. Sophie greeted her and then put a plate of freshly baked blueberry muffins in front of her. Ellen felt like royalty being waited on like this. "What else would you like for breakfast?" Sophie asked. "This will be plenty for me," Ellen replied.

Jake had finished the morning chores including cleaning stalls already. He sat down and Sophie brought him a breakfast fit for a king. As they talked she watched Jake eat and couldn't believe he could consume so much food with the small frame he had.

It was time to leave and Jake carried her bag out to her truck. They all exchanged hugs as if they were close relatives and then Jake and Sophie waved as she drove off down the driveway. Ellen honked and waved out the window as she turned onto the main road.

Ellen figured the trip to be about a three hour drive if traffic was light enough. She planned to use the time to figure out just what she would say if she could talk to Steven this time. She wondered if he knew anything about Hawk and the mare yet. How much if anything did he remember about any of it? She assumed she would get all those answers soon even if she needed to stay for a few days. She drove on and replayed in her mind again the accident she had witnessed. Steven was lucky to be alive but could he make a comeback, or would his injuries and memories forever hold him back?

Chapter 5

THE DRIVE WENT easily for the time of day and allowed her to miss any real rush hour traffic. Her friend, the radio, kept her mind from focusing on her upcoming encounter. The weather was great and that made the drive even less of a drudgery. As Ellen approached Lafayette she was tempted to continue directly to the hospital in Indy but she knew she needed to stop and check on the mare. Her plan was to probably stay nearer to Indy so she might visit Steven and his doctors as needed.

As Ellen pulled into the stable where they had left Stella she noticed that the vet's truck was there. She hoped that she was by chance coming at a time when the vet was just checking on her and not for any real problems. Ellen got out of the truck and walked to the barn. She walked down the aisle but noticed that Stella wasn't in the same stall they had last seen her. She walked into the arena where she now saw the vet observing as one of the Mexicans lunged Stella.

The vet turned and greeted Ellen. "She looks good. She is actually a very nice mover. She certainly moves like a bigger horse. She's very light and elegant once she gets going. She's a real fooler." The vet seemed excited to give Ellen his lunging evaluation of the mare. Ellen was impressed as she watched and then asked the vet if he had seen anything at all since he had checked her the other day. The vet told her he was amazed that she came through the whole trauma with just a few scratches. "It amazes me that the big one never had a chance and this little girl walked out of the whole thing." The vet said as he packed up his stuff and got ready to depart. The Mexican took the mare back to the aisle and tossed a cooler on her. Ellen stopped and thanked the young man and decided that she knew enough about the mare's condition and so she departed for Indy.

She was now on the final leg of her journey and all her thoughts focused on Steven and the questions she was sure she would have to answer. Honestly she had no idea what to expect. She wasn't even sure how alert he would be or what he might remember. Fact was she wasn't even sure if he would know who she was. Ellen just knew one thing. She felt she had to be there for him to help in any way she could and yet she couldn't even say what made her feel that way. The time went by quickly as she debated with herself about what she was doing.

Before she knew it she was at the exit for the hospital and just a few minutes from the parking lot. Her mind now questioned as to how or why she was in this situation. She had put her life aside and traveled hundreds of miles to check on and help someone she barely knew. After all, her first real conversations with Steven was just days ago in a chance gathering with other friends. She remembered watching him as he spoke to all those who asked him about his successful weekend. She felt she actually enjoyed watching him talk and the reactions of those around him. He appeared in command but in no way controlling. He didn't brag about any of his accomplishments as so many do. He was a quiet but very conversational.

Ellen walked toward the hospital entrance and took a deep breath. She so wanted to do this but was she being too invasive after just meeting this person. How would he take her presence or would he ever even acknowledge her efforts? Then she asked herself if any of her self-inflicted queries were even valid or was she was really doing this out of the goodness of her heart. She thought back to the accident and how Mary and Sue looked at her as she committed herself to becoming a part of this man's hopeful recovery. Possibly they both wondered who had appointed her 'Florence Nightingale' and assigned her this particular case.

As she walked up to the receptionist desk her mind flashed back to her previous visit that now felt like months ago instead of a couple of days. There were new faces behind the desk. She asked the younger woman behind the desk for a visitors pass to see Steven Wilson. She walked away for a moment and returned with a pass and stated, "You must be his sister that was here the other day." Ellen was surprised by the connection the young woman had just assumed. The receptionist seeing the puzzled look on Ellen's face said, "You've been the only visitor and because of ICU we keep that information."

Ellen just smiled and took another breath. "You know your way?" the receptionist asked and Ellen without thinking just nodded.

As Ellen walked toward the elevator to go to the fourth floor her mind drifted and was blank now. Her motor skills seemed to be in charge now as she pressed the elevator buttons and exited on the fourth floor without a conscious thought. She had arrived at ICU without thinking about her steps. A nurse greeted her at the entrance of the ICU department and asked in her pleasant voice, "Can I help you?" Ellen held her hand out with the ICU visitor pass in it and explained she was here for Steven Wilson. The nurse looked at her and said, "He was moved to the Neurology department on the third floor." Ellen took a deep breath and recalled being told of his move when she called. She thanked the nurse for the information and felt foolish for being in the wrong place. They both smiled as the nurse gave her instructions to get to the neurology department.

Ellen was much more alert as she took the elevator down to the third floor. After she exited she went to the nursing station to find out Steven's room number. The nurse at the

An Event to Remember ~ 49

desk gave her the room number and pointed down the hall to where she would find it. Ellen just thanked her and started down the hall to Steven's room.

Ellen entered Steven's room not knowing what to expect. She walked into the private room and saw a completely different Steven than she had seen days earlier. He appeared to be asleep as she came closer to the bed. His head dressing had been greatly reduced in size but still covered his forehead but now exposed his entire nose and eyes. She saw now that his eye on his left side was a bit swollen but also very black and blue. His leg was elevated with all the rods showing, his left arm in a newer looking cast and he still wore his oxygen tube. He was on an IV and had two monitors attached but a tray alongside his bed indicated that he was now capable of eating or at least drinking. She stared at his pitiful looking condition as he lay there. She began to move closer to the bed while the image of him in the victory gallop came to mind. Just looking at him she firmly believed that his full recovery was imminent and that he would experience the feeling of success again.

She reached forward and touched his right arm as if to say, I'm here for you. He pulled his arm away as she touched it causing her to jump back. It was as if she had no expectations to be shown signs of life in that way. The arm was just a reflex action she told herself but now she was even more taken back. "Are you another new nurse or another tech who has come to poke at me?" Steven asked. Before Ellen could even comeback with a response Steven spoke. "You don't look like any of the ones that I've noticed before." His voice was so soft and his speech was broken a bit as he tried to get his thoughts out. "I'm not a regular that you have seen. I don't even work here. I came to visit and see how you're doing. Do you remember me from the Event or from the bar where we met and talked after the Rolex?" Ellen asked. She didn't get any answers as Steven now appeared to be asleep and not with her any more.

Ellen was at first a bit puzzled that suddenly she had lost him during this brief conversation. One of his nurses was coming in to check his vitals and to give him some additional medication via his IV drip. The nurse asked Ellen if she had been here very long. "You're his sister I understand," said the nurse in a very pleasant way. Ellen hesitated a minute and then just answered with a simple, "Yes." "Are you from town or nearby or did you come in from out of town?" The nurse continued trying to make pleasant small talk. Ellen then told her that she had come back in from New York where she lives. The nurse looked at her with a puzzled look. "You said that you came back from N.Y., were you here earlier? I haven't seen you here before today." The nurse asked.

She felt a little like she was being drilled by the nurse for information but couldn't see any reason for it. Then things started to fall into place as the nurse finished her duties with him. "I just think he's so very hot." The young nurse exclaimed. This nurse obviously had a thing for him even in his present condition. Ellen was surprised at the nurse's comment but then thought she had spoken so openly because she thought Ellen was Steven's sister. Ellen herself thought that he was a great looking guy but hadn't really thought of Steven in a romantic way. Or had she. Was it her admiration for his riding and accomplishments that had brought her back here, or were there some feelings inside that she hadn't given recognition to? Ellen quickly convinced herself that it was purely her compassion as a fellow rider that had driven her to jump in and help take care of matters. After all she had plenty of her own things to be concerned with and her intentions were to help him until he was at least more mobile. Then she would return to her life and business while having gained a great friend and helped a fellow competitor.

The nurse had left the room and Steven still seemed out of it in a coma-like sleep. Ellen decided to go back to town for something to eat and to check into a hotel nearby. She checked in and before very long she had fallen asleep on the bed. When she woke it was already past seven o'clock. She unpacked her stuff and went for a good soak in the tub. She lay in the tub and reflected on all that she had witnessed and experienced during the past week or so. A lot of it all seemed impossible and again she began to question herself as to why she felt the need to be so involved.

Ellen went out for a fast food dinner and then came back to the room and watched some mindless TV. She was amazed at how sleepy she felt again and went back to bed by ten o'clock.

It was 6:00 a.m. when the alarm went off and the radio then came on with some country music. She just lay there a few minutes curled up in the covers and listened to the tunes. She finally crawled out of the bed and slid into some jeans and her muck boots. She had decided to go and check on Stella and then she could clean up and go see Steven and hopefully spend a good day with him.

The drive to the barn seemed easier as she was more familiar with where she was going. The horses were just being fed as she arrived. Ellen spoke to the barn help and asked the normal questions. "How long has the barn been here? Have you worked very long? Do most of the horses belong to the barn owner or others? Do many of the horses compete?" The lone Hispanic young man wasn't very good yet in English and he must have felt bombarded by her string of rapid-fire questions. José tried to give her the answers she was looking for but was rescued by the fact that Stella had finished her breakfast. Without giving any more attention to Juan's attempted answers, Ellen simply moved on to be with Stella.

Ellen pulled Stella from her stall and put her on cross ties in the aisle. She then walked to the front of her and offered her palm for the mare to smell. After a few sniffs the mare gave Ellen's hand a couple of good licks and then looked into Ellen's eyes. Ellen then leaned forward and gave Stella a kiss on her muzzle. Stella looked at her with a bright

52 ~ *Steve Farkos*

eye that seemed to have a twinkle in it. Did the mare actually remember me pulling her out of that trailer she wondered? "I know girl. Trust me I don't think I will ever forget you either," Ellen told the mare.

Ellen brushed Stella up and checked her all over. She picked her hoofs and noticed a small amount of possible thrush in her one foot and took a moment to treat it. Looking at her hooves she felt she might be due for a trim soon also. She then walked Stella out and put her into the large grass paddock up front. Ellen found José and spoke slowly enough with plenty of hand motions to convey her message to him. Bring the mare in about 2 o'clock she said while pointing to the mare and then her stall. She motioned again from the paddock to Stella's stall with a sweeping motion and then pointed to the clock on the wall specifying 2 o'clock. Once she felt certain that José had understood she got back into her truck and started off.

Ellen went back to the hotel for a quick shower. The maid had already cleaned up and Ellen felt a little bad as she kicked her barn shoes off and left some barnyard dirt and shavings about as she took her socks off. She tossed her barn clothes in a heap and jumped in the shower. She enjoyed the hot water and the pressure that the hotel shower offered so she decided to wash her hair and played with the shampoo as she did. She was in a really good mood today and for no identifiable reason. She was still singing as she stepped from the shower and wrapped a towel about her head and another around herself. She then spent time going through the clothes she had brought to find the ones right for the day.

It struck her as funny that she had brought some clothes that she hadn't worn for some time and a few she hadn't ever worn yet. The selection was obviously not from the normal everyday barn wear. She decided on a pair of Khaki pants and a soft green button front sweater that she had only worn once before. Then she put on a fine chain-type silver necklace. As she looked at the necklace she realized she was doing something that people back at her barn would classify as highly unusual. She smiled as she looked at herself in the mirror and thought to herself that she was looking pretty good. She now realized that her hair was still quite damp and she worked it with the towel some more. She finally figured she should just put into a ponytail, as it wasn't going to dry without a hair dryer, the hotel's being broken and hers left at home. She took one last look in the mirror and smiled but also felt that the ponytail had hurt the sophisticated look she had hoped for. The reality was just as it appeared, a woman who spent all her life caring for and riding horses trying to look a little nicer in these clothes and jewelry.

Ellen walked into the hospital and this time left the reception desk with the correct information on her pass. She walked briskly to the elevator and wondered on her trip to the third floor what changes Steven had made since yesterday. As she walked in she saw Steven in the bed with the back slightly elevated. As simple as it seemed it gave her the impression that there was improvement. He was still wrapped as he had been yesterday. His leg was elevated in a pulley and his eyes were closed in sleep as she reached the bed. Once at his bedside she looked at him with a great admiration. He was a handsome looking man even with the evident bruises and swelling. His lower lip was that type that was just a bit bigger kind of a pouting look yet placed over a strong looking jaw.

Then Steven woke and slowly opened his eyes. With his free right arm and hand he gently removed the sleep that remained in his eyes. "Hi. It's you," he said with a slight smile. "You were the one that was here yesterday that I thought was a new doctor or nurse. You said you weren't, though, right?" Ellen just nodded her answer. She was quite excited that he spoke so much more clearly than yesterday. "It's nice to hear you so much better today. I 'm really happy that you recalled our meeting yesterday since I wasn't sure you would," she said. Steven smiled and then said, "I actually don't remember much but I do remember you."

Then she heard footsteps behind her. It was the younger nurse from yesterday who showed some excitement about her patient here. "Good day Mr. Wilson, it's nice to see you a bit upright." Ellen felt that the nurse acted as if she wasn't even in the room. The nurse kept talking to him as Ellen stood by the bedside.

Steven then asked, "What was your name? I'm sure you told me yesterday but honestly I just can't remember what it was."

Before Ellen could speak the young nurse answered his question. "Oh. My name is Elizabeth but everyone calls me Beth," the young nurse stated with a grin.

Then Steven in an apologetic tone said, "Sorry, I meant the other young lady."

"I'm Ellen," she replied but then the nurse turned and asked in a sharp tongue, "Excuse me but I thought you said you were his sister." Steven gave Ellen a puzzled look and so Ellen then directed her response to him. "I knew from our previous meeting that you had no family. I saw the accident and helped there as much as possible. I decided that night I would do what I could to be here for you. Hell I've been back and forth from my barn in upper New York state since you've been here. I lied that first night you were here so I could check on you 'cause I didn't know who else might." Ellen was convinced she had acted in a most caring manner but was embarrassed that the young nurse knew her claim to be Steven's sister was false. The young nurse left a bit disgusted and feeling that she probably had competition for Steven's attention.

Steven now asked that Ellen again explain how she knew him. He wanted to know if anyone else had been hurt. He also now asked her about his horses. "Are my horses ok? I was hauling two when the accident happened. Do you know where they are? Now I remember. You were in that Bar and Grill I had stopped at." He wasn't giving Ellen a chance to answer any of his questions, which right now was fine with her. "You rode at the Rolex, right? And you had your friend or boyfriend there who had also rode. You all had a lot of people with you." Ellen skirted the real issues for the moment by answering his last queries. "Patrick was the other rider you met. All of our friends and grooms were with us. We had been there a while and you joined us by chance. And for the record, Patrick isn't my boyfriend. I came to help you out however I can, as an admiring rider who was a witness to your horrible accident. The truck driver that came across the median that night and hit you they said died before the actual impact. I believe they said he had a heart attack."

Steven was silent now. It was obvious that he was reliving the moment and feeling the pain of that night. His heart felt heavy as he thought about the driver of the truck. Now he clenched his fist as readied himself for the impact as his mind was recalling the parts of the night he could remember. His fist now squeezed so hard that the clip he wore on his finger and the IV port on his hand both exploded away. That was enough to have the nurses running as it set off an alarm on the machines he was still attached to. The young nurse, Beth, was fast to ask Ellen to leave the room. Ellen did but didn't want to. She was happy, however, that she didn't get the opportunity to explain what had happened to the horses, especially Hawk.

It was a seemingly very short ride back to the hotel. As she drove she was just so happy to have not had to tell him about Hawk yet. After seeing his reaction to the memory of the accident she wasn't sure he was any more ready than she was to talk about it. As she entered her room she wasn't sure how or when she would approach the issue.

As she walked into the bathroom she caught sight of her hair in the mirror it was the most frizzed out ponytail she had ever seen. She laughed as she thought of what that young nurse had been thinking about the way she looked. She made a vow to herself that she wasn't ever going to let

56 ~ *Steve Farkos*

her guard down around Beth again. Beth definitely hoped to get closer with Steven. Ellen was certain that her own objectives were much purer than the young nurse's and didn't want her to have any chance after being ordered from Steven's room that afternoon.

That night she called home to Mary and gave her an update. Mary's first question, of course, was how Steven took the news about Hawk. Ellen then explained how he had reacted to remembering the accident and let Mary know that it was still an open issue. Ellen of course then also felt it necessary to give Mary her evaluation of the young nurse she had decided she just didn't like.

Mary reported that everything on the home front was quiet and good and then she asked about Stella's condition. "I actually have seen the vet and watched her run and play. We're all amazed that she was involved in the same accident that created so much damage and carnage. She seems to be a really nice horse with a great attitude."

After they talked Ellen went and secured another fine dining experience from the Wendy's just down the road. She brought her bag of food back to the room, kicked off her shoes and turned the TV on. As she flicked through the channels in search of something good to watch she was barely focused on what was there or even the taste of her food. Instead she thought about Steven and wondered if he would ever totally recover and again be the strong Eventer he had so far proven himself to be.

Ellen had finished her gourmet meal when the ten o'clock news came on. She listened waiting for the weather segment to come on. As she half listened to the local news she was suddenly brought to a very alert and focused state. The woman reporter was giving an update on the terrible accident that had occurred on I65 just over a week ago. She mentioned the driver of the pick-up truck and trailer was Steven Wilson who had just completed a successful showing at the Rolex down in Lexington. They said he was in stable condition but also mentioned he had lost at least one of his show horses. The reporter then went on to say that the coroner had finished his full exam and was certain the semi driver had died before the collision. The coroner suspected that he had died of a heart attack after falling asleep and waking as he bounced off the road out of control and seeing he was about to crash. The police added that the driver did have an alcohol level that was just enough to have helped him to dose off. The reporter didn't give the truck driver's name but said his family had been located and informed. She then mentioned no family was located for Mr. Wilson and they had sadly discovered the entire rest of his family had perished in an accident a few years ago. Ellen trembled as she feared Steven might be watching the same news program and would now be aware that at least one of his horses had died in the crash.

Ellen decided to call the hospital. She gave the room number to the operator and hoped that Steven might answer. The phone rang several times and then a nurse answered. "Hello." Ellen asked the nurse if she was with Steven. After the nurse said she was, Ellen asked if there was any way she might speak to him. "Oh sure." the nurse said. "He doesn't see many people and I'm sure he'll love the attention." With that the nurse handed the phone to his good right arm and told him there was a pretty sounding young woman on the other end wanting to talk with him. "Hi Steven, it's Ellen. I've come to see you the last few days but I had to leave kind of abruptly today."

"I remember." He said in his weaker voice. "I was sad that you had to leave." Ellen felt good when he said that and also realized that he didn't seem to remember what they had been talking about at the time. As their conversation continued she felt certain that he had not caught any of the news story. She was relieved at least for now. After they hung up she began to formulate just how she might begin to explain it all to him. She decided that she would tell him about the newscast but not the details the coroner had reported about the truck driver. She just didn't see a need for it now but understood it might prove important in the future. As she lay on her bed searching for the right words and phrases she would use she fell asleep.

It was about 2:00 in the morning when she awoke and realized that she was still in her street clothes. She got up and slid a nightgown on and brushed her teeth and rinsed her face and back to bed she went. It took only seconds for her to be fast asleep again. During the night she once again dreamt of the accident. Everything was so vivid. The dream kept returning to her visions of Hawk and the horrible state and position the collision had left him. She woke soaked in sweat and tears in her eyes. How was she ever going to tell Steven? A question she still had no answer for.

Chapter 6

THE HOTEL ALARM went off at 7:30. It had been the most hours she had dedicated to sleep but it certainly didn't feel like it. It seemed that she had one of the shortest nights of sleep since all this had taken place. She wasted no time getting up, as she wanted to make sure she looked just right today. The trip had used up a lot of the cash that she had brought and she felt she needed to go back home and make sure everything there was OK. She was no different than other stable owners. No matter how good your help was and how much you could trust them you always worried about your place and your animals.

Ellen went to the hospital and was ready for Beth the nurse to see her again. She had dressed special today. She wore a short skirt, new blouse, with her hair done just right and then some simple jewelry for accents. She knew it was going to be the last visit with Steven for a while and she wanted to leave an impression with the young nurse and, while she was at it, with Steven too.

The only thing that still was weighing on Ellen's mind was having to tell Steven about Hawk. She had tried, as she got ready to find the best way to bring it up. She was actually in a good mood other than that concern and it was a beautiful day. Besides looking really good today she wore a wonderful attention getting smile. As she walked into the hospital a few passers-by wished her a good day and smiled happily back to her.

As Ellen walked into Steven's room she was surprised by what she saw. It looked like a funeral parlor with all the flowers that were all over the room. Even as she started to wish him a good morning another two floral arrangements were on the way in the door. Steven was propped up in his bed and looked in amazement around the room as it filled up with flowers and balloons.

"Good morning. Is there something special going on today that I'm not aware of?" Ellen asked. Steven took his eyes off the latest delivery and looked at Ellen. "You look great. Maybe I'm the one that needs to find out what's going on. If I didn't know better, I would assume I was watching my own funeral preparations. I promise though that I'm actually feeling much better." Ellen thanked him for the compliment that he had snuck in his dissertation. She did think he was acting better and showing some humor. He still wore his IVs and oxygen but seemed to be sitting up better and much more alert.

"It's nice to see you again. Maybe you could read some of the cards for me so I know what this outpouring is about." He suggested. Ellen agreed and walked across the room and sat her purse down and went to the biggest flower arrangement. She picked up the card and quickly read it to herself. It was suddenly obvious that this sudden outpouring of good will had been brought on by last night's TV news. Ellen then read the first card out loud. "'Steven, even though we don't know you we are wishing you a speedy recovery.' It's signed 'Fellow Eventers at Westbrook Stables.'" She picked up another card. This card was from the Davidsons, who had also competed at the Rolex. Steven was now becoming more curious as to why this was all happening now. Ellen picked up another card and started to read it without the caution she had started with. "Steven we saw the TV news last night about your accident..." Steven interrupted her asked if Ellen knew what TV newscast had been on last night. Ellen paused for a minute and then said she had seen the broadcast. Steven seemed shocked.

Steven wanted to know what was said about the accident and wondered about the timing. Why would it be reported over a week after it might have been more timely news? Ellen felt that she was now in a corner and would have to tell Steven some of the newscast. "Steven, I think that there are several reasons why it made the news and touched some people. They talked about how it was freaky accident and mentioned the death of the semi driver. They told people that you had just completed a competition at the Kentucky Horse Park. Many know what the 'Event' was and see you as a sports hero." Steven still couldn't believe that information was enough to have so many people, who probably don't even know him, send so many well wishes. Ellen took a deep breath and then warned Steven that there was more he should know. Even though she didn't feel ready to expose the other information she started again. "Another thing that the news mentioned was that you were in the hospital after the devastating accident and that you had no family as far as anyone knew." Now Ellen began to cry which touched Steven yet he wasn't sure why. Ellen fought the tears but knew the impact of the information she still had to deliver. "Steven, I'm not sure how I can even say this to you." She cried more as she reached for his hand. Steven couldn't imagine what Ellen was so tortured by. He tried to settle her but encouraged her at the same time to let him know what was tearing her up now. Ellen looked at him and wiped her eyes with the sleeve of her blouse. "I am so sorry to have to tell you this. I've been putting it off till you were better. Hawk didn't survive the accident, only Stella did." Steven gasped and grabbed her hand so hard she thought he would surely break it. Then there was a flood of tears that silently ran down his face.

"Hawk's dead?" Ellen then tried to wipe his eyes as she told him that she was the first one to see him after the accident. "I helped to get your mare out and then went back in to try to get Hawk up and out. There was no way he would be going anywhere." With that statement she began to cry again.

They both became silent now. Both had swollen eyes from the tears they had expelled. As if they hadn't handled more than their share for the moment Beth, the nurse, came strolling in. It was her day off and she was just coming to visit Steven and to see if there was anything she could do for them. Ellen and Steven continued to face each other while they held hands and tried to absorb all the news and feelings. Beth bubbled over to them as if they were both just dying to see her. Beth was dressed to make an impression and Ellen now caught her with an eye.

Steven was really shaken by the news and continued breathing shallow and rapidly with his eyes kept shut. "Are the two of you OK?" Beth interrupted with. Ellen turned to here with a glare and asked, "Aren't you working today? Why are you dressed that way instead on in your scrubs?" Beth informed her, in a matter of fact attitude that she wasn't working and she just came in to see how Steven was doing.

Ellen just turned and in a not so friendly tone said, "This is not a good moment for you to be here right now. We are sharing some horrible news that you wouldn't understand. Please leave now and come back later. Please."

Beth was upset with being asked to leave but something told her she shouldn't fight it. She turned away and started toward the door, "I'll leave for now but I'll be back in a while." She was determined to get things her way because she had planned her day off to be spent with Steven.

As things started to settle Ellen apologized to Steven for not giving him the whole of what she knew right away. She explained that she wanted him to be stronger than that first day that she saw him. She also admitted that she didn't think that it would be any easier to deliver the news no matter how long she might have been able to wait.

"I understand how difficult this was for you. Can you tell me anything of what you saw when you found him? Do you know who took care of removing him?" Ellen looked at him and softly said that she couldn't and didn't want to describe anything more than she had about finding him. Steven was disappointed by her answer but let it go for the time being. "Can you tell me how the mare, Stella, is doing?" Ellen perked up because this was the first chance to get good news out today. Her voice now had life as she told him how she had helped to pull her out. We took her to a farm in Lafayette where we were stabling our horses overnight. She explained that Stella was still there. The vet has checked her over a couple of times and also adjusted her. "I paid for the whole month's board and asked the vet to occasionally check on her if he was in the neighborhood. I paid the vet for his visits and insured him that we were good for anything that she would require from him. The best is I watched her being lunged and she looks great."

Steven was happy to hear about the mare's condition and told Ellen he would pay her back as soon as he could get his hands on his stuff especially his wallet and checkbook. Ellen wasn't worried about the money now. Then she told Steven that the police probably had his wallet now and any other personal items from the truck she had left with Jake at the house.

"I will be leaving today to go back to my farm. I've been here about a week and I need to go and make sure my place is ok. I will stop to see the mare and I'll check with Jake and Sophie to be sure things are going well at your place. I'll assure them that you are doing better now and give them a number to call you. We can talk then about me getting Stella to them soon also." Steven was surprised at her organization and extra effort to get things done and taken care of. Steven tried to let her know he was thankful for all she was doing for him, Stella and his place.

"I'm sorry that you have to leave. Actually I think I'll miss you being around. Do you know when you'll be coming back?" Ellen wasn't sure how soon she would be back. She wanted to talk with the doctors and get a possible time line for his recovery. Reality was she wished she didn't have to leave at all. Ellen excused herself after she squeezed his hand and told him how happy she was that he had made it through the accident.

64 ~ *Steve Farkos*

Ellen stopped at the nursing station to inquire how she could get a hold of Steven's doctor. The nurses were nice enough to check if he was in the hospital. Once they discovered that he wasn't, a nurse gave Ellen the two numbers that could most likely get them connected. As she left the nursing station and headed to the elevator she saw Beth getting off the elevator and heading toward her.

Ellen felt annoyed but was prepared to not say anything. "Are you leaving now?" Beth asked. Ellen just replied, "For now." She hoped that Beth might wonder when she would be back next.

Ellen drove back to the stable where Stella was being housed. She had every intention of changing before she went there but time was escaping all too fast. As Ellen got out of her truck the two Hispanic grooms that were working stopped what they were doing and one whistled loudly. Then the two chatted in a low tone and chuckled about what they were saying. At that moment the barn owner came around the corner on a horse he was working and reprimanded the two in Spanish. The two quickly disappeared and found their way back to the jobs they were assigned to. The manager then rode up to where Ellen stood near her truck. "Sorry about that. You do look mighty nice and I'm sure their eyes don't get to see someone looking this good very often." The manager said as an apology and compliment at the same time.

Ellen let him know that she had come to see the mare before she left. She explained the vet would be checking on the mare whenever she could. Then she told him that she would be traveling back to New York but she hoped she would be returning in a week or so. After seeing the mare she said good-bye to the manager and returned to her truck. As she pulled out she devilishly waved to the two grooms and then laughed to herself as she drove off.

Once she had packed her suitcase and gathered up her barn stuff she was off. She planned to stop over night at Steven's farm and to update Jake and Sophie on Steven's condition. She wanted to make sure they could take the mare in as soon as she could make arrangements to get her there.

As she pulled into Steven's place Sophie recognized the truck and immediately came out to greet her. Jake was finishing up chores and joined them as soon as he was done. Ellen was hungry and realized that Sophie hadn't started anything yet. "I have an idea," she said. "I'd like to take you out to dinner." At first Sophie was excited but then became concerned as she stood there playing with the apron she had just put on. "I'll need to change and clean up. Look how nice you are today." Jake then echoed her thoughts but he really liked the idea about going out especially since Ellen had offered to take them.

"Come on honey we can get changed quickly and I can give Ellen some wine or beer while she waits." Ellen agreed and said she would love a glass of wine. Sophie disappeared immediately and Jake was right behind her after he had gotten Ellen a glass of wine. Ellen sat down in a large over stuffed and beat looking older chair. It wasn't pretty but it was really comfortable and the wine really made her feel relaxed and content for the moment.

Jake was the first to reappear and poured himself a small glass of wine and asked if he could bring more for Ellen. Because of her early morning and her stressful visit with Steven she thought it was better not to consume anymore without some food. Sophie then entered the room. She was truly a beautiful woman. In less than twenty minutes she had reached a look that had taken Ellen at least an hour and a half to obtain this morning

"Sophie you look absolutely beautiful. I love your dark hair and the way you put it up.

I feel like maybe I should have freshened up more now," Ellen said smiling.

They went out for a nice dinner and Ellen brought the couple up to date on Steven and the mare. Ellen had a tear come to her eye as she told them how Steven had taken the news about Hawk. Jake actually showed emotion as she told him about Steven's reaction. They all enjoyed a good meal and conversation and then they headed back to the house.

Sophie asked if Ellen might stay another day. "I really can't. I need to get back home and that's a long ways from here. I want to make sure everything is good there and then I'll be coming back. I'll bring my trailer so I can haul her back here or to my place after Steven and I talk more about it. On my way I hope to talk with Steven's doctor to see what all they might have planned. Maybe you can get to the hospital to see him while I'm gone." Sophie agreed that they needed to find the time to get out to see him while she was gone.

Ellen woke the next morning and headed back toward home. She planned on stopping overnight somewhere near the eastern border of Ohio. She knew that it would be less than half way but she felt it would allow her a peaceful night's sleep before the final leg of the journey.

On the way Ellen tried several times to reach Steven's doctor on her cell phone.

It was the fourth attempt that finally paid off. The doctor had that professional tone in his voice, the one that's supposed to put you off if at all possible. Ellen wanted information and wasn't going to let him go until she knew all answers she was after. "Good morning, Doctor Kindle, to you also. I need some information regarding one of your patients, Steven Wilson." The doctor broke in immediately and wondered her connection to the patient. There were restrictions that prevented giving out information to people that weren't family or other professionals involved in the case. "I'm his sister and I will be watching over his physical therapy once he is released," Ellen answered quickly, hoping that it sounded as natural as it did when she used it to get into the ICU unit. Once again it worked and the doctor asked what information she needed.

"My biggest need at this point would be to have some type of idea as to when he might be released. I guess, more

An Event to Remember ~ 67

importantly what will be his condition when you do release him? I will have to come back from New York to bring him home and he will have to travel to get back to his place. Will there be medical support that I will need to arrange for him?" Ellen asked in her rapid-fire way of speaking.

The doctor told her that he would probably be kept in the hospital for another week at least. "We can probably pull a few of the stabilizing pins out from his leg depending on the next set of x-rays. He will probably have to keep a few in for a couple weeks and then he will need to go to a hospital here or where you will have him to get them removed. He will be off the oxygen yet this week. His ribs will be very sore for another month but the damage to his lung was minor and his ribs will take time but there's really nothing we can do to help. The last scan we did on his head showed that the swelling was beginning to subside. We will watch that carefully to be sure it has before he would be released. His arm will be another month and then it will just be therapy to regain his strength. Guess what I'm thinking at the moment is that it will be a week to ten days till we release him from the hospital. He will need to go into a hospital to have the leg pins removed. His arm cast will be ready to come off about the same time. His leg cast will need another month after that. I feel confident there will be little else to be aware of besides making sure he doesn't bang his head again for a bit. I think once you have him settled the best thing is to have the new doctor send us a fax and we can fax him all the medical records and any x-rays via email." The doctor then excused himself for an emergency and hung up.

At the hotel that evening Ellen sat down and set up a paper with the pros and cons to keeping Steven at his home in St. Charles or her place in New York. After reviewing her pros and cons she still didn't have much of a solution. Neither had substantially stood out, in fact her arguments for New York were selfish mainly just to make it easier for her.

The one thing that bothered Ellen was that she knew a very good orthopedic near her home that several people she knew and herself had great success with. In Illinois she was sure there were many good ones but she was uneasy about picking someone she didn't know. Ellen wanted him to recover and be a strong eventer again, wishing only the best for him. She was also now realizing that she knew little about him or about doctors in his area that could help him.

Ellen started off the next morning and was able to make good time on the final leg of her trip. Mary heard her truck as she pulled into the farm. Ellen drove past the house toward the barn where Mary was. Ellen jumped out of the truck and enthusiastically embraced Mary and kept thanking her for all of her help. Ellen walked through the barn and looked in at each of the horses. "How's my big guy?" Trick never even turned to look at her. It was like he was mad that she had been gone or he wasn't happy working for Mary. Ellen was surprised at his lack of attention toward her. Mary then told her, "He's been a bit funny since we came back. He's been slow to eat and moody in his manners." Ellen didn't respond to what Mary had just told her. Instead she headed back toward the tack room and threw some treats in her pocket.

Once back at Trick's stall Ellen rustled the plastic wrappers on the mints she had put in her pocket. Trick's ears perked up and he swung his head around to view his owner.

"Oh. So now you know who's out here. Silly boy you'll have to work to get what I have in this pocket." Ellen slid the door bolt back on his stall and put a halter on the beautiful animal. She then took him by his halter and walked him into the indoor arena.

Once in the arena she sent him running with the crack of the whip she had picked up on their way in. Trick opened his stride up as if he was in a huge open area outdoors. It seemed like he was covering the length of the arena in a mere four strides. Ellen then yelled in a loud, firm tone,

An Event to Remember ~ 69

"Trick, Whoa!" Amazingly the big horse slid to a stop as if he was a western reining horse showing his stuff. "Good boy. Now walk here and I'll give you a treat." Ellen said as she motioned to herself. Trick obediently marched toward her and came to a stop facing her. He was perked in his ears and seemed almost to be smiling as Ellen gave him two of the mints she had and stroked his muzzle. Mary marveled and said she wouldn't have believed it if she hadn't seen it for herself. "He's like a different horse now. He's all happy to see his owner and rider, I think. He really did miss you."

Ellen played with him for a while longer having him do little tricks to earn the mints. As he jumped over the cavelleti that was in the middle Tricked looked at her as if he were awaiting her approval. After a few more tricks and now an absence of mints Ellen called the horse back to her hugged him and then walked him back to his stall.

Ellen was feeling a bit shaky about the debate she had been having in her truck while she was returning home this morning. Here was her competitive partner and friend and she hadn't even considered him when she made her pros and cons list. She asked herself now. Why was she so bent on being the caretaker for this man she knew so little about? Again she couldn't answer the question. Ellen and Mary then walked back to the house after removing Ellen's bags from the truck.

Ellen brought Mary up to date on Steven's condition and told her about his place. "Jake and Sophie live at the farm and are the nicest couple. Sophie does the entire housekeeping and Jake keeps the barn and the property spotless. I know you would love them both. I don't think they often go far from the farm." Ellen told her. Mary didn't say much and Ellen realized that she might not have been vocal enough about all Mary's effort while she was gone. "I wonder if Steven feels as confident about his place in their hands as I do about having you in charge here. I am really fortunate and blessed to have you." Suddenly a little smile came unto Mary's face and Ellen felt she had made a

70 ~ *Steve Farkos*

good save with her comment. Ellen smiled too, proud of herself.

Ellen took time that evening to get Mary's opinion about her further care for Steven and where she should do it. Mary was shocked. "We're at the beginning of your show season. Are you not showing this season?" Funny, it seemed that Ellen had never even thought about that aspect of things. "I don't even know. I hadn't even thought about that," Ellen said. Ellen got up from the table and didn't say anything more. Mary sat at the table a few minutes and tried to figure out what had come over Ellen. Little more was said that night and the two women went to bed. Ellen tossed about into the night once again trying to understand why she was so intent on being Steven's caretaker until he could compete again. Suddenly she asked herself, if he even wanted her involved. How much did she really know about him? Did he have a girlfriend? No one seemed to be looking for him but how was it that this good-looking gentleman didn't have anyone to look after him?

The next morning Ellen called the hospital and asked to be transferred to Steven's room. A woman answered the phone and it only took a few words for Ellen to realize that it was Beth who answered the phone. "Is Steven there?" she asked in an irritated voice. Beth paused for a minute and then said she would put him on.

"Good morning, Steven, I was wondering if you had a few minutes to talk. I'd like to find out if I can be some more help. I will tell you that I had another wonderful visit with Sophie and Jake and I told them how well you were doing. Then I also told them how good the mare was doing," Ellen said. Steven told her that of course he appreciated her help and wasn't sure how he could repay her for all that she had already done.

Ellen then told him about her conversation with the doctor and the schedules he had projected. "I would like to be there for you. We need to talk logistics but I think since we both are in the same field that I can offer some things and understanding that others couldn't." Steven was a little shocked by her generous offer. Beth, who was standing nearby, could tell there was something going on that she felt she should be involved in. "What? What?" Beth asked Steven. He didn't answer but asked Ellen to call back again after visiting hours so they could talk more.

Ellen hung up and sat there wondering if she had lost her opportunity to help this person she was so driven to aid. She was convinced because of their shared occupation and having competed together that she could offer more toward his recovery because of her understanding. Ellen never seemed to acknowledge any romantic feelings toward him but her desire to look nice when visiting Steven and her growing dislike of Beth told a different story.

Ellen knew that there was one way to clear her mind. She pulled on her riding breeches and grabbed a vest in case she needed it. She was half way out the door when Mary was coming in for breakfast. "You haven't put the coffee on yet? Let me guess you were on the phone with Steven." Mary smiled at her while Ellen ignored her and went out the door to the barn. "Do you want some help getting ready?" Mary yelled out the door to her.

Ellen didn't respond so Mary just went in and put a pot of coffee on. Ellen walked in and pulled Trick out of his stall. Mary hadn't turned the horses out yet because it looked like a bad storm was coming in. Ellen did just a fast brushing and picked Trick's feet. Before the coffee was probably done in the house Ellen had Trick saddled, bridled and walking into the arena behind her.

Ellen mounted and allowed her horse to stretch for a few laps around the arena. Trick was bit inattentive since he was still thinking about the hay he had not finished. As the horse became more tuned into Ellen she gathered up her reins and asked the big horse to trot. As she began to put him together in a more collected trot Mary walked into the arena to watch her. Ellen and Trick were now floating across the arena on the diagonal and they were doing a beautiful extended trot. "Looking good!" Mary yelled into the arena. Ellen was smiling now, as it was obvious that her mind was now on her ride and the pleasurable feeling partnership she had with her horse. Ellen was having fun and now started doing a series of flying changes as she rode around the perimeter of the indoor. For not having worked together for a good week plus they looked like they could go to a show and kick some butt.

Ellen brought Trick to a walk and allowed him to stretch forward. Mary couldn't say enough good things and Ellen had a huge smile on her face as she took in all of the compliments. "Do you want me to walk him out for you and take him back?" Mary offered. Ellen reached forward and gave the gelding a pat on his neck and then looked to Mary. "No thanks, for the moment anyway. Trick gets to do what he likes best now. I'm going to take him out and give him a little gallop and maybe even a cross-country fence or two." Ellen responded. Mary then asked if she should trade out saddles if she planned to jump. Ellen declined and figured that she would be all right in her dressage saddle for the little she was planning to do.

Mary opened the sliding door of the arena to let Ellen and Trick out. As she opened the door it showed the changing weather. The wind had picked up and was blowing small debris around the driveway area. The sky was becoming very dark and there was rumbling of thunder in the distance. "Are you sure you still want to go out?" Mary asked. Ellen assured her that she was only going out for a few minutes and she'd be back before Mary knew it. Mary had planned to go out and watch them do their thing but now wasn't sure. "Ellen I'll wait here and you can dash in if the storm hits sooner than you plan." With that said Mary pulled the door part-way shut and watched as the two went to the back acreage where the gallop path and cross-country fences were.

Ellen could feel the wind blowing against them now. Trick pushed bravely against the wind fearlessly because he knew where they were headed. As they neared the gallop path they picked up a trot to get to the path faster. As soon as they reached the path Ellen cued Trick to pick up a canter and in just a few strides the horse advanced into a gallop. Ellen made no attempt to pull him back but instead tried to get off his back in a two point even though she was still in her dressage length stirrups.

This was Trick's favorite thing. He was made to gallop. Ellen smiled as they cut through the wind and a light blowing rain that had started. Trick's gallop felt incredible As he stretched out his stride and lowered his back as he did so. As they reached the back of the property Ellen began to gather her reins up and asked Trick to shorten his stride. She then turned him into the center of the path of the property were there were many different cross-country obstacles. Trick's eyes brightened and his ears perked forward with excitement, as he knew he was going to jump. Ellen cued him and took one of the smaller fences at a controlled gait. Trick flew over the fence with no effort at all but Ellen now remembered she was not very fond of jumping in her longer dressage length stirrups.

The rain started to come down much heavier. Ellen decided to cut across the property in the straightest line possible to save time. Trick opened his stride up into a full gallop. The rain made it harder for Ellen to focus forward as the reins became and everything was accepting the rain as if it were a sponge. Ellen maintained her straight line and took another fence in her path. She was in sight of the barn and now gathered Trick back up a bit.

Suddenly there is a flash of lightening less than twenty feet in front of them. The light was blinding and the thunder shot off next to them. Trick twisted and buckled downward in a rolling motion. Ellen was launched and took a hard, wet landing but was thankful not to be on or under Trick as he took still another tumble. Ellen got herself up and started toward Trick. He was lying there motionless at the moment. Visions of Hawk came to mind and she cried as she ran to Trick. The ground was already saturated and slippery. "Trick! Trick! Come on fella we need you to get up." As Trick heard her voice he strained to turn enough to see Ellen coming. She now smacked the dressage whip against her boots and insisted that the horse get up. The horse had obviously been shocked by the fall but now gathered himself and got back up. "Good boy! Are you OK buddy?" she asked.

Another strike of lightening hit a cross-country fence up the hill behind them. Trick whinnied a good-bye to Ellen before taking off to the barn. As he ran for home Ellen was certain that he was slightly off in his gait.

Mary caught Trick and quickly put him on a set of cross ties and threw a cooler over him. Then Mary rushed out into the rain to find Ellen. She hadn't gone very far when she saw Ellen running back to the barn. "Are you Ok? Come on get in the barn." Mary said. In another minute Ellen arrived soaked through and through. As she stood there catching her breath, Mary brought a cooler, wrapping it around her. "How's Trick? He looked a little off as he ran back to the barn. Does it sound like the rain's let up?" Ellen asked. Mary took a fast look out the doorway and told her it was like a light mist now. Mary instructed Ellen to go up to the house and get some dry clothes and she would start taking care of Trick and checking him out. Ellen agreed and went to the house to get some dry clothes and to dry herself off.

Chapter 7

ELLEN QUICKLY DRIED off and returned to the barn where Mary was tending to Trick, who was still wet and steaming. "How's he looking? Have you seen anything that would have made him tender as he ran back?" Ellen inquired. Mary looked up from where she was squatting near his front leg. She had been drying the leg with a towel and cleaning it up. "Here. Look here, I'm pretty sure we have small splint. He's a bit sensitive to it but he's much more sensitive to the shoulder." She said as she pointed to the shoulder above that leg. Ellen came around to where Mary was and felt the bump on his leg. She ran her hand over the spot several times and then agreed that it was a live splint. As the dampness lessened it was now possible to feel a little heat on the leg. Ellen now stood up and probed the massive shoulder where Mary had experienced some reaction from the horse. Mary watched as Ellen kneaded the spot near his shoulder joint. Trick sucked his shoulder inward attempting to avoid pain he was feeling as Ellen pressed on the spot that was hurting.

Ellen and Mary finished drying Trick with towels after they took the wool cooler off of him. The towels were able to dry much more than what the cooler was capable of drawing away. Ellen then pulled out one of his lighter show sheets and put it on him while Mary went about mixing a poultice. As Ellen finished attaching the leg straps of the sheet Mary started to poultice and wrap the injured leg. Once she had completed that leg she wrapped the other

76 ~ *Steve Farkos*

front leg also since that was considered to be the best practice.

"We'll need to give him at least a week off with just some short walks. I'll give him Bute tonight, probably two grams, and again the same in the morning. After that maybe we'll just give him a gram a day for the next three days. I'm actually more worried about that shoulder. I'm hoping it's just a bruise and nothing more. I don't want him to be off work too long. We'll probably not jump for the next two months, but I like to try and keep him in condition with flat work." Ellen said hoping that they would still be ready to compete in the fall especially in Pennsylvania and Kentucky. The two women then went up to the house and sat with a glass of wine and ate nearly a whole loaf of the French bread Mary had bought the day before. The conversation was focused around the spill that Ellen and Trick had taken but even that was short lived. Ellen then announced that she was going to the shower to warm up and clean up. Mary sat for a while after Ellen left the room, wondering about some of the strange behavior Ellen was demonstrating? What is this driving Ellen so strongly to help Steven? It seemed to Mary that everything was being put on hold because of Ellen's new self-appointed responsibility.

After they had both showered and dried their hair they both had the same idea as they came to the kitchen at the same time. "Ah a sip of wine for you too I assume," Ellen said. They both sat down and talked and sipped their wine. Before they realized it they had finished the bottle of wine and hadn't gotten to any thoughts about Steven and what Ellen thought she might be doing. Ellen did tell Mary that she expected to be sore in the morning from the fall and stated how stupid she was galloping back to the barn especially with the ground conditions. "Live and learn." Ellen then wished Mary a good night and headed off to bed.

Morning came with a bright spring sunlight blasting through Ellen's bedroom window. Mary was in fixing breakfast and the smell of coffee and bacon could have made a bad man turn good. As they sat for breakfast Ellen thought it was a good time to bounce her latest ideas off Mary. Mary had hand walked Trick after she fed and reported that he was sore on that shoulder but she felt he was already better where they had found the splint. Ellen was happy to hear about his improvement but thought for safety sake they might call the vet out to see if there was something special they should do for the shoulder.

As they started their second cup of coffee Ellen started to be more specific about the plans she was putting together. "Mary, I thought about this most of the night so I feel pretty certain that this is what I want to do. I'm sick about what happened to Trick today. I'm also feeling somewhat obsessed with helping Steven however I can. I want to get everything back on track for him now. With Trick off, I'm planning on going back to help bring Stella, the mare, either to Steven's place or back here depending on what his plans for her are. I want to help get Steven home and get him settled and see how Jake and Sophie handle all of the extra needs that he will have." Mary then asked as Ellen took a breath "How long are you talking about being gone? Do we have any extra horses scheduled to come in for training and what do you expect me to do with the four that are in now?" It was like a volleyball match as they traded questions and answers back and forth. "Mary I am not trying to bury you. I will be here for the next week or so and then I plan on leaving. I will probably be gone for a few weeks then. What gets accomplished during that period of time will determine what the weeks after may call for." Mary again was going over issues in her mind that were being generated by Ellen's ideas. "Well I just want to say I will not work Darien without you here. You know he and I just don't get along and he's the only one in the past ten years who has hurt me. I just don't like him and I don't care how much potential the world thinks he has." Mary said firmly. Ellen agreed to the Darien thing but couldn't see any other issues that they needed to worry about.

78 ~ *Steve Farkos*

They sat in the kitchen for the next hour and went over details she had now thought of and notes she had made for when she would be gone. "We'll be done with that Childress gelding we have in now and we can have them pick him up. I will put extra time in on him since I won't be working with Trick I'm sure for at least another month. Other than that we don't have much to worry about in the training we owe for now." Mary asked what else she would have to be concerned about. "Without you here how do you want me to handle any training inquiries? Remember that's our main source of income for the barn this time of year. I can handle a portion of it but if people think you're not going to be here much they may shy away."

They discussed all the aspects for another hour and seemed to agree on all the plans they had now put in place. Mary was in some ways excited about the chance to run things and be responsible for the barn and its reputation. Ellen was happy to see her willingness to help her and felt certain that everything would be fine.

"Ellen, I have to ask you, though, why are you doing all this for someone you barely know?" Ellen paused for a moment and then stated her answer both to Mary and for herself. "I think that I feel that I must do this first because I was the first to see him at the accident and the one who discovered Hawk. I felt a connection with him when we sat and talked at the bar the night of the accident. I've silently followed his career the last few years and I guess I admire him for all that he has gone through to get where he's at. I'm not after him. I want to help him and know him as he recovers and again rises to the top. Knowing that he doesn't have any real family to help or support him is a factor for sure also. I just want to be there to see how he picks his new horse and see him make it back to the top of our sport again."

Mary listened and then said that she felt like she understood the whole thing a little better. Ellen felt for the first time that she had a better sense of what was driving her. Either way they had agreed on how they planned to handle things. Now the next step was to have Steven agree to and understand her desire to help.

That evening Ellen called to the hospital again to see how Steven was doing. Again she was irritated when Beth answered the phone. After a short exchange of meaningless greetings and other words Beth handed the phone to Steven. "Hi, Steven. How are you doing today? Have they changed any of your meds or taken you off the oxygen yet?" And then she threw in an unsuspected question as she said, "Is Beth your roommate now?" With that said Steven gave a little chuckle and then answered most of Ellen's questions. Once he had satisfied her health related questions he then said in a softer voice, "Regarding that other issue, I'm not sure to be honest. Seems like it. A bit strange, yet on the same hand kind of nice." Ellen was happy to hear that things were progressing and getting better but she wasn't exactly tickled with the idea of Beth always being there. As they talked she could tell in Steven's voice that he was doing better and seemed more comfortable since they had taken him off the oxygen.

Ellen small talked with Steven as she heard Beth getting pushy in the background trying to get Steven off the phone. Steven wanted to talk more with Ellen about the accident and horses but knew it wasn't working now. Steven looked at Beth and then said into the phone. "I'll give you a call later so I can catch up with you about the accident more." Steven figured that this would give Ellen the message that he wanted to talk more to her but without the extra ear over him. At the same time he thought that Beth should be getting the hint that he would want some quiet time later but he was giving her the moment now. He had begun to see an obsession growing in Beth. He didn't understand it but it was kind of a fun ego boost to have someone so enamored with you while you were all bandaged and laid up. On the other hand he saw Ellen as a new friend that was willing to help him recover, health wise and horse wise, without looking for anything in return.

Ellen hung up with a promise that she would call back in the afternoon. As she went about some of her chores she wondered if Steven thought she was an annoyance in any way. She thought maybe she was trying too hard to help and maybe like Beth was pushing herself in where she wasn't needed and didn't belong. Then she couldn't help but wonder why it bugged her so much that Beth was expending so much effort to be around him. She couldn't help but feel Beth was more than a little attracted to him. She just couldn't see Beth as someone that he would be involved with. Silly, she thought. I can even see myself with someone like him. He's was coming into his own and now will have to build himself back up to that point. He's become a star in our field and why would he ever even notice Beth or even me for that matter? He's got women both in and out of the sport chasing him. So why does it bother me so much about Beth? If I'm truly going to help him I'm sure I'll see a plethora of women trying to gain his attention. Can't let it bug me, just got to get used to it, I guess, or not be so intent on helping.

It was about four in the afternoon when she called Steven back. He was very tired it seemed and that made sense when she found out Beth had only left a short time ago. "Is this a good time for you? Ellen asked. "I really hoped to talk about ways that I might be able to help you get home, regroup and get back in the saddle. I thought that there might be something I could do to help you with that new mare you got. I just want to talk about it all and see if you even want my help."

Steven coughed and then spoke, "I really would like your help but I'm intrigued by why you want to do any of it. I have some farm help, nice people and hard workers, who you've met. I have no idea how long my recovery may take. I feel I want you to help since you were the face that I first saw after the semi hit and it kind of haunts me that you were also the first to see Hawk. If you want money I think you're barking up the wrong tree, is all I can say. I'm just really not sure why it means anything to you."

Ellen had listened to him but couldn't give a strong argument why. She explained that it was something she felt she had to do, almost like she was commanded to. Steven laughed in a polite manner and then said, "Well whoever has commanded you to, I'd like to thank him." Ellen then jumped in and said, "I think it's settled then. So let's get down to business and set a plan as to how, where and eventually why." Then she laughed. Steven then told her he liked her sense of humor and now looked forward to having her to help.

He agreed to the first part of the plan. Ellen would come back the day or two before the doctors planned his release. By that time she could have made adjustments at his farm that would make it easier for him to get around both the house and with luck the barn. She suggested some things that might make it easier for him to get around and he seemed to agree with her ideas.

Then her plan would be to move the mare from the barn where she was to his place. She felt that they could pick her up on the way back to his place. At first Steven showed a bit of nervousness at the thought they would be traveling with a trailer behind on his first road trip after the accident. Ellen sensed his concern and immediately tried to get him to think positive. She then told him that she and everyone who knew him expected that the first real step in his healing would be for him to have a solid positive attitude. She told him that every action and thought was to be positive if he wanted to make a comeback. Steven's smile could be seen over the phone as he teased Ellen about being a taskmaster. "At least you're better looking than those the movies always depict." Ellen was surprised by his comment but now smiled herself. She wondered if he meant his comment as a compliment too.

She reassured him again that they would travel just fine. The only question she had was how she could make him most comfortable on the ride. Maybe I could work the mare a little for you if you want. Steven didn't seem too worried about that as he informed her his intentions were to just get her going enough for sale. Ellen didn't offer any more thoughts about the mare after he said that.

Steven seemed tired as they talked and so they agreed to discuss it more tomorrow and they said good-bye and hung up. As they talked the next few days they decided that they would start the rehab efforts at Steven's place. Jake and Sophie had made a trip to the hospital and were enthusiastic about Ellen coming to help. Both Sophie and Jake seemed impressed with Ellen and the commitment she had already shown to get Steven back on his feet.

Ellen called every day to talk with Steven and to see how he felt he was progressing. She also called the doctor about every third day in an attempt to keep a finger on Steven's progress and possible release schedule. Ellen and the doctor discussed often the challenges she might experiences as he began to recover. She wanted to know what to watch for and what might be unusual but normal in his recovery.

It had been over ten days since she had been there but on this day the doctor told her that he could in fact be released tomorrow if she was ready. Ellen asked the doctor not to tell him that yet because it would take her until the following day to get there.

Ellen hung up and called to see how Steven was feeling today. To her dismay it was Beth once again who answered the phone. It had happened several times while she was gone and she was baffled by her seemingly constant presence. She told Steven that the doctor thought he would have some good news for them tomorrow. She could hear excitement in his voice. Steven was definitely ready to get out. After Ellen had talked to Steven she called and talked to Sophie and let her know that she would be bringing Steven home in two days.

An Event to Remember ~ 83

Mary helped Ellen hitch up that evening so Ellen could get an early start. The two ate dinner and covered any details they felt were necessary. "Do you have any idea how long you are going to be gone?" Mary asked. "Do you think you'll be coming home for a visit after a period of time?"

"I'm not sure how long I will be gone. The doctor said it would be several weeks for him to be operational and stronger. I will pick him up a wheel chair right away, but it will be a while before he has strength enough to do anything. I know I won't be able to stay away from here that long so I will be coming back once we've established some good routines. I guarantee I'll want to make sure I get back to check on Trick and you."

The next morning Ellen left pulling the empty trailer with her. She left as the sun was just coming up but she had no plans on stopping overnight in Ohio. Her plan was to make it to Steven's farm and spend the night with Jake and his wife. Ellen had traveled about five hours and then made a stop to stretch and get some coffee and a snack. About another two hours into the trip it began to rain and the winds picked up and sideways against the truck and trailer. As she passed another car or truck she would feel a strong pull on the trailer as the suction created by the wind tried to take the trailer from her.

The rain and wind continued for the next hour. After the storm was passed Ellen realized how tense she must have been driving. She felt fatigued in her arms and shoulders. She took another exit and decided to go in and relax at the diner that was there.

She had covered about nine hours of her trip so far. She slid into a booth and sat sideways with her feet up on the seat. She ordered coffee and a piece of pie. She was fighting her eyes wanting to close when a voice broke in. "Hey, pretty lady you're looking pretty wiped out." It was a tall truck driver standing at the table's edge attempting to engage her in some small talk. Ellen was a good-looking young woman but she was never into herself. Ellen didn't

84 ~ *Steve Farkos*

go out much since her riding took top priority over pretty much everything. She dressed in jeans or riding pants most of the time. She never dressed flashy even if she went out with her friends for a night out. "Have you been traveling all night?" Ellen turned to sit correctly in her seat and looked at the driver. "No. I left at sunrise but I got tired fighting the storm I went through and the wind was playing games with my empty trailer." The driver now slid unto the seat across from Ellen. "You're pulling a rig. You look too young and pretty for that type of career." The truck driver then introduced himself, "I'm Larry. Do you have a name or do I just keep calling pretty lady?"

Ellen was annoyed that he had just sat down but the fact that he was so chatty made her more alert and awake. "I'm not pulling a rig, just a horse trailer. It's empty now so the wind was playing games with it. My name's Ellen and who invited you to sit down any way?" Ellen gave him a slight smile and then sipped her coffee. Larry then asked her permission to sit there and wondered if he might order a coffee too. Ellen gave him an affirmative nod and started into her pie. They small talked about destinations and the reason for each other's trip. Ellen realized now that she had been there for more than an hour and waved to the waitress for her bill.

"I need to get going I want to get into St. Charles, Illinois before ten tonight." Ellen grabbed for her wallet but Larry snatched the bill from the waitress and handed her a ten-dollar bill. "I want to pick that up. It's not often I get to have a conversation and coffee with a pretty young lady named Ellen." Ellen thanked him. Larry got up, wished her a good trip, winked and said farewell. As he walked away Ellen took a good look at him and realized he was not only a nice guy but he was handsome and well built. Ellen felt good about her extra stop now and was energized by her meeting of Larry.

Once she was back on the road she called Mary and told her about her coffee with Larry. Mary teased her and then went on to tell her how good Trick was today after she had turned him out. Ellen was happy to hear that and suggested Mary try to lunge him tomorrow.

After she had hung up with Mary she decided to call Steven. Steven answered right away and Ellen was happy it was him. "I'm on my way there now. I'll be picking you up tomorrow and taking you and your mare home. If the doctor hasn't told you yet he will before the day ends." Steven was excited about the news and turned away from the receiver in his hand and spoke. "I'm getting out tomorrow." Ellen could hear him say in an excited voice. Ellen couldn't resist and asked whom he was giving the good news to. It was Beth and Ellen just sighed and then ended the call.

Ellen arrived at Steven's place about 10:30 and both Sophie and Jake welcomed her. Jake was excited to show her what he had done. He pointed to the porch and showed the long ramp that he had made for Steven to use with a wheelchair. Ellen was impressed and admitted that she hadn't even thought about one. Sophie excitedly told her that they had gotten a wheelchair from someone they knew in town and they didn't have to buy one.

"It's a good one, too," she said in accented English. "Jake tried it out on his ramp and made it look easy." Jake suddenly had an embarrassed look while the two women just smiled.

After eating the warmed up leftovers that Sophie had saved for her, Ellen excused herself and went off to bed. The long day and drive had taken a toll and sleep was now her focus.

Chapter 8

ELLEN WAS EXCITED about the day. She woke early and made a good effort to look her best. She was very aware of her hair after Steven had seen her in her frizzed out mess. She looked good even without make up but she did put a little on this morning. She pulled a new pair of jeans out of her suitcase and put them on. Maybe not what you would think of for a hospital visit and picking up a friend but she knew on the way back they would be picking Stella also. She came out and Sophie had breakfast made and already on a plate for her. "You look very pretty," Sophie told her. Ellen was starting to wonder what was different that people suddenly were using the word *pretty*. Sophie was now the third person in as many days to use the adjective. Ellen never thought of herself in that way as rarely was life about her in her focus. To her she thought that life was being with horses and being helpful to people.

The house and the barn looked great. Jake and Sophie had made little changes and everything was as clean as a whistle. Ellen was excited about picking Steven up. Ellen made the trip to the hospital faster than she had ever remembered. As she pulled into the hospital parking lot, Ellen smiled as she thought what most people might be thinking as she pulled past the main door pulling the trailer.

She ended up having to park, toward the back of the lot so there was no way she and the trailer would be blocking anyone. She walked with good feeling in every footstep into the hospital. She was truly having a feel good day as she entered the hospital.

Ellen walked to the hospital rental office where she had reserved a wheelchair to take to the house. Ellen was more than a little excited that Steven had agreed to her plan of helping. Once she had signed all the rental papers she headed down the hall to the elevators.

As the doors opened on the third floor her heart seemed to speed up now with anticipation of the experience she was about to undertake. Reaching the room Ellen took in a deep breath and slowly expelled it as if she was riding a transition. She pushed the wheelchair ahead of her into the room and announced. "Your ride is here your highness!" But the wind and excitement was taken out of her sails as her eyes now focused on Beth sitting on the edge of the bed and holding Steven's hand. His eyes flashed a look at her but she was slow to read its meaning. Did his look mean 'Oh you're here!' or 'I didn't ask her to sit here.' Either way she didn't care now. Instead she now assumed the role of a director and got things moving.

"Beth, be a doll and gather any of the better flowers still alive and any presents that Steven has collected so you can take them down." Beth just gave Ellen a look and then started her assigned task. Ellen noticed all of the wraps and bandages had been removed from Steven's head and face. He looked quite normal again as almost all of the swelling had also gone away. He was a very handsome gentleman she thought.

"Let's get you into this chair, Steven." After helping maneuver him into the wheelchair she started to collect his duffle bag with his clothes and looked to see that all his personal stuff was ready to go. Ellen looked to Beth and saw her struggling to carry all the stuff she had organized to go. "Beth, don't forget to grab all the cards he has received over the weeks I'm sure he'd like to see them again sometime. Seriously Beth, go get a cart or something to get all of that. Working here I'll bet you know where you can get one. I am going to start downstairs and we'll wait for you near the entrance so you can keep an eye on your 'man' as I go get the car." Ellen was feeling sort of good giving directions to her.

Once Beth reached the lobby Ellen had her wait with Steven as she drove the truck up.

It was humorous to watch the faces on the others around the parking lot and near the lobby as they looked in shock as the truck and horse trailer pulled up to the lobby door. Ellen parked and walked around to prepare to get Steven in for the trip. Beth loaded all the extras in the back seat and Ellen opened the front door and flipped the console up making the front seat like a bench and no longer bucket seats. Beth rolled Steven closer to the truck door as Ellen finished the front seat preparation.

Steven tried to stand but wasn't very sure footed standing on his one foot as he tried to balance his cast leg forward. He swayed and swung around and grabbed the door for balance. "You OK? Hang on a second. This may be tougher than we would have guessed." Beth chose that minute to give Ellen a look for her lack of plan to get Steven into the high set truck.

"Had you not thought of how you would get Steven into your oversized vehicle? Your truck seat must be a foot and a half higher than a normal person's car." Steven ended the conversation, "Ladies! I'm doing the best I can to balance here but I need some help to get in there." Ellen wrapped herself around Steven's midsection and instructed Beth to watch and grab his cast as they began to maneuver him. Steven shifted around so his back end was now positioned in line. Steven slowly let go of the truck door and reached above his head to grab the handhold above the door. Once Steven had a hold of the handgrip he started to pull himself upward. Ellen grabbed around him and added her effort to lift him. Beth fought to control his leg as Steven thrust it about as he attempted to jump up. The one pin still in Steven's cast poked into Ellen as she was lifting and Beth tried in vain to control the leg that seemed to have a mind of its own. Finally, after what appeared to be a three stooges performance, Steven's butt slid onto the seat. He pulled himself backwards deeper in the seat and started to laugh. "Should we open the window so my leg can ride along?" The ladies looked and laughed also. Steven's full cast leg was stiff as a rock and pointing out the door like a linebacker defending the door jam. "How will you close the door?" Beth asked. We could have put him in the back seat but where would you put all of that stuff?" Then Ellen reminded them they needed to put the wheelchair back there also after they got it folded back up. Steven laughed and repeated his idea of hanging his leg through the window. Ellen looked into the cab and told Steven to pull himself as far back into the console area. "Go as far back as you can. As long as I can drive we'll be OK."

Steven wrestled himself backwards until he felt the seat change as it reached the driver's area. Once he had reached it he slid his leg forward a bit and it did just barely fit in. There wasn't much more than an inch between his toes and he dash. "Hope you're a good driver." Steven said to Ellen with a smile on his face. "Wait a minute." Beth said as if a light bulb had just come on above her head. "Steven can ride with me in my car and we'll follow you. This is my day off so I could just drive him home and then I could see his place that he has told me so much about." There was suddenly a knot in Ellen's stomach, but it would probably be easier for Steven. "I'm staying here. I got in and I'm staying here until I reach home, but thanks for the thought. Next time we'll know better but I did feel we put on a good show." Steven laughed which helped the ladies realize that he wasn't mad but was ready to go.

They said their good-byes and thanks as Ellen climbed into the driver's seat, but Beth had a look of determination on her face that said she wasn't giving up. As Ellen put her seatbelt on she felt Steven's shoulder press against her arm. "Are you going to be alright? I'm sorry. I didn't think about your leg not bending." Ellen was concerned about his comfort but he assured her that after the past few weeks in the hospital bed this was like being in heaven.

It was a short drive to the barn where Steven's mare had been kept. On their drive Steven repeatedly thanked Ellen for all her efforts. He also made her feel better as he told her if Jake had picked him up they would have had a similar struggle with his truck.

They pulled into the barn area and Ellen reassured Steven that she would load Stella as quickly as possible so he wouldn't get claustrophobic. Steven appreciated it but asked her to walk the mare up near his window so he could see her. Ellen agreed to his idea as the barn manager now came up toward the truck.

Ellen and the barn manager walked to the barn where Stella was stalled. Steven tried to see as much of the property as he could. He had never been here before and just wanted to take it all in. It was a barn owner thing. One didn't want to miss anything that might make sense to add to your own place. Ellen walked the mare up where Steven could see her and then slowly moved her about so he could see her from all angles. Steven smiled and gave her a thumbs up and Ellen went to the back to load her on the trailer. The mare loaded without issue. Ellen was impressed by the mare's attitude about loading when she considered what the mare had gone through in the trailer accident. The barn manager had stopped for a moment to talk with Steven. Steven was really happy about how good the mare looked. Steven and the barn manager shook hands and then they pulled away to finish the trip to Steven's farm.

Jake and Sophie were sitting on the porch as Ellen and Steven pulled in. Ellen thought she should take the mare out to the barn first but Steven insisted on getting out. As

Ellen pulled up to the house Jake and Sophie rushed to the door and opened it to let Steven out.

"Mr. Steve welcome home," Sophie said as Jake opened the door. Both stopped as they surveyed the situation. They hadn't envisioned the boss looking like he did. Ellen came around to the passenger side and opened the back door to get the wheelchair out. As Ellen opened and locked the chair into position Steven started to hedge his way out of the truck. He reached a point where his leg was sticking straight out and another few inches would have tipped the scale and the leg and cast might have yanked his pelvis forward in a very painful way.

Ellen directed the operation and in a few minutes they had Steven in his wheelchair. As soon as he, Jake and Sophie had exchanged loving greetings and happiness for his life and return, Steven turned the chair and started toward the barn. Steven made the wheelchair go as if he had spent hours practicing. Sophie followed Steven as Jake helped unload the mare. "She's a nice looking one. I have a stall set up for her. I also took down Hawk's nameplate off his old stall. That was the right thing to do?" Jake asked in a respectful tone. Ellen and Jake came into the barn as Steven sat in the aisle looking at Hawk's old stall. Steven began to cry and put his face into his hands. This was probably the only sense of closure that he might get. Ellen motioned to Jake to take Stella and walk her around to the other door to bring her into her stall. Ellen walked up to Steven and put an arm on his shoulder. "He was a great horse and a hell of a partner." Steven was living the ending through what Ellen had told him about the accident. His heart was having a hard time letting go of the best partner he had ever known or had.

Steven straightened up and Ellen suggested that they go back up to the house and get him settled. Jake needed to feed the horses and Sophie walked ahead to get the stuff from the back seat and into the house. When they reached the house Steven stopped wheeling his chair. "Wow whose idea was it to put the ramp here. Let me see if I can do it." Steven repositioned his chair and started up the ramp. Ellen followed close behind and explained that she and Jake had talked about it but Jake had taken care of it by himself.

Steven had made it about two thirds of the way up and then came to a halt. Fatigue and his long hospital stay were taking a toll. Steven tried to start up again but was unable to get rolling again. The incline had him beat. Ellen reached forward and took the handles and was about to push when Steven spoke up. "Please don't I need to do something myself. I need to feel I can take care of myself again." Ellen let go of the handles and Steven strained to make the chair go forward. He was going nowhere and suddenly the chair began to roll backwards and as he tried to stop it the chair began to flip over. Ellen again grabbed the handles and needed all of her strength to keep him upright. No words were exchanged but Ellen now pushed him the last few feet up to the porch.

Sophie had gotten his bedroom ready so they wheeled him directly to his bedside. "You need to rest. You've had a rough day and need some quiet time." Ellen then helped him into his bed. After he had sat on the bed she lifted his cast leg and helped to swing it on the bed and then elevated it on an extra pillow.

Sophie brought in some soup and an apple and set a tray across his lap. Ellen sat on the chair near the bed and watched as he finished everything as if he hadn't eaten in a week. She then took the tray and told him to rest and she went back to the kitchen. She walked back to ask if there was anything he'd like special for his first dinner. She found Steven was already sound asleep.

Jake came in and told Ellen he had parked her trailer and unhooked it. Ellen was grateful especially since she hadn't even thought about it since they had taken the mare off. Sophie, Jake and Ellen sat and had some soup and tried to decide what would make Steven happy for dinner. Jake was sure any food Sophie cooked would easily surpass anything the hospital could have offered.

The next few days were mainly spent in adjusting to new routines. Steven was proficient by day three as far getting himself up and down the ramp and out to the barn. But Steven always felt helpless when he needed to wash. It was more than once he sought help from Sophie and was more than a little embarrassed.Feeling helpless wasn't something Steven liked. Jake went about his normal tasks and in some of his free time he would devise tools that would help Steven get in and out of his wheelchair without help. Ellen began to help with the horses and she started to ride Stella. Ellen was impressed with the mare and felt it was a good way to stay in shape.

The next week passed with little incident. They all went about their jobs and Steven got stronger as they let him fend for himself more and more. Then one day after Ellen had finished working Stella she walked toward the house to tell Steven how great the mare had done. Ellen had taken her over some cross-country fences in the back. The mare was great and her scope was unbelievable. Ellen was excited to share her news with Steven and hoped it would encourage him to start thinking beyond his loss of Hawk.

As Ellen entered the house via the back door since she was still wearing her riding boots. She expected to see Sophie in the kitchen but instead she heard voices in the living room. She walked through the kitchen and as she entered the living room she saw Steven, Sophie and Beth all drinking coffee and sharing stories and laughter.

"Ellen, please come in. I'll get you a coffee if you'd like." Sophie was always happy to see Ellen. Sophie and Ellen had already become good friends and Sophie was always sweet and pleasant. Beth looked around as Ellen had come in. "Oh Hi! I didn't realize that you had moved in here." Ellen was ready to spring across the room just to give that woman a swift kick but instead she held her ground and started telling Steven how great the mare had been. Steven was pleased and wanted to know all that she had done with her but Ellen excused herself to go back to the barn. "I'll be back in later and we can talk more. I also need to talk to the doctor this afternoon about your next appointment."

Ellen was not very excited about the visit Beth had surprised them with. She was aware that Beth had called a few times but assumed by now that Steven would have seen her as a flake and a thrill seeker. Ellen went about grooming Stella again just to pass time. As she groomed she began to realize that this dislike she had for Beth and the belief that she wasn't good enough for him might just mean that she had hopes that there could be more than just a friendship between her and Steven. She dismissed that thought almost as quickly as it had occurred. Ellen talked to the doctor that afternoon and found out that Steven needed to come back in ten days and with luck they might remove his large cast and pins. The doctor thought they might be able to replace it with a smaller cast on the lower leg and a wrap with stays around his thigh. If nothing else the doctor felt this should give him some better mobility.

Ellen brought the others up to date on the doctor visit at dinner and then announced that she would be going back home for a few days. She told them she needed to check on things there but promised to be back in time to take Steven to his appointment. "I don't wish for you to leave, Ellen. Can't you just check things on the phone?" Sophie inquired. Ellen insisted it was necessary for her to leave for a while. Neither Jake nor Steven said anything but watched Ellen as she left the room. Beth was silent during the conversation but now offered that she could use her vacation time to help in while Ellen was gone. Steven just said that there wasn't much she'd be able to do so he thought she should save her personal time for more important things.

Later that night as Ellen sat in her room brushing her hair before bed she heard a knock at her door. As she turned to look toward the door she realized that Steven's wheelchair had already pushed the door part way open. Steven rolled in as Ellen offered a greeting. "I was a little surprised by your announcement at dinner. I thought that you would have mentioned it prior to announcing it. Are you OK? You have seemed so happy and we are all happy to have you here. I think Jake and Sophie feel you are a long time part of the family." Ellen listened carefully but didn't respond for a moment.

"I love it here and I do feel that I've been able to help but I have a farm too and I worry about things there. My desire to help you may be a bit uncanny. But I need to go for a bit and you seem to be able to get plenty of help." Steven realized that there might be some jealousy about Beth showing up but he didn't make a point of it. "How soon do you plan on leaving? What does it typically take you driving back?" he asked. Ellen told him it was a two-day trip even though she had driven in one shot once but then she felt worthless the next day. Her preference would always be to make it a two-day run from now on. Steven said a good night to her and thanked her for all she had done. He made her feel good when he told her that he would have never agreed to anyone else helping. "You understand things and the business," he said as he wheeled out of the room.

The next day was as usual as any other. It was after dinner when there was a slight turn of events. Steven asked Sophie to bring him the envelope that Jake had picked up in town during the day. As Sophie returned Steven looked to Ellen and said. "We talked while you were out riding today and I decided that we needed to show all our thanks for your help. Sophie this involves you too. Hand that envelope to Ellen, please," he said.

Ellen accepted the envelope but was concerned that it could be money, which she would be offended by. As she opened it she realized it was tickets of some nature. "These are airline tickets for New York. They're for you and Sophie." Sophie was shocked at what she heard and immediately looked to Jake. Jake smiled, as he had been part of the surprise. "I thought the least I could do is save you a couple of days in your travels. I understand that you need to go back. This should save you two days but we also had an alternative reason too. We figured you'd have to come back here if we had your truck and trailer." Ellen smiled but then also pulled some money out of the ticket envelope. What's this for?" Ellen said a little mad maybe. Steven then explained that the money was for a cab or to rent a car to get from the airport or home. He said that they had put some money in there for her, Sophie and Mary to go out for dinner. Sophie's never gone anywhere or had a vacation and we figured she should see more of the US. Sophie was very excited and Ellen was just in awe that they had done all of this. Ellen thanked him and checked the flight information on the tickets.

The next day the ladies got packed and were busy planning what they might do extra when they were at Ellen's. The next morning Steven was left home while Jake drove the ladies to the airport. It was all new to Sophie since she had never flown before and it was fun for Ellen as she helped Sophie and explained things to her. Sophie was having so much fun it made the flight seem very short and it allowed them to further their friendship.

They had a little over an hour drive to reach Ellen's place. Mary was there as if she had been waiting all day for them. They went into the house and settled for a bit and had a snack and some coffee that Mary had waiting for them. The three then toured about the farm. Ellen was excited to see Trick and asked Mary for an update on his recovery. "He seems to be doing pretty good. Yesterday was our first hack for about 40 minutes with lots of walking. He was pretty full of it at first but settled nicely. I wasn't going to push it at all for another week or two."

The ladies got all dressed up that night and went to a private golf club restaurant where Ellen's father had been a member for years and she was given an honorary membership after his death. Ellen rarely went there but thought it would be perfect for the night.

It was a fun night. They drove up in the rental car and the valet opened the doors for the three women. They were all dressed up in summery dresses and looked outstanding. All three of the women were in their late twenties and all were very attractive, especially tonight as they wore clothes they weren't often seen in. As they walked into the club Mary noticed that a group of men took a good look at them. They were early and had planned on having a cocktail in the bar. As they walked in it seemed the entire room took note of them, both the men and the women.

Ellen ordered a bloody mary, Mary then ordered an apricot stone sour, and Sophie just said she'd have the same. Sophie then told them she had never had a cocktail just wine in her past. Mary and Ellen laughed and were sure they would have a fun night. The three princesses had a wonderful dinner and shared a bottle of wine. They returned home with Sophie talking every minute while they drove.

Back at the house they sat in the kitchen and had another glass of wine. It was obvious that Sophie had enough to drink for the night but she sure wanted to talk. Ellen decided to take advantage of Sophie's talkative mood.

"Has Steven had many girl friends since you've known him?" Mary was surprised by Ellen's question. "No, not many but he did have one he cared for very much. She died after a bad accident on her horse. He said it was a reckless mistake on a broken horse. It was an instant and he never said good-bye. Once she was gone many tried to get his attention but he keeps a wall around himself it seems. He hurt for a long time I think. In front of Hawk's stall the other day was the first time I've seen him show any emotions again. He's always pleasant and fun to be with but hides his feeling deep inside." Sophie stopped and took a sip of her wine and then Ellen really jumped in with a question that Mary read a lot into. "So do you think he has a thing for Beth? She seems to have her hooks on him doesn't she?" Mary realized that even though she wouldn't

98 ~ *Steve Farkos*

admit it Ellen definitely had a thing for Steven. Sophie's answer was humorous but also was reassuring to Ellen. "Mr. Steve would never be happy with someone like Beth. She's too girlish and wanting. She is only capable of small talk and he knows that already by things he has said to Jake. I think he maybe likes you but I shouldn't say that, Jake tells me. But I do." Ellen didn't say anything and Mary just gave a look to Ellen. Mary already knew that Ellen would be the last one ever to admit she had feelings for a guy especially in a romantic way. Sophie was now really feeling the effects of her fun night and excused herself and headed to the bedroom.

Mary bugged Ellen about the conversation that just taken place in front of her. Ellen didn't seem to have much to say but she also made less of an attempt to deny the fact that she was pleased that Steven might like her. Somehow it felt good even though she didn't feel it was necessary.

Before they flew back to Illinois, the three spent an afternoon in New York City. Sophie was in awe as they wandered the streets and saw the busy city. She couldn't believe the size of the buildings and the hordes of people. Both Ellen and Mary enjoyed showing Sophie the city. Mary dropped them at the airport and they all seemed sad about having to go separate ways.

After they returned to Steven's Ellen made a point of teasing Jake about all the fancy dudes that were checking out his beautiful wife at the club. Jake smiled at her and reminded her and Sophie that he was very aware how lucky he was and Sophie rewarded him with a wonderful kiss and hug.

Steven was moving about well in his wheelchair now and would come out to the barn to visit the horses but also to watch Ellen work Stella. He had seen the mare work once before he had bought her but was amazed at what he was seeing in her now. He had originally bought her with the intention of selling her but now thought she might stay. He was happy with Ellen's riding and had her occasionally ride the others that were there. He decided for the time to have only Ellen work with Stella and Jake was fine with that.

Steven decided to work with Ellen to improve her flat work and make her more aware of her jumps especially in the cross-country area. Steven would have Jake drive him out back so he could help Ellen on the many obstacles that were hidden around the acreage. The farm offered just about every type of fence and combinations that a rider might face.

Ellen felt that she was at an ongoing clinic. She was feeling improvement every day and found herself really enjoying the mare.

Steven's doctor appointment went well but it was disappointing to him when the doctor said he would need at least another month before he would be walking well or riding. The truck ride home was quiet as Steven contemplated what his mental condition would be as he was to be on limited exercise for another month.

The next week saw Ellen riding well and Steven doing even more coaching. They clicked as a coach and rider and it was obvious to Jake that Steven was enjoying coaching Ellen and seeing the progress that she was making. The mare was muscling up as they worked and she was looking really good. She was very supple and agreeable as Ellen worked her.

At dinner that night Ellen announced that she was planning another trip back home since it would be another month before Steven would be walking and starting a more rigorous routine of rehab. No one said anything at first as they were surprised by her announcement. Steven broke the silence and joked about Sophie not going this time because he didn't want her to get anymore corrupt for Jake. Jake and Sophie smiled and Ellen smiled but indicated her disappointment. Steven then got serious, "Ellen what would be the main purpose of you going back at this time? Ellen answered telling him that she missed her place, didn't want to overstay her welcome here, needed to evaluate Trick's status and thought she could start planning her show schedule. She did promise that she would be back for the doctor visit and then would plan how to use her time effectively to get Steven going and in the saddle again.

"Well!" Steven started. "This is what I have been thinking. I am so impressed at the progress that you have made with Stella that I wanted you to take her to an event. I want you just to compete at training level. I feel you are working at advanced level with her but I don't believe she would be fit enough to do more yet." Ellen was surprised and pleased about such a plan but felt she needed to take care of things at home and she explained that she hadn't ever done an event without Mary there as her groom and encouragement. "Ellen, your horse is just coming back. He's not ready and he will require some good focus to go into rehab. The time off is not hurting him. I will fly you back again to make sure that things are lined up at your place. That way when I fly Mary out to help you at the show you will be confident that everything will be in good hands. All you have to do is say yes."

Ellen was surprised, to say the least, as was Jake and Sophie. Ellen looked at Steven and said she wanted to answer him now but needed to wait. She wanted to say yes but felt she needed to call home and talk about it before she agreed. She would still need to go home but there was a lot to plan and take care of if she was going to do this. Steven agreed and asked Sophie to call and set up a flight for her to go home in a couple of days and asked that the tickets be delivered. It was all happening pretty fast. But Ellen couldn't help but be excited.

Ellen spoke with Mary that night and then she went to Steven and agreed to the plan. The next day Ellen rode with a new enthusiasm, maybe a little bit much. It took a while to settle Stella into the relaxed working mood that she had been showing as of late.

Ellen flew back home and she and Mary met with her friend Sue who had been with her at the last show and the

An Event to Remember ~ 101

scene of the accident. She would be in charge while Mary was away and Mary would hire an extra hand to help out. Susan had good horse knowledge and sense but wasn't an active rider these days.

Once Ellen returned to Steven's place she took her turn to drop a bomb his way. "After I met with Mary and we all agreed to take on the show Mary came up with a condition that I agree with. We decided it would be fair that after I show Stella, you, Mary and I will go back to my farm and you could help me start my horse back." Steven, Jake and Sophie all were surprised but Steven instantly agreed, which made Ellen very happy. In the last month they had removed Steven's cast and he was walking pretty well after the first week without help. He walked around his property every morning to work on his endurance and balance. He began doing some weight training to regain the strength he had lost. He knew he couldn't ride until he had his body fit again. Ellen sometimes watched and encouraged him as he pushed for the results he wanted. As much as he missed riding, he was enjoying teaching Ellen. He also couldn't stop wondering if he could ever enjoy and trust another horse as he had Hawk.

Ellen and Stella were going great. Steven was so proud of how they were performing and was now looking forward to the show in Indianapolis. He knew that they were ready and he was now wishing they had entered at the prelim level. Ellen's confidence was high. She felt like she had been riding the mare for a year, and Stella was easy to partner with. She had a great work ethic and a desire to please and please she did.

It was a week and a half before they would leave for the event. Steven felt he had accomplished a great amount in the training of these two in the short time they've had. He still walked with a slight limp that he hoped would soon disappear. They had just finished their morning workout. Stella steamed as she was lathered and wet in the cooler morning weather. Ellen dismounted and was clearly very excited about the ride she had just had. Steven walked up to her and gave her a huge hug. "You're ready." He said proudly. "Now it is time to get Mary up here and the two of you can get everything ready for yours and Stella's debut."

Chapter 9

MARY ARRIVED EXCITED and was met at the airport by Ellen and Sophie. They tossed her stuff in the back of the truck and drove to Steven's place. Mary was as excited as Ellen about the event. She quickly brought Ellen up to date on how well Trick was doing while Sophie asked a hundred questions about Mary's trip.

It was a quiet meeting as Mary met Steven again and Jake for the first time and now could put a face with his name. After dinner Ellen and Steven showed Mary around the farm and introduced her again to Stella. Mary took to the mare right away as she nickered when Mary rubbed her hand over the mare's soft muzzle.

The next morning things were all business as Mary got more acquainted with the mare and little subtleties that might make a difference when handling her at a show. Mary watched as Steven coached Ellen through her dressage paces. "Don't throw away all your contact for your lengthenings. Use a lighter half halt and use your seat." Steven instructed. On her next pass the improvement was definitely noticeable. Mary was impressed but also noticed how well the mare was working for Ellen and how well Ellen worked with Steven.

Mary was getting excited about this new team showing down at Indy. For the next few days they worked on final stages of show prep and the packing required. They were going to use Ellen's truck and trailer and that made Mary's job easier because of her familiarity with how they had always packed in the past. Mary had brought all of Ellen's show clothes from New York. Sophie pressed her show shirt and stock tie and made sure that everything was spotless. That night Ellen checked through everything and

104 ~ *Steve Farkos*

checked it off on her list then gave the OK for final packing.

Steven walked into the room where they all were. "Check everything twice to be absolutely certain we have everything we'll need. We're putting things together in a short time to make this work. All the stuff from my trailer is gone. Make sure we have all the tack we might need and back up like we used to carry. Ellen do you have a stud kit in your trailer?" Suddenly Steven stopped all his thoughts. "We have regular shoes on Stella now. I've got to get our blacksmith Tom out tomorrow to set her up with new shoes and have them tapped for studs."

Jake did a complete check up on the truck and trailer making sure we were good to go. He was methodical as he checked the oil, lights hook-up, hitch, tire pressure and he loaded the grain we would need and got the hay loaded behind the cab of the truck. Everything had checked out but he noticed we didn't have a carrier for water. Steven had always taken some water from home in case his horse was slow to accept the water at the show. After talking with Steven they decided that they wouldn't worry about it for this trip but would see how fussy the mare might be.

Mary went about checking everything inside the trailer. There was a lot of tack and accessories that belonged to Trick so Mary worked to organize it and put it out of the way. She checked the first aid and medical box to see if they were in need of anything right away. Then she checked for poultice, wraps, liniment, stuff to wash with and tack cleaning soaps, conditioners and rags. The box of studs had fallen out and now she searched to make sure she had a full set. It was important to know they would have a complete set for whatever the turf conditions might require.

Thursday morning the day they would be leaving for Indianapolis. They all woke eager to go but they didn't have to rush because it was only about a four-hour trip at max to get to the horse park. Sophie had breakfast all ready and Jake came in from feeding and loading another bale of hay

An Event to Remember ~ 105

he felt they should take. They sat and started breakfast but Steven hadn't joined them yet. Sophie and Jake sat and started to eat. "Where's Steven?" Ellen asked. Sophie then told her that he had left early to make a fast run to town. Shocked, Ellen asked whom he had gone with. Jake then explained that he had borrowed his truck and went by himself.

Just as they were finishing breakfast Steven walked in and was all smiles. "Where did you go?" Ellen asked even before wishing him a good morning. "I went to the bank and I drove for the first time since the accident." Steven was feeling pretty proud of his morning's accomplishment.

They went about the final preparations after breakfast. Jake went and grabbed a wool cooler for them to take and Mary started to wrap Stella for the trip. Ellen brought hers and Mary's suitcases out and put them into the trailer tack room. Steven was finishing his packing and gathering his cameras. Tom had finished her new shoes and they were about to load Stella when they realized that Steven still wasn't out yet. Ellen suggested that Mary just let Stella graze until he made it out. Ten minutes later there was still no Steven. Ellen asked Sophie, who had come out to wish them well, to find out if he was ok. Sophie returned in a minute. "He's on the phone with Beth and appears to be having a hard time hanging up." Needless to say Ellen's mood suddenly took a negative turn.

Steven walked out and realized that everyone was waiting. Mary and Jake started immediately the loading process. Steven tossed his gear into the tack room of the trailer and put his cameras in the truck. "Are we all ready?" he asked. Mary answered as she locked the back door of the trailer behind Stella, "Ready to go and have some fun while we show off this new team." Steven laughed at her enthusiasm. Ellen in the meantime just settled into the driver seat and started the truck. As soon as Mary and Steven were in she put the truck in gear and pulled out.

Ellen honked the horn as she saw Sophie and Jake waving behind them in her rear view mirror.

Mary talked excitedly to Steven from the back seat while Ellen just drove and didn't seem to have anything to say. Traffic was light and the trip ended up only three and a quarter hours most of which time Ellen didn't seem to have much to add to the conversations. Mary knew her well enough that she didn't push any buttons and Steven wasn't about to chase her for more conversation either.

They pulled into the horse park and were able to locate their stalls right away. Steven had also ordered a tack stall so he began to set it up while Mary and Ellen unloaded Stella. Once they had her unwrapped Mary spread shavings, hung buckets and filled water while Ellen took the mare for a walk. When Ellen returned the stall was ready and she put Stella in so she could help organize the tack stall.

Steven had the tack stall set up and functional and just needed help to unload the hay.

His one arm was still weak enough that it was a challenge to lift anything that weighed over forty-five pounds so Mary helped him and then they were pretty much finished with setting up their area.

Ellen and Mary walked to the show office and picked up her packet. She would be number thirty-one for the weekend. She put the packet in the tack stall and pulled out Stella's bridle tag and placed it on the hook near the bridle and then took the course map out and took a look at the listed obstacles.

"Oh good. You grabbed the course map. I was going to suggest that we walk the course now and we can walk it again tomorrow after your dressage test. Actually there will be plenty of time to walk it as many times as you'd like tomorrow since your dressage test is at 9:34," Steven said eagerly.

Ellen questioned if Steven should walk the course, thinking that it might be just a little too much for his leg. "Mary and I have walked a lot of courses and she typically

An Event to Remember ~ 107

takes a photo of every fence so if there are questions later it becomes easier to work out any questions." Steven was determined to go and Ellen made it clear that she wasn't going to walk a lesser pace just because he was along. Steven was becoming a bit perturbed at Ellen's attitude and he was sure he knew what was bothering her. "Mary, I like your idea of taking photos of every fence. It makes a lot of sense. And I will go on the walk just to see how you plan things and if I can't keep up I'll finish on my own." Mary was trying to figure out now which of the two of them was more stubborn.

The course walk went well and Steven managed to keep up, but not without effort. His leg was talking to him as he was stressing it a bit on the uneven and rolling terrain. There were only a few fences that Ellen lingered at to consider the approach and any change of footing questions there could be. All the other fences she felt would ride straight-forward and should be a lot of fun.

After the walk Steven unhooked the trailer and brought the truck back to the stall area and then sat resting on the open tailgate while the ladies bathed and grazed Stella. Once they had finished they fed Stella her evening meal and topped off her water. Now it was time to locate their hotel and check in.

At dinner that night Ellen and Steven did discuss a few of the cross–country obstacles and both agreed on how they felt the one option fence should be taken. Ellen was definitely getting excited and was ready for the challenge. Once they were back at the hotel Steven felt it was important to break the ice that he still felt was chilling the air between he and Ellen. Mary went into their room first and then Steven took Ellen by the arm and let her know that he wanted a moment to talk to her.

"Ellen. I have a strong sense that you are upset with me for something and I'm not 100% sure why. I don't want to do this event and have anything holding you back from showing all that you've been working for. If I have upset you let's clear the air and get on with things. We're both professional and out for the same goal here." Ellen agreed and then just let her feelings out in her attempt to clear the air.

"I've tried to accept your relationship with Beth but quite honestly she annoys me. It really was too much that we all waited for you so we could leave just so you could finish talking to her. We were ready to load and go yet you couldn't put her off and call her back. You could have called her from the truck if you really needed to."

Steven responded and was obviously a bit aggravated by the whole thing now. "I'm sorry for the holdup, but I was trying to put some distance between that woman and all of us. She has called almost every other day since I've been home. I have put her off most of the time by saying I was working with you and Stella. Any other time Sophie has run interference so I didn't have to get hung up having to talk with her."

Ellen was more than a little surprised by this news. She had no idea that Beth was calling that much and that Steven was actually aggravated by Beth's relentless efforts.

Ellen grabbed Steven's hand and thanked him making things more understandable by sharing that information with her. Ellen wanted to say more but just couldn't or didn't feel she could at this time.

Steven realized that this information had cleared the air and again he offered a simple apology for delaying things as he had. He then gave Ellen a hug and whispered in her ear. "Trust me I'd rather talk with you. Believe me. Now focus on what we're here for and get some sleep you need to put in a good dressage test tomorrow. I always say, "Make dust don't eat it." He said smiling. "I want you at the top or at least very near the top after your dressage. Now go get some sleep." As Ellen turned to enter her room Steven just gave her shoulder a gentle squeeze.

They all left the next morning early to prepare for Ellen's dressage test. It was 5:30 a.m. and Ellen hadn't slept much

An Event to Remember ~ 109

as she continually ran her dressage test through her mind. She had ridden every transition several times during the night and now was excited and ready to go. Mary fed Stella while Steven started to check over all of the clean tack. Ellen gathered all that was needed for braiding and brought it down to Stella's stall. Ellen topped off Stella's water and then she and Mary were going to begin braiding.

Mary set the stool near Stella's neck and the mare remained perfectly still and quiet. As soon as Mary started the first braid the mare danced out of Mary's reach. So Mary readjusted her position and started to weave Stella's mane in a braiding motion. Again the mare danced away from and then backed toward Mary knocking her off the stool.

"Ellen I think I will need your help. I've never had much luck braiding a moving target. Have you ever tried to braid her before?" Ellen hadn't ever tried before since there had never been any reason to. She came into the stall and put a lead rope on Stella's halter and started talking to the mare. The mare seemed settled enough so Mary once again started the braiding process. As Ellen talked to her the mare seemed content. It was when she started the fourth braid that the mare again protested. She shook her entire neck as if she had a horrible itch or something. Mary was showing some irritation now as her frustration mounted. "At this rate you may miss your class." Ellen decided to try something she had seen at a T-Touch Clinic she had attended. "Let me try something I saw at a clinic once." She told Mary. Ellen reached up and slowly started to massage in a circular motion the space between the mare's ears, right on the poll. Just seconds after she started she told Mary to give it a try again.

"So far so good it seems. This is supposed to be a way to calm and relax them. I do think it's working. Within minutes Mary was able to braid the length of the mane and only now only needed to pull the braids up and tie them. Stella was finally finished being braided and the braids were beautiful and perfectly spaced, a trademark of Mary's talents.

110 ~ *Steve Farkos*

Before it seemed possible Ellen was dressed, mounted and starting her warm up. Steven had gone over to watch a few competitors ride to evaluate the competition. He watched in silence as Ellen went through her warm up. He was pleased and didn't find a need to say very much. It was about five minutes before her ride time and Ellen stopped by the rail to have Mary wipe the dust off her boots and she took the moment to question Steven. "Well how do we look? You have hardly said a word. It feels pretty good though." Steven looked at her and said. "I've been enjoying the ride you're having. Try being a little softer on your canter departs and remember not to throw her away when you ask for that lengthened trot. I really think you're good to go. Now go show that judge what you've been able to show me." He gave her a big smile and a tap on her boot.

Steven and Mary walked to the side of the dressage arena and Steven prepared to take some video while Mary pulled out her camera. Ellen circled the arena waiting for her starting bell. As the bell rang, Ellen started toward 'A' while both Steven and Mary raised their camera in perfect timing to one another. Ellen and Stella made a very attractive pair and now Steven's hopes were that her ride would go as good as they looked.

Their ride was going beautiful and Stella looked supple and happy as she floated around the arena. Now came her half circle back in canter. Steven started to mumble directions as he continued to film. "Be patient. Hold her. Hold her. Now!" He said in a very low voice. Then he uttered a strong "Yes" as she managed to nail her flying lead change at exactly the right moment. The rest of her test rode as well as the first except that she got an early lead change on her second half circle back and change.

"That was a really good test. I was proud of you and Stella out there especially in your second lengthening. It was the best you've ever done. Your second lead change was a bit early but they may not mark it down much." Ellen smiled as she was excited about her ride and she could tell

An Event to Remember ~ 111

that Steven was pleased also. Mary went on and on about the attractive partnership they made. "Well that was a good showing for phase one. Let's go walk the cross-country again and then we can hand graze the mare for a bit."

After they had walked the course again, they took time to grab some lunch and decided to go watch some of the lower level dressage tests that were going on. Steven was amazed at the really good quality of horses but was fast to express his disappointment in a lot of the riders and lack of effort in their presentation and accuracy. "I wish I could have an hour with these riders and just show them how much better the scores could be if they would groom their horses and themselves better," Mary then added.

Overnight there was a huge downpour. The radio talked about 3" of rain but it seemed like a lot more as they walked to the truck and the parking lot was still ankle deep. The showground, near the stabling area, was flooded in some spots and in other spots where the water had receded there were collections of manure and shavings. They had left two chairs out overnight and it was a sure bet they wouldn't be sitting in them for a while.

"Well at least Stella didn't drown last night. Her stall looks pretty good." Mary said. "And the tack room seems damp in spots but dry overall."

Even though the conditions were sloppy Ellen and Steven went to walk the course again. "I thought you weren't going to walk with me this morning," Ellen said to Steven. He explained that although he was feeling the course walks from the past few days he wanted to see a few of the fence approaches that might have been compromised by the heavy overnight rain.

They were both impressed as most of the course was in really great shape. The soil was sandy enough that it had handled the rain quite well. The water complex was deeper than they remembered so Steven instructed Ellen to take her shoes and socks off and rollup her pants to wade in to check the depth. "Had you been thinking you could have gotten your Wellies out of the trailer and not had to go wading barefoot," Steven said with a laugh. Ellen walked the route she would take through the water complex. She had rolled her pant legs up past mid-calf but as she approached the far side she felt the water engulf her rolled pant leg. "It's really deep over here." Ellen yelled out. Steven then had her walk it again making it into a large bending line. The water level stayed more consistent but it would mean that she would need to take the exit fence at an angle.

When they returned Mary had Stella all brushed and was starting to put the studs in her shoes. "Mary, you are a dream," Steven said. "Can you show me the studs that you chose? The grounds are not as bad as we thought. There's only two fences and the water complex I'm worried about them slipping at. Here let's put the studs in this configuration and use the two biggest mud ones on the outside of the rear feet." Mary agreed with his plans but then she broke out laughing as she saw Ellen's pants all soaked.

As Ellen's go time came nearer Steven and Mary started her with a warm up session and then just left her to finish her warm up without them. Steven and Mary then went in the truck and drove around the property where they would have a shorter walk to reach the water complex. As they were walking out they could see some of the early prelim riders now on course. Steven looked at Mary and told her in a very confident voice that Ellen and Stella could have handled this course at the prelim level, he was sure.

On the way walking to the water complex Mary noticed that Steven had started to limp. She decided not to question him about it since they were nearing the water complex. They stood and watched as the last two prelim riders negotiated the obstacles. The prelim riders had an obstacle in the middle of the water that Ellen wouldn't have on her course. It was obvious to Steven that the deep water was pulling hard on the legs of the horses as they took the middle obstacle. He was happy that he and Ellen had agreed on the bent line approach, as he was certain the prelim horses had made the middle area of the complex even worse.

Mary was excited as they saw the first training level rider now approach the water complex. Steven watched as the first two horses through struggled to keep their pace and leave the ground as they jumped out. "Do you see how those horses are fighting their way through there? They're jumping out of there as if it was molasses. Those horses have another eight fences to go I guarantee they'll have time problems or just really be fatigued for the last few fences. I hope Ellen takes the route we agreed on and I hope Stella will be good about jumping out over the fence at such an angle. We really don't know that much about her in a situation like that.

The next four horses came through, the fourth of which struggled in the water and slipped to a halt launching his rider. The young girl rider hit the cold water and sprang up as fast as she had fallen, accompanied now by some really choice swear words. "God that had to suck. I can't even imagine getting dumped that good and that water is deep enough to really soak you," Mary noted. Then Steven pointed out that the horse acted like he had no desire to leave the water as he just stood there. Now a couple of spectators went into the water and helped to get the horse moving out. "I think that horse knows how mad his rider is right now. He probably thinks he's safer staying put." Steven laughed at Mary's thought.

There had been a hold put on course during these issues. Steven kept looking at his watch and hoping that Ellen had not been started on course. In a few moments riders were released again. They watched the next two riders coming through and the second one had a refusal on the jump in and again on the jump out. It was obviously the fourth refusal for the rider she now walked off the course. Mary now grabbed at Steven's shirt and pointed off toward the top of the hill.

"Here she comes and look at her! She looks great. That's a nice horse. Look at the stride I wouldn't have guessed her to be able to cover ground that easily." Mary's voice gave away all her excitement. They watched as the two came down the hill. Ellen now sat taller and began to collect Stella up. "Good girl. Good girl. Now ride your plan." Steven was excited to and watched as Ellen dropped her shoulders back a little and drove the mare to the first fence. Stella's ear perked forward and she left the ground. The pair proved faultless over the first obstacle.

Now Ellen asked the mare to bend outward in a large bending arch. The crowd reacted thinking that she was pulling out or lost control. The mare cantered through the water with no change of pace. The plan was working and now they needed to make the exit obstacle. Ellen gave Stella a harsh half halt to insure she was listening. The crowd seemed convinced that Ellen had made a bad move as they angled toward the last obstacle. "We're about to see what that mare's made of." Steven muttered. Ellen now focused over the fence, opened her inside rein and gave the mare a kick with her outside leg. It was as if they had practiced it a hundred times. The two flew out of the water and over the fence making the crowd gathered around the water complex go into wild cheers and applause.

Steven swung around to Mary and hugged her. "Let's get to the finish line. Mary started to run toward where they had left the truck. After about twenty-five feet or so she realized Steven wasn't running. Mary looked back to see him limping. "Go ahead and get to the finish line. If I'm not back when you have Stella untacked then come to find me. Now go and tell her how proud I am. Hope the rest went as well as that complex." Mary took off again feeling funny about leaving Steven.

Mary reached the finish line as Ellen was handing over her pinney. She had already loosen her girth and taken her

An Event to Remember ~ 115

vest off. Mary barely had the truck stopped and parked and she jumped out of it and ran to Ellen. "You were spectacular at the water," she yelled as she came in earshot of Ellen. Ellen was smiling and was very excited. "It was Steven's idea for the water complex. But Stella was amazing. I had so much fun and to go clean our first time out in these conditions is just unbelievable. Hey. Where's Steven at?"

Mary then told Ellen that Steven was limping badly and asked her to go ahead and help you and if he wasn't back by the time we had Stella taken care of we should come to pick him up. Just then a golf cart came rolling to a stop near Stella's stall as the ladies were untacking the mare. "Were you clean?" Steven asked from the back of the cart. Ellen gave him a thumbs up as she walked to him very excited but also concerned about him.

One of the horse show officials was driving the cart and had spotted Steven limping back toward the barn. It turned out that Lisa Watkins, who was the show's technical delegate, and Steven had competed during the years and she was very pleased to have been able to help him out. Steven had told her about the accident and his loss of Hawk. Lisa got off the cart and met Ellen and Mary and then asked if they had a dry chair for Steven. Lisa and Ellen gave a hand to Steven as they got him into one of the chairs they had set in the sun to dry. Too much too soon on his now weak leg had caught up to him.

"Are you alright? We need to get you back to the hotel. Mary and I can finish things here in a short amount of time. We can feed Stella just before we go and Mary and I can come back later again to check on her." Ellen was showing a true concern for Steven.

"That all sounds good but don't take any short cuts with Stella, she earned some good treatment for her efforts today. The conditions looked really bad at a few of those fences, especially after other horses had been over the course. I'm really proud of both of you."

Steven wanted Stella settled but then he was all for the idea of getting back to the hotel as his leg was now complaining strongly to him.

That night they ordered room service since Steven didn't care to go out and it would insure that he would be able to pay for everything without the women having any objections. Ellen and Mary had just thrown on some comfy clothes and their hair was still damp from the shower as they knocked on Steven's door and waited a moment for him to get to the door. Steven had cleaned up and wore clean jeans and a knit shirt. "Wow! No one told me this was going to be slumber party too." Steven was feeling better after a shower and extra ibuprofen. The ladies smiled and then Mary whispered to Ellen that she liked Steven more and more as she got to know him. Ellen gave her a playful punch in the arm and a warning grin. Steven closed the door behind them and limped across the room to sit back down.

No sooner had they sat down than room service knocked at the door. Steven asked Ellen to let them in and he grabbed some money for a tip from his wallet. "Just sign the tab and give him this for a tip." Steven said as he handed her some cash.

The meal was outstanding and all of them had been a lot more hungry than they thought. Steven had ordered a bottle of wine that was really hitting the spot. They talked about Ellen's good ride and she gave them a good descriptive review of how the ride they hadn't seen went. Ellen then changed the fun conversations and asked Steven to explain just how his leg was feeling. After they talked about it, Ellen suggested that Steven stay behind tomorrow and let his leg rest. He would have nothing to do with that at all but promised to go back to the doctor when then got back.

Mary threw on some clothes and went back to the barn to check on Stella. It was common to do so, plus they had fed her earlier than normal and Mary was going to give her another couple of flakes of hay. Ellen stayed behind and

An Event to Remember ~ 117

talked with Steven and then retired back to her room. Ellen was concerned about Steven's leg even though between the wine and Ibuprofen Steven walked pretty freely across the room as he wished her a good night.

Throughout dinner with all the happiness and cheer they were sharing about the success of the day they also realized they hadn't checked the scoreboard. Ellen realized, as she got ready for bed, she had no idea where she was placed in the standings. Ellen now tried calling Mary to see if she could check the standings after all the cross-country results had been posted. Ellen wasn't able to reach Mary and called Steven's room to let him know they probably should leave earlier than planned since they didn't know the standing. Her placing would determine her 'order of go' and that could affect their timing in the morning.

"I don't think we have to go much earlier than we planned. I'm sure your program said they would be running in reverse order. With your clear cross-country round and certainly a better than average dressage test the worst would be that you'd be in the middle of the pack. Maybe a twenty minute difference than we'd planned." Steven felt pretty confident that Ellen was at least in the middle of the list of competitors but was probably willing to bet she was near the top.

Ellen was anxious as she waited for Mary's return. With the issue of Steven's leg they had forgotten to check the standings. Worse than that both Ellen and Steven always had a habit of not checking dressage scores or placings until they had completed cross-country, which they had not done today. So she now sat there with no idea of her standings and only hoped that Mary might think of checking.

Mary came in and said that Stella was fine. "She was happy to get the extra hay and she had drunk all her all of her water. I hung another bucket and put some electrolytes in both buckets after I filled them." Ellen then interrupted her. "Thanks for being on top of things. I tried to call you. None of us ever got the standings and tomorrow's stadium will be run in reverse order. We'll probably have to leave earlier in the morning to be sure we're there in plenty of time."

Mary laughed at Ellen's concern. "You don't give me much credit do you?" Ellen looked puzzled by her comment, but before she could say anything Mary grinned and told her. "I went and checked the board before I drove back. You had a 27.8 on your dressage test and you're in second as someone I don't know had a score of 26.5. I wish I would have seen that test cause I really didn't believe anyone would have a better test than you had."

The score excited Ellen since it was a few points better than she had ever scored with any other horse she had ridden at that level, even Trick. " I wish I would have seen that first place test also. That's a hell of a good score. I feel pretty good about second."

"You mean second after dressage. That first place rider had a refusal and 2 time penalties on her cross-county. Currently you're in first place and the woman behind you has a score of 34.3. So you'll be riding at the end of your division." Mary was smiling the entire time as she related the scores and placings.

Ellen was excited and really wanted to tell Steven the news but Mary suggested that he could be asleep and thought morning would be soon enough to give him the good news.

Ellen called Steven as soon as she woke. She thought she might be waking him but decided she couldn't wait any longer. To her surprise, Steven was awake and was having a cup of the coffee he had brewed in his room. Steven was thrilled by the news, but he too was sorry he had missed the test that had beaten Ellen in dressage.

Steven still wanted to leave early since they had not walked the stadium course yet and there would only be one opportunity to do so before her division. He also thought that they could watch some of the prelim rounds to see how

An Event to Remember ~ 119

the course was riding; the only likely difference would be the fences would be lowered for her division.

It was a beautiful day. The sun was warming everything up and the stadium ring was a sand based arena and the footing was perfect.

Mary was getting Stella groomed and cleaned up perfectly. She had bought a new set of leg wraps and the white wraps shown beautiful against Stella's dark bay legs. Steven and Ellen walked the course and agreed that there wasn't anything very tricky about it. There was one turn back that Ellen thought some riders might have trouble with but she felt confident that she and Stella would nail it perfectly. It was obvious to Steven that Ellen's confidence and trust was growing and becoming stronger every day. The two were forming a very solid partnership that was sure to bring success.

Mary walked Stella from the stall and today's braids seemed even better than yesterday's and today she had stood perfectly by herself. There wasn't a single hair out of place. Stella's coat gleamed in the late morning sun. Ellen looked as perfect as the mare. Everything was cleaned and looked perfect. Steven took a rag and did a fast wipe of Ellen's boots and wiped even the soles of her boots.

Even the warm up area was in perfect shape and Stella's wraps stayed amazingly white for a change. Several horses before Ellen pulled rails early on. And as Ellen had predicted the turn back line saw two bad refusals, including a rider down. Steven slowed the warm up until they had reset the fence and helped the fallen rider out of the arena. Everyone applauded to see that she was OK and knew full well it was something that had probably happened to the majority of them, at one time or another.

Ellen was at the in gate and as the rider before her finished her round she was now motioned in. As Ellen rode in the announcer read her name and Stella's. He then added Steven Wilson who was the mare's owner was here today. The audience rose and applauded a true welcome to Steven.

120 ~ *Steve Farkos*

Most all the horse-loving and event-following people present were aware of what had happened to Steven and Hawk in the accident.

Ellen was engulfed by all type of feelings as the bell sounded announcing her round could begin. Ellen took a deep breath and picked up a canter. As she approached the starting gate she whispered to herself. "Focus now." Her first fence was a bit ugly, as she wasn't carrying enough pace. Ellen gave the mare a squeeze and Stella responded perfectly and adjusted her pace. The rest of the fences flowed even the turn back that had caught two of the riders. Ellen was smiling as she made the turn to the last vertical. Everything looked perfect as Mary and Steven watched. As Ellen took off Stella grazed the top rail and in a delayed motion it bounced in the cups and then fell to the ground. Ellen was upset as she heard the crowd let out a horrible sounding sigh.

Ellen came over to where Steven was standing. "It's OK. It's your first go with her. You just didn't ride that last fence and I've seen that happen more often than I want to remember. Mary said you're still good as there was more than four points between you and the second place horse." Ellen still said nothing, just listened.

They called in the horse and rider pairs that had placed. They then announced the placings and a steward handed each their ribbons. Ellen hooked the first place ribbon on Stella's bridle and posed for a picture with the organizer and sponsor as they held up the cooler they had won. The music began and Ellen led the victory gallop around the ring.

On the way back to the barn Ellen was pretty quiet. Mary and Steven reviewed the weekend and knew the ups and downs that they had seen. All in all it was a good show, good results and a great start for Stella's new career. Steven even made it known that he now intended to hold onto the mare and not sell her. Then he turned to Ellen. "Why are you being so quiet? I would think you would be happier

An Event to Remember ~ 121

than all of us. You did it, while we watched and look how happy we are."

Ellen looked directly at Steven and said. "I know that I disappointed you in Stadium today. I became part of the crowd as I felt the joy of you being there. I know all you've been through and I thought it amazing that the crowd honored you so. And because of all that I didn't focus all the way to the finish." That said Ellen cried. Steven and Mary reassured her they were very proud of her and what she had accomplished in the short amount of time.

Chapter 10

As they returned to Steven's Jake and Sophie who waited to hear the results and everything about the weekend met them. Mary helped unload Stella and then handed her to Ellen, who said she wanted to put her up. Mary then sat with Sophie and Jake and gave them the details of the weekend. Steven followed Ellen to the barn and brought in some of the stuff from the trailer.

After he had brought in some materials he walked into the aisle where Ellen was finishing getting Stella ready for her stall. Steven walked up to her and held out the cooler and first place ribbon and told her he wanted her to have them. Ellen was taken back a bit and didn't really feel right about taking them.

"It's normal that any winnings, no matter what they are, always go to the owner," Ellen stated. Steven agreed that was the norm but he'd only ridden Stella once and bought her with the intentions of selling her. "It was you who have put the work into her and now I feel that we should shoot for a couple tougher ones. I want you to ride her. Honestly I think it may be a while before I can ride very effectively." Ellen was surprised by his announcement and came to him, hugged him and thanked him for his trust and confidence in her.

Steven gave her a kiss on her neck and told her he believed in her as a rider but also as a friend. Ellen felt a rush of warmth go through her body. She felt great as she took the cooler and ribbon and set them aside for the moment. "I need to feed her now since everybody else is already eating and she's been really good and patient while I

An Event to Remember ~ 123

made her wait." Steven agreed and turned to go get some hay. Ellen put Stella in and went into the feed room to get Stella's grain. As the grain crunched into the grain bucket there was a nickering from down the aisle. "Who was that? Sure didn't sound like anyone that I know in the barn," he said. At that moment the mystery nicker came again.

Funny how barn owners and those who see their horses daily get to know their every sound. It's also true about the horses knowing their owner's and caretaker's footsteps or voices. More soft knickers greeted Ellen and Steven as they approached the end of the aisle. As they looked into the last stall they saw a horse that they didn't recognize. The more they looked at him the more curious they became. This couldn't be a horse sent in for training. This horse was underweight and scarred from battles with other horses probably. Ellen went in the stall; the horse was loving and kind with one of the kindest eyes she had ever seen. Steven on the other hand was less interested in his kind eye and more curious as to why he was in his barn.

They walked back to the house to check with Jake to see what he knew. "Mr. Steve, they found him down the road just after you left on Thursday. They brought him here and we have checked everywhere for an owner but so far no luck. So Sophie and I have just fed him and turned him out for only short periods. He was really weak when we first got him brought to us. He's much perkier now. I meant to tell you when you first got back but everything else was happening and I honestly forgot." Steven then told them all that he wasn't running a rehab center. Ellen looked at him and then made an effort to convince him to get the horse stronger and then either find him a job or a new home. Mary and Sophie agreed and pleaded with Steven to help the poor guy out. Steven agreed but at the same time was very hopeful that the real owner might turn up.

"If he's going to stay Jake I want you to get the vet out and get him vaccinated and checked over. I cannot afford him getting others sick. Looking at him, I will guess that he hasn't been kept up to date on anything. Pull a coggins test on him also. He looks like he's been loose for some time yet if he's been out he should be fat from all the spring grass available. It doesn't make sense to me."

His arguments made sense to all of them but they still felt it was important to take him in and give him a life. Jake went to contact the vet and the others finished unpacking from the trip.

That night at dinner Mary wondered what the plans were regarding her going back to New York. It was decided that she would go back in two days and that Ellen would stay a while longer. Ellen would stay and go to the doctor with Steven to see what he could or couldn't do.

The doctor took a look at Steven the next morning and made it sound pretty simple. "You are doing a lot on a leg that still has at best 80% of the strength it had before. Your quads are the weakest. They atrophy faster than any other group of muscles and take longer to get back to full strength. You need extra exercises to rebuild those muscles to be as strong as your good leg. Bottom line was that you were overdoing it based on the current condition of that leg. It's going to take time. You can't accomplish it all over night and you can't overdo it without setting yourself back," the doctor told Steven.

On the way home Steven decided that they should campaign Stella for most of the remaining local season. Ellen, however, did have concerns about not being at her farm enough and about her own horse, Trick. "Ok. Let's take Stella to your place and go to some events in your area on the east coast. I'll go with you and I can help you with Trick and whatever else you need as a payback for all you've done for me," Steven offered unexpectedly.

Ellen was surprised and at the same time excited about the idea. "Let's look at the omnibus and see what will be available to enter that might make sense and then we can make plans."

An Event to Remember ~ 125

After they reviewed the omnibus they found two events that were easily reachable from Ellen's place. One was in upper state New York and the other was in Pennsylvania. They decided to run Stella again at Training and then in Pennsylvania they would move her up to prelim. Even Mary was excited about the decision since she would be there for it all and she also enjoyed working with Steven and watching him coach Ellen.

Mary flew out a week ahead of Ellen and Steven. Jake and Sophie were ready to take care of things but were wishing that they could go along with the others. Steven gave them instructions not to take in any other horses while they were gone and to see if they could fatten up the mystery gelding and put some light conditioning on him. Steven and Ellen with Stella in the trailer headed off to New York. They had made arrangements to lay over in Ohio at a friend of Steven's who had a small ranch. Ellen was amazed at all the contacts that Steven had established across the country.

They were making good time and were only about fifty miles out from their Ohio destination when Ellen's truck just died. They were perplexed, as there were no previous signs, of any kind, that anything was going wrong. Steven got out and took a look under the hood but didn't see anything that might be obvious to a non-mechanic individual like himself. Ellen got on the phone and called Triple A Auto for assistance. When they arrived they were quick to identify that the oil pan had a leak underneath and the engine for all practical purposes was blown. Ellen was speechless and didn't know what to think. Jake had even checked the oil after they had returned from Indy. Triple A called for a bigger tow truck that could pull the truck and trailer to the nearest town that would have a dealership that might be able to help them out.

Once they reached the dealership Steven paid a generous amount to rent a truck from their used vehicle lot. This was not a common practice but the dealership owner was very

126 ~ *Steve Farkos*

sympathetic being a horseman himself. They were back on the road in just about two hours after reaching the dealership.

They reached Ellen's place late the next afternoon. Mary was there to greet them and had Stella's new stall ready. Once they had everything brought in from the truck Ellen took Steven out to show him around. Mary was bringing Trick in as they approached the barn. "That's my guy, Trick. He's a good horse and Mary says he's ready to work again." Steven walked up to the gelding and patted him on the neck and offered his hand to be sniffed. Trick licked Steven's hand and then nickered. Trick seemed to be giving Steven his stamp of approval. Ellen and Mary both laughed at Trick's unusual approval.

The next morning Ellen went out early and started her work out with Stella. Her plan was to work her early and then put a ride in on Trick. "Mary, do you think Ellen would be upset if I got on Trick and hacked him about to see what he's like? I haven't been on anybody since the event in Kentucky but I am feeling ready," Steven said as he stood there in a pair of breeches that he had brought with him. "I'm sure she wouldn't mind. My guess is that she would appreciate your evaluation. I rode him yesterday so I'm sure the two of you will be OK," Mary told him. Steven was happy and at the same time smiled inside at Mary's concern as she mentioned she had ridden Trick the day before.

Mary helped to get Trick ready. Steven was excited and probably would have been excited to get on any horse after these past few months. As he swung up into the saddle he felt a bit uncomfortable as the barrel of the horse was now stretching his leg in a way it had not gone for months. He shifted his seat a few times to see if it would make a difference. After walking and adjusting his position for about ten minutes Steven cued Trick to pick up a trot.

Steven trotted about on the grass nearest the barn as Mary watched. He liked what he was feeling. It was an incredible feeling to once again be on the back of a horse. Trick was a nice horse and he had good balance, the only thing Steven would have wanted was a bit more sensitivity to his aids. Steven now trotted off toward the outdoor arena in the back near the tree line. Ellen was walking with Stella on a long rein when she became aware of Steven and Trick's presence. Ellen's smile could be seen from a good distance, as she was happy to see them both doing what they were meant to do. "Hey, mister. You're looking good up there but where's your helmet?" Ellen said teasingly. Steven picked up a canter and did a small circle around her and then broke back to a trot and took Trick over a log fence that was near the arena. Ellen cheered as Steven rode back to her. They walked the horses out together and talked about Ellen's upcoming events.

The next few days they worked horses together. Steven continued to school Ellen and was pleased with the consistency she was showing. He was also excited about how well he felt Trick was going. At the end of one of those sessions Steven asked if they could switch horses. He had not ridden Stella since he had bought her but he was more interested in seeing if Ellen could feel a difference in how her horse, Trick, was going.

Both were more than a little pleased. Although Stella felt small for him, she was sensitive to all the aids and was an absolute pleasure to ride. Ellen had done a great job.
Trick showed happiness as Ellen sat into the saddle. He knew her well but he had respected Steven's aids as Ellen now felt him lighter than she remembered. "We should do this more often. I am impressed at how Trick feels right now. Thank you."

The days went on and many an afternoon Steven spent time on the phone in the study in an almost secretive way. One morning as they were approaching the first event Steven asked after breakfast if he could borrow the truck for the day. He said he needed to go back to the dealer and check on the repair job and timing of her truck repairs.

128 ~ *Steve Farkos*

Ellen saw it as a chance for her to work more horses and restock the trailer with little things like meds, poultice, wraps and new outdoor rug for the tack stalls they always had.

Steven didn't return until after dark. Everyone was in the house and Steven walked in and sat down and wondered how the day went. Ellen of course wanted to know the status of her truck more than anything else. "They had your truck just about finished and almost back together. It looked good to me but I'm no expert as you learned on the road the other day." Ellen wanted to know how much longer they would have to rent the truck they had. It was nice enough but when it's not yours you just do things differently she thought.

The next morning was the morning they would do the final preparation for the New York event. Mary was coming in from morning chores and Ellen was finishing making a pot of coffee and had put some scones in the oven. Mary was grinning like a cat that had just put a dog in check. "What's up, Mary? You're beaming," Ellen said but Steven was across the room, not visible to Ellen, with his finger pressed up against his lips. "Oh I was just thinking about how much fun we would have at the show again. I just have a really good feeling about this weekend," Mary said, still grinning. They all sat and had the warm scones and coffee. Mary offered to clean up the kitchen so Ellen could get out to have a lesson with Steven. Ellen agreed and went back to her room to get something. Steven winked a thank you to Mary. She couldn't stop just bubbling with excitement at what she had seen.

Once Ellen returned and was ready Steven let her lead the way out the door. "What's this?" Ellen screamed in excitement. There before her was parked a brand new truck with a large bow on it. It was a beautiful quad cab in a deep blue. On the doors her farm name "Burlingham Stables" with a logo and a line that read "Eventing Professionals" was printed in metallic gold. Steven was smiling in a very proud way as they went down to get a closer look. Mary was right behind as they inspected every inch. "I can't afford this," Ellen then said in a very excited yet firm and worried voice.

Steven then explained that her repairs were going to run nearly $8,000. Ellen was shocked at that news. Then Steven explained. "Your engine was shot. The interior cloth seats were showing some good wear but I still got a $16,000 trade-in value. More importantly I have spent every extra minute I could since we've been here getting tough with my insurance company and their lawyer who was dealing with the trucking company from the accident. I've been given a range that their figure will fall into once they agree on a market value for Hawk." Ellen interrupted because she didn't understand what any of that money had to do with her.

"Ellen, I will never be able to repay you for all you have done for me. You hardly knew me but you've taken on so much. Look at all that you've sacrificed from your life already to help me. This is my gift to you as a thank you. I don't even consider it enough to be honest but I will tell you I hope that we will be friends and fellow eventers forever. You don't have to worry about anything, I even put the title in your name."

Ellen turned and hugged him and gave him a kiss on his lips and thanked him over and over again in her excited state. Steven was surprised by the kiss but said nothing and showed little reaction to it. "Take it for a drive, here's the keys." Mary asked if she could go and Steven wished them a nice ride as they both got in. Ellen was blown away by the leather interior and all the special features especially the heated seats and built-in GPS.

The next day they went as planned to the up-state New York event. The truck was the big talk as they drove that morning and Steven was thankful it was a shorter drive as his mind was already on the Event. Steven was pleased with his surprise and was so thankful for all Ellen had done. He

130 ~ *Steve Farkos*

knew realistically all the money and time she had given up to help him with no apparent rewards in mind.

Ellen's event went well but did not end as well as the one in Indy. Her dressage score was a 33.5 and that had her in second place. Cross-country went well but she picked up time penalties that then pushed her into third place. The stadium round was tricky and there was one turn into an oxer and then to an airy vertical that caught Ellen as she pulled a rail. Quite a few riders in the division either had rails or time penalties. After it was all said and done she had moved back into second place. Steven felt the whole ride was off a little since their last outing.

Ellen was disappointed but both Mary and Steven kept reminding her that this was only her second time out with the mare. Ellen reminded them that the next show in Pennsylvania she was signed up for prelim. She tried to tell them that it just didn't feel quite the same this time out. They applied a poultice to all of the mare's legs and changed it daily for the next couple days. They gave her the time off and felt that maybe they had pushed training wise, plus the ground was really hard this month because of the lack of rain. For the next few days Steven suggested it might be good for Ellen to work with Trick.

Trick was really doing well. Steven enjoyed instructing the two but was a little jealous since he had been enjoying his rides on Trick. Trick knew his job and that was an important factor to a rider coming back from a severe injury. It was like a little insurance policy to be riding on a well-educated veteran horse.

Once Ellen started working Stella again in preparation for their first prelim event, they were left with less than two weeks of work. Steven chose to work on the dressage test since it was quite different than what they had been doing. Being a level up, the judging criteria would be stiffer also. The shoulder-ins needed to maintain the same rhythm and angle from start to finish. A bigger problem seemed to be maintaining the counter canter as long as required since

An Event to Remember ~ 131

Stella kept anticipating the upcoming change and doing it before she was asked. Steven finally asked Ellen to dismount and he got on Stella. He attempted the same movement with the same result occurring. He knew it was the mare and not Ellen after a few other tries with similar results. He was finally able to keep the counter canter as long as he needed and more. Steven dismounted and asked that Ellen remount. As Ellen walked Stella and adjusted her stirrup length he explained how he had finally accomplished the correct ride.

"I know it's not the correct way of training but remember we only have a few days now before you have to perform the move. After I had made the half circle back I took a little firmer hold on the rein that was my original outside rein. I drove more with my seat after the turn and put even more weight into my inside seat bone. Basically I guess I was forcing it. It's not my way of doing things but sometimes we don't have a choice.

It took Ellen several tries but finally she got the mare to hold it. As is the case often, the one lead came much easier. It felt funny as she rode it but she was determined to use the method if that was what she needed to execute the movement in the test.

Steven took every opportunity to ride Trick and he was enjoying him a lot. A few times they would switch horses for a short time. Steven was a firm believer that the competing rider should be the only one to ride the competing horse the last two weeks before an event. So many times those last two weeks he watched as Ellen rode both horses as he often felt she was missing riding her big guy.

They arrived in Pennsylvania for the Cobblestone Farm Event. Once they were set up and Ellen had pulled her packet, they decided to walk the Cross-country course at least once that night since this event was being held on a two-day schedule. The format would be different this weekend also since they would be running Dressage and

132 ~ *Steve Farkos*

Stadium on Saturday and Cross-Country on Sunday. It seemed like more two-day events were running this format and by doing so eliminating the pinning of awards and victory gallops for the sake of saving some time. Mary wanted to go along on the walk to see this course since it was a new event for all of them.

The three of them started off on the course walk. Steven and Mary chatted as they walked along. Ellen was quiet but attentive at the fences as she and Steven concurred on the approach and technique to be used at each one. The water complex once again showed a good technical challenge as they surveyed it. There was a hill up to a fast decline followed by a good three-foot drop into the water. Once in the water there was an option going left over two corner fences set about two strides apart. The straighter option was wide looking sea serpent model showing an arched back with the head on one end and the tail on the other end emerging out of the water. It was clearly marked that the raised back was the place to jump. It would be a challenge as it was a skinning with an airy opening at the bottom to draw the eye of the horse.

"This is a hell of a jump. I can't imagine too many that will take that direct route. Do we know who the designer was for this course?" Mary asked but neither Steven nor Ellen had the designer's information. Steven walked around the complex to view it from several angles before he said much. "I know that you haven't done that much with Stella and this jump is looking really tough to you. After watching the partnership that you have developed with her though I think you should take the direct route." Ellen looked at him as if he was nuts. Before she had an opportunity to say anything Steve was verbally dissecting the entire trip through the complex as he saw it. "What about the exit fences? Ellen asked. "That's a combination set at two strides in max height." Steven was quick to agree with her assessment of the exit fences but then said, "Take a look at the direct route. It's a straight line and if ridden well will

An Event to Remember ~ 133

give the horse a good approach to the exit line with a possibility to develop the strong stride you need. If you take the option line it will ride easy, but look at the turn you'll have to make in order to do the combination coming out. The first fence will ride like a chip and the two strides in between will then force a huge spot to make it out or a disastrous stop." Mary was witnessing the first disagreement between the two of them. "Let's finish the course walk and we can talk about it more later before I walk it again," Ellen suggested.

The rest of the walk went well with no big surprises. The only other question they had was the coffin combination that was set into a low spot. The approach was on a downhill run which is considered the hardest approach to an open ditch but after talking about it Steven and Ellen were confident that it would ride well.

They finished the walk and Mary went to walk Stella and set up her dinner. Ellen decided to walk the cross-country course again even though Steven felt that walking the stadium course would be smarter since it would be ridden first. Ellen insisted on re-walking her course now and she politely stated that she wanted to do it on her own.

Ellen went on her way and Steven walked over to the stadium area and walked it before returning to the stable area. Mary was now trying to get Stella's dressage equipment ready as Ellen had called and wanted to ride her when she returned. Steven was pleased to hear that and felt it might help settle the nerves that Ellen was showing now. After Ellen put in a relaxing hack they settled Stella in and drove to the hotel to check in and have dinner. After dinner Mary wanted to take the truck and go back to check on Stella, top off her water and throw her a flake of hay. While Mary was gone Steven and Ellen shared some wine and talked about the courses. "I think you and Stella will do great in Stadium tomorrow, we'll walk it together after the advanced riders go and they allow a course walk. We'll warm up ahead of time and Mary can hold her while we walk it. There's one weaving triple line that we'll talk about but I really don't see any issues. How did your second course walk go?" Ellen just looked up over her wine glass and simply replied fine. "Are you that worried about the course? You two are proving to be a great partnership and I believe 100% in the two of you. You need to go out there and be positive in every stride. You have to clear your mind of any negative thoughts. I would never ever ask you to or demand that you do anything that the two of you weren't ready for. I believe in you and I care about you." Ellen looked up at him after his last comment. "I'll be fine," she said and then excused herself for bed. Mary walked in moments later and then offered her good night to Steven and went off to check on Ellen.

Ellen seemed to fall asleep faster than normal, so there was little conversation between them. She was in a good sleep when the hotel wake-up call got her and Mary moving the next morning. After a quick breakfast of coffee and yogurt, they were headed to the barn.

Once again Mary had prepared Stella to perfection. Ellen was still a little quiet but both Steven and Mary left it alone. Ellen mounted and went to the warm up area. Ellen and Stella were warming up great. Steven offered a few helpful hints and obviously they were accepted and resulted in slight improvements that added to the polished look of the two as they finished their warm up.

Ellen came down the centerline and absolutely nailed her halt. As her test progressed Ellen began to smile as she was realizing how well her ride was going. Then came her first half circle back and she seemed to hold her counter canter with no problems. Steven whispered to Mary that side was her easy way. Moments later Ellen performed the mirror image just as perfectly. As it rode every bit as well the second direction Ellen's smile was now getting bigger by the moment. Her test ended and the entire crowd of spectators came to a roaring approval of the test they had just seen. As she passed the judge after her final salute he stood and

An Event to Remember ~ 135

leaned out of the box and smiled. "That was the test I've been waiting to see all day. Good job!" Ellen left the arena with a glow about her that Mary had never seen before.

Steven had run over to be near the exit that Ellen would be coming out through. As Ellen dismounted he grabbed her and hugged and lifted her off her feet. "You were spectacular. It was a pleasure watching that test. It flowed perfectly beautiful." He finally put her back down after Mary showed up and reminded them they could celebrate later.

Stadium rode much like Steven had thought. Several riders pulled rails as they did the triple fence bending line. The change of direction for the third element cost riders a rail for probably half of the class. "Watch the next few riders. The problem is that these horses are fit and they haven't done cross-country yet and they are overly eager to go jump. They're coming in too fast especially in that line. I want you to take one more vertical for warm up and show me, at least twice in a long approach, that she's listening completely to you."

Steven watched as Ellen did what he had asked. As she rode near him he told her she was ready and wished her luck.

They announced her and she entered the stadium. Stella's ears perked with anticipation now. The judge rang the bell and Stella lifted into a beautiful canter. The time allowed was one minute and thirty-five seconds and Ellen finished through the timers at a minute thirty. The round was clear and had looked like a perfect equitation round, with the rider and horse in a perfect rhythm as they completed the course.

The day had been a huge success and the three of them were full of verbal replays of the day. After her dressage test and clear round Stella was in first place with an incredible score of 26.2 with the next closest rider at 35.4. Once back at the hotel they all cleaned up and Steven treated them to a fine dinner at a fancier Italian restaurant. Spirits were high

136 ~ *Steve Farkos*

and Steven made an effort to not talk about the cross-country course coming tomorrow.

As soon as Stella was fed her morning rations Mary went about putting her studs in. Ellen excused herself and said she be back in a bit. After about twenty minutes, Steven who had been holding Stella for Mary asked if she had any idea as to where Ellen had gone. "Don't say that I said anything but she mentioned something about jogging her course and watching some of the advanced riders negotiating the water jump." Ellen returned about twenty minutes later and started to prepare earlier than normal for her ride. They all went about their tasks to get Stella and Ellen ready but in a much quieter way than normal.

Steven wanted Ellen to warm up for a good thirty-five minutes. He wanted the mare to be loose and this would be her first and only ride of the day. The warm up went well and when Ellen was about five or six minutes out of the start box Steven wished her good luck and said he was going out on the course to photograph.

Mary met up with Steven as they both had the same idea and were headed to the water complex. "Do you think she'll do it your way? Or do you think she'll take the longer option? I'm just not sure if she feels confident enough for this one," Mary said as they watched the first of the prelim riders come through. The first three riders all took the longer option and two of the three picked up penalties at the exit fences. Then there were several riders who took the direct route only one had issues at the exit fences and one had an issue with the water entry. "Here she comes." Mary said to Steven. He lifted the camera and watched as she slowed Stella down. She dropped from her two point into her seat, shortened her reins and legged her over the first element. She legged Stella into a rolling canter and then pulled her crop out in one hand as she held the reins in the other.

Stella was well aware of the crop that Ellen held ready now but it wasn't needed as Stella cleared the center of the obstacle. Ellen softened her rein and let the mare go for two huge strides and then cautioned her back with a strong half halt and then sent her through the exit combination.

The crowd went wild as they now galloped off to the next fence. Steven was so excited he dropped the video camera. Once her division ended and placings were announced, Ellen went to the office and picked up her first place ribbon and trophy. There was nothing but happy talk as they packed up and loaded for the trip home.

On the drive home Steven made it very clear how happy and proud he was that Ellen had chosen the direct route and then rode it as the champions he now believed they were proving themselves to be.

Chapter 11

The next morning Steven woke early and went out to the barn. He tacked up Trick and got on for a ride. He went down the road for some different scenery and to further see Trick's courage after not being anywhere but the property for several months now. Once he had found a nice stretch of road with a good grassy shoulder he rose into a two point and stayed in it until his leg began to complain figuring he had traveled a good two miles. He walked Trick for about five minutes and then turned him around. He knew the ground he had covered was safe so he now asked the gelding for a canter. After a dozen strides he asked for a gallop and he enjoyed the breeze in his face and the smoothness of Trick's gait. After the first mile he brought him back into a trot and then to a walk as the big horse was heaving just a little trying to catch his breath

Steven was really enjoying the gelding and was feeling pretty safe with him. As Trick caught his breath Steven rubbed his neck in praise. They were now approaching a bridge that went over a creek. After they had crossed over it Steven decided to take Trick down along the side of the creek on the mowed area next to tall corn crop. He walked along the creek for probably a half of a mile or better and then he saw what he was hoping for. The bank along here was a bit higher and the creek was close to twice the width of any part they had passed so far. The water wasn't very deep in this section since the creek bed was so much wider. Steven could see the bottom since the water was very clear as it came running through. He visually marked the spot where he was standing and inspecting the creek bed. Turning around he went back a good football field's length and then turned around started a trot and then developed a controlled canter. As they reached the spot where Steven had checked the creek bed he demanded a sharp turn and a jump into the water. Trick never hesitated a single step. The gelding showed no fear and didn't react negatively to Steven's unexpected and intentionally harsh request.

Steven and Trick jumped out on the other side and after a few strides came to a halt. Steven praised the gelding over and over as he turned him back toward the water and asked him to step into the creek. Once in the creek Steven and Trick walked along until a fallen log cut their path short. Steven was thrilled with his ride and with Trick's work ethic.

Ellen was waiting for their return and was happy when she saw the smile on Steven's face as they got back to the barn. "He's a nice horse. He isn't as smooth in his gaits maybe as Stella but he's very close. He's balanced and has a wonderful work ethic and I do think he's gotten more responsive to the aids. I was thinking for a comeback I'd like to take him to my first event if you'd let me," Steven said confidently after his ride. "Of course you can. After all whose horse have I been riding and showing? I'd love to see you show him and I am sure you'll make all of us proud," Ellen said.

Mary was walking up now and teased them both since she was hearing the word "show" again and they had really just pulled in yesterday. Steven now started to dismount and as he touched down on the ground his leg gave way and he tumbled backwards. Both Ellen and Mary jumped to help him up as Trick stood like a statue right where Steven had halted for him for his dismount.

"Are you alright? Did you do something to injure that leg again?" Mary asked. "No nothing new I just probably pushed it harder than I should again. I'm ok and don't change your mind about letting me show your horse. Look at him and what a good gentleman he is," Steven said as he patted Trick on his neck.

That night they talked about what possible events they could go to and not have to drive too far west. Mary suggested that they look into the fall event down in Tennessee. Ellen had never been there but Steven had competed there a couple years ago. They decided that Steven would need to compete at Training level much the way Ellen had started Stella. Ellen would go prelim again and see if she could compare this new event with the fantastic weekend she had just completed. Steven suggested they could take both horses to his place and that they could give them a couple days lay over.

Ellen was getting excited and thought that it would be fun to show together. She and Steven were in a whirlwind conversation when Mary interrupted. "It all sounds so exciting and cool but what about me?" They both looked at her and Steven said without a second thought. "You'd be with us of course. It wouldn't be an event for Ellen without you and I was looking forward to being pampered by you too." Everyone was smiling and joking when Mary broke the mood. "Who's going to take care of your farm while we're gone? You made it sound like we'd be gone for at least a couple weeks."

It was an awkward moment as the three paused and had nothing to say. Steven spoke first. "Well here's what I think we need to do. Contact Sue and find out what it would cost for her to come in for a month to take care of the farm. She could move in and if necessary have her boyfriend too and if that doesn't work we'll hire a helper for the farm work." Ellen then added her thoughts. "Sue has a job and probably wouldn't do it for the month. Since we're taking Trick there would only be three horses and the dog to watch. The horses could stay out almost all the time as long as they got grain twice a day and they have water. I just don't know if she would do it. She worries a lot about her social life and a month might be too long for her." Mary had nothing to offer as she was only hoping a solution could be reached because she really wanted to make the trip with them. Steven wasn't about to give up on the idea. "Call Sue and get her initial reaction. I'd also like to talk with her about the financial part of things." Ellen agreed to call her later when she should be home.

Later that afternoon Ellen got a hold of Sue and asked her to stop over that evening. It was about seven o'clock in the evening when Sue made it over. They invited her to have a glass of wine and caught up on things since their last visit. Sue wanted to hear all about Ellen's last two events. As Ellen finished talking about her experiences, she then told Sue about Steven riding Trick. Sue was surprised to hear he was riding Trick as Ellen rarely had let anyone on him besides Mary.

Ellen then explained why they had asked her over. She told Sue that Steven was going to event Trick and that they wanted Mary to come along to take care of them. Sue was very surprised by what they were planning. Sue was very concerned about how it could work with her job as she only had one week's vacation left and had hoped to use that in the winter to go skiing in Utah. Steven then made the effort to ensure the deal would work and be worthwhile. "Sue, I figure if you would get up early enough you could grain the horses and check water and do the same after work other than that it shouldn't be too bad. And to make it worth your while how does $350 a week sound for your efforts?" Ellen and Mary were surprised by the offer since they had never discussed any of the finances. "I figure that should cover your time and additional gas it may run you. So what do you think?'

Sue was surprised by Steven's generous offer, but admitted that she would have done it for less. She admitted

142 ~ *Steve Farkos*

to enjoying being at the farm and figured she'd get a little riding in while she was doing it. Ellen and Mary were excited at her acceptance of the plan. Mary saw it almost like a vacation and she was really enjoying shows when the three of them were together.

For the next week they all made plans and checked to be sure that everything was covered for what Sue might need. Mary carefully packed the trailer using a checklist to be certain she had everything that the two horses would need. Ellen and Steven worked the horses and made plans to have the farrier tend to their feet before leaving.

Steven called and let Sophie and Jake know of the plans. He also asked about the gelding that they had taken in before leaving. Jake was excited about the recovery the horse was making. Jake felt he had put on some good weight but was even more pleased with the animal's personality and manners.

Even Sue was planning on making everything work out perfectly. She called Ellen and let her know that another friend of theirs had lost her job and now agreed to check on the horses during the day and make sure things were good until Sue could return from work.

Ellen knew that Becky, their friend, lived over an hour away and the travel might be a real drain on the plan. "Sue, why don't you see if Becky can stay at the farm especially during the week? She would have computer access for job searches and would be able to have the weekends to herself. See if that works for her," Ellen suggested.

Everything seemed to fall in place and even Becky agreed happily to be part of the experience. The rest of the week passed rapidly and before they knew it they needed to pack the truck and load the horses.

"Ellen, I almost forgot, we need to drop off your title for your old truck and pick up the title for the new one on our way." Steven explained. Ellen disappeared for a time and returned with the paperwork Steven had requested. As she reached the truck to put the papers in Ellen gave Steven a

An Event to Remember ~ 143

huge hug and a kiss on the cheek. "I just wanted to thank you again for my truck. It is still hard to believe that it is mine." Steven just looked at her and smiled saying nobody deserved it as much as she did. Steven seemed to enjoy the little emotional exchange that had just occurred.

The trip was going well and the three were excited about all the time they would have together to work as a team. They traded off on the driving so that they would be able to make the trip without any overnight stop. "We can give the horses a break when we get something to eat and we will give them a rest and offer them water when we stop at the dealership to take care of the titles."

They pulled into the dealership and parked the trailer near the front of the lot. As they walked into the dealership Mr. Palmer, who owned the dealership, greeted them. He walked up to Steven and shook his hand in a warm greeting. Ellen and Mary thought that Steven must have known him for years. Steven introduced the two of them to Mr. Palmer and then handed him the title from Ellen's old truck that they owed him. Mr. Palmer offered them all coffee and then asked if Steven would mind coming into his office for a minute to sign a few papers that he was holding for him. The ladies thought nothing of it and sat and enjoyed the coffee.

Steven emerged from Palmer's office carrying an entire folder of stuff. He walked up to Ellen and handed her a piece of paper for her to sign. "That's your title for your truck so you need to sign it." He held the folder as she signed the back of the title. He then put it into the folder for safekeeping. Ellen couldn't imagine what else was in the folder but figured she didn't need to know probably.

They all walked toward the front door as they walked out Steven handed Mary a set of keys as if she would take the first shift of driving. That wasn't the case though, because as they walked out they saw a new blue dually that looked similar to Ellen's new truck but with the extra fancy wheels and tires. "That's my new truck." Steven said. "I bought it a week ago when they were able to locate it. Mary you can drive it first and then we can switch again in a while." Mary was excited and figured that he wanted to ride a while with Ellen alone. Steven explained again that the insurance money was covering it all now but he was sure more money would be coming from the trucking company. The once Ford man also admitted that after driving Ellen's new Chevy truck he made his decision to get the same.

They all headed out and Mary was in heaven as she followed in the new dually. Mary was in a fantasy about being the top groom and traveling in style as they went from event to event in a first class way. At least for the moment it was true. This was really the life, she thought.

Ellen was blown away by Steven's new purchase. "It's not like I'm out just blowing money. I've paid a hell of a price for everything I have. I lost my parents and sister and for the most part I never touched any of that money. Now I've lost Hawk, my truck and trailer. And between my insurance and the monies being offered so far by the trucking firm's insurance company, I have to replace my truck and trailer and eventually Hawk if I intend to compete at the level I was at."

Ellen just sat and looked at him as he spoke. She felt a pressure in her eyes as she held back her tears. She couldn't even imagine if all of these tragedies had happened to her. Ellen had no immediate family. Her parents were older when she was born and they had both passed on in recent years. It was how Mary had become such a big part of her life and that was why she always felt like she was a sister and always treated her like one.

Steven looked at Ellen and could tell she was fighting tears at the moment. "Ellen, it's hard to talk about the last few years that I've had but I'm beginning to see it all differently now. I guess when you really think you're going to die you see things in a different light and begin to maybe act differently than you had for years before. I acted as if I was the only one to care or be concerned about anything for

An Event to Remember ~ 145

years after losing my family. We were all very close and did everything together. I put a wall around myself 'cause I didn't want to ever feel that destroyed again. I was always polite to others I just didn't want to get connected. Jake and Sophie came a while after I had lost my family and they did help me get through a lot of things. They're very special individuals but I really don't open up my feelings very much, even with them."

Ellen was really taken by what Steven was saying. She reached across the console and searched for his hand. She then took his hand and squeezed it as a sign of her compassion. Steven wrapped his hand around hers and held it with feeling.

"Ellen, I thought I was dead for sure after I got hit. I was hardly conscious when I thought I was seeing an angel or bright spirit of some kind. As they worked to get me out of the truck I passed in and out of life it seemed. I just kept looking for that angel every time I started to come to. I didn't know for another week or two that I was looking for you. Then you showed up at the hospital and I saw that angel again. The drugs made me so out of it. As I recovered and heard stories about you always being there I knew that you were the angel. Since then you've been there for me and helped me in every way possible and have never asked for anything. You are a true friend and like no one I've ever known before. This truck is nothing compared to what I feel you deserve as a person. I'm just hoping that I will always have you as my friend." Steven was choked up as he finished but he had spoken from his heart for the first time in a very long time. "I don't mean to seem forward but you have come to mean a lot to me and I really respect and trust you. You have given so much of your time and efforts to me and never looked for anything in return. That's just rare. Really rare." Ellen was actually feeling a bit awkward now. Was Steven saying more than she was thinking or was she thinking less than she knew? Ellen knew she liked him and admired him but really never thought of it as more than that. And she wondered now if Steven was trying to tell her that he had feelings for her more than just as a friend.

The thoughts that Steven was now sharing made Ellen realize that he had feelings stronger than friendship for her. Ellen had been subconsciously avoiding seeing her own feelings. True, she admired him and saw him as a special friend but now wondered if, in fact, she had feelings similar to what Steven seemed to be talking about.

It was late that night when they all pulled into Steven's farm. Jake had been called ahead of time and both he and Sophie met them as they drove in. Jake and Mary took the horses to the barn and then Sophie and Ellen took care of the wraps and putting additional hay and grain in the stalls the horses would occupy. Steven did a fast clean out of the trailer and then closed it up and walked to the barn. It was about 2:00 a.m. and Steven suggested that they take care of the tack and vehicles in the morning. "It's really late, we can take care of everything in the morning and make it a more leisurely day." Steven felt it would be a good time to catch up on things.

When morning came they all just took care of the necessary chores and left the horses graze and have the day off. Jake really liked Trick and Trick had become best buddies with Stella after their marathon trailer ride together. The two of them enjoyed the large paddock where they spent the day playing, grazing and sun bathing through midafternoon. Steven and Ellen pulled all the tack from the trailer and Sophie sat in the shade and started to clean and recondition everything. Mary went about reorganizing the tack room and getting it ready to handle the two riders at the next show. Both Mary and Ellen had become too used to taking over the entire tack room of the trailer but now the space was going to be shared with another rider.

For the next week Ellen and Steven worked the horses and also hacked the two older geldings. Steven really had Trick going better every day. Jumping-wise he was keeping everything simple and low. "Are you and Trick ever going to go over some larger fences? We did sign you up for training and not beginner novice," Ellen said laughingly. "Seriously, don't you think we should have the two of you go over some fences more like the ones you'll be seeing at the event?"

Steven told her that this was typical of the way he always trained. He assured her he'd take Trick over some more realistic stuff before the show. He was looking to establish obedience and adjustability for now. Ellen realized that he was very serious in his methodology. As they talked they rode toward the back of the property. Once they were about half way out Steven motioned to Ellen to follow him. Steven picked up his canter and Ellen did so also. Steven then galloped a short distance and then brought Trick back to a controlled canter again. He looked behind to see Ellen having a bit more to contend with as Stella was getting worked up chasing Trick up the hill. Steven then turned Trick sharply to the left and took a huge skinny log, something you might see at prelim level. Ellen attempted the same turn, but Stella was now on her own program and not attentive to Ellen. Steven pulled up and watched as Stella blew past the fence. The frustration on Ellen's face was more than obvious. Ellen made a large loop back and took the fence now in good form.

Ellen rode up to where Steven was waiting. "Ouch. Twenty point penalty." Steven mused. Ellen wasn't happy that she had missed the fence but made it out to be Steven's fault. "I'm sure if you were second and I had Stella galloping to a fence with Trick coming behind you might not have the same control as you demonstrated while leading. They're pack animals and Stella just wanted to keep up with Trick and not get left behind."

Steven agreed that Stella and Ellen had shown good control in their forward going partnership at their events. He also felt that the control was partially due to the fact that the pair was on course alone. Ellen was a little hurt by the implication Steven had made. She felt that she did a good

148 ~ *Steve Farkos*

job keeping Stella's attention whether they were alone or amidst other distractions including other horses. Steven saw that she might be upset and that by no means was the goal he was after. "Ellen, have you ever fox hunted? Have you ever jumped in a pack?" Ellen hadn't done either. "Don't forget that I haven't been riding this horse all that long." Steven was trying to make a point for the sake of training but Ellen seemed to be taking most of this as personal and negative instead of seeing a goal to work toward.

"Ellen, go back down a ways and pick up a gallop. Then go to the fence the same way we did, but as you gallop, check behind you and get a glimpse of Trick as you make your turn to the fence." Ellen was determined to get Trick wound up and wanted him to give Steven a real ride. She rode farther back because she wanted to really get Stella going. She picked up a canter and quickly developed it into a gallop. Steven made a point of starting right behind her. Stella was building some good speed. Trick was right on her tail as Ellen looked back the first time. Now as Ellen looked back the second time she saw Trick falling back, obviously responding to a cue from Steven. Ellen called out to Trick as she pushed Stella on even more. The fence was now a little more than thirty yards away. Suddenly Steven had Trick coming full blast again, Ellen began to steady for the fence and Trick was still coming. Trick was just about on Stella's tail as Ellen attempted to make her final adjustment to the fence. At that same moment Steven asked Trick to come back to him. Stella took a huge spot and easily cleared the fence but pushed Ellen high out of the saddle. Ellen turned around to see if Steven was going to try the fence. He did and did it as an equitation hunter with total control.

Both of them pulled up together. Ellen's heart was pounding from the rush of the big fence. Steven was calm as he asked Ellen if she had noticed the control. "We not only sped up but then came back to take the fence just behind you." Ellen acknowledged seeing it but wanted to give the credit to Trick and her training. Steven was now

An Event to Remember ~ 149

feeling more competitive than he normally allowed to show. "Tell you what," he said in a matter-of-fact tone that Ellen wasn't used to hearing. "Let's switch horses and do it again."

Ellen agreed and they took a moment to change horses and adjust their stirrups. Ellen was smiling as she felt that this would be a piece of cake. They both started back toward the barn so they would have a good area to get the horses going. "I'll be going first so I hope you can hold that big guy back once he gets going," Steven said and with that cued Stella into a canter and then immediately let her gallop. In seconds he heard the thundering hoofs of Trick coming up behind. They weren't even two thirds of the way to the jump area and already Ellen and Trick were in passing gear and Ellen was struggling to slow him down. Steven didn't back Stella off; instead he pushed her as if they were in a race. Now as they were closing in on the fence Steven asked Stella to come back and she responded correctly. Trick charged on and slowed just enough to find his spot at the fence and jumped it big and flat. Steven followed with a nice round fence and then came quietly to a halt and waited for Ellen's return.

"Ellen wasn't smiling much as she came back to where Steven and Stella were waiting.

"You made your point but I also want to say that I've never had a problem slowing Trick down like I just did. I swear you've changed him." Steven laughed and explained again that most of her riding was always alone or when she rode with someone else it was usually a hack. Once he got going you started fighting him to come back with the reins and I guarantee you without realizing it you were tightening your legs to brace. Ellen was actually impressed at what Steven had demonstrated to her.

"I am impressed and I know that I was bracing a bit especially near the end. I was impressed as you got Stella back and took the fence so nice and round again. You're probably right about riding alone. Trick isn't used to dealing with that competitive scenario either but you managed to control him. I want to know how you prepared him for that when all you've done is ride alone with him."

Steven smiled and said it was really simple. He explained that you must know how to maintain his attention and how to get it back instantly. "Probably more importantly you have to retrain yourself to have your conscious overrule your subconscious. In other words when your subconscious and raw instincts tell you to fight and or brace you must be able to overrule that, give a strong reprimand and then soften again. It's not easy and it will be one of the toughest things you try to change in your riding. But as long as you are trying you will be improving." They got back to the barn and were greeted by Mary and Jake who were ready to take the horses to clean them up. "Did something happen out back? These horses are really lathered and wet and you've switched horses," Mary asked.

Ellen told them that they were doing some tough training and Steven just nodded in agreement. For the next week Steven worked with her on some techniques to keep or be able to regain Stella's attention. As she practiced her dressage Steven would occasionally cause a distraction to see how fast she could recover the mare's attention. Ellen was feeling improvement and now began to see even a change in the mare's expressive movement. She was grateful to Steven for getting her to see weaknesses in her training and giving her ways to improve things.

It was time to pack up for Tennessee and as they finished the trailer it looked more packed than ever. Mary told them if they were going to do a lot of this they might have to consider a larger trailer. "Hopefully your times will be far enough apart, otherwise we'll be bumping into one another. It seems as you move up the levels you also require more room for all the equipment you need." Steven told her that she was right and with the hope of showing together next year he had ordered a new trailer that would be available in the next month.

An Event to Remember ~ 151

The following day they arrived at the event grounds ready for another adventure. After they unpacked and checked in at the office they wanted to walk their respective courses. They found the same start gate that would be used for both of their divisions but after the first two fences the courses went different directions. Ellen's prelim course went off to the right whereas Steven's would turn off to the left.

"Ellen I would like to walk your course with you and then you can walk it again while I walk my course. I haven't ridden this course in a couple years and I want to make sure there aren't any big surprises." Ellen agreed to Steven's thought and they headed off together to survey her course.

There weren't any big surprises but the three steps going down in the deep woods surprised Ellen. "Do you think I need to do anything special as we head down this set of stairs? At my go time there will be a big difference as we go from the sun in this open area to the deep shadowed area of the woods where the steps are. After that last step it's quite a fall off as the ground continues on at a steep grade." Steven looked at her and then simply reminded her about the work they had been doing. "Keep her attention and if she trusts you, like I think she does, this will ride easy for you. This complex will define a true partnership and I think you'll do great." They finished walking her course and didn't run across anything else that she seemed to have concerns about.

Ellen walked her course again as Steven walked his course for the first time. They met where the two courses had their finish lines. Ellen was now confident about her course and Steven also felt good to go with his course. Ellen asked Steven how he felt about his course. "I feel confident about the course. It will be a good comeback course for me. The fences are all smaller and there aren't any technical questions that I saw. So I think it was wise to start back at the lower level and I trust that Trick and I should have a great run."

152 ~ *Steve Farkos*

The first day ended well. After dressage Ellen again was in the lead by a lot with another great score. Steven had put in a good test but was fourth in his division after dressage. Ellen went clean on cross-country but picked up two penalty points for time faults and still held on to her first-place ranking. Steven also went clean and was able to move up one place to third after the rider who was ahead had a refusal at the water jump.

That night they reviewed their courses and Steven told Ellen what a pleasure Trick had been on course. He also teased Ellen about her continual improvement in their dressage. After dinner that night Ellen excused herself because of a headache she was fighting. Steven and Mary decided to go to the hotel bar and have a glass of wine. As they talked Mary wanted to dig deeper to learn more about Steven. After they had talked for about an hour, Mary asked Steven if he had ever been married or engaged. At first Steven was taken aback by her question. Steven took a few minutes and then answered her queries. "I've never been married but I was almost engaged." Before Mary could question what he had just said he gave her the answer he assumed she'd want. "I dated a woman for nearly five years and was ready to commit, ring and all. She had finally understood my horse passion and was showing interest in all that I did. I thought the time was right but I was wrong. Just before I was going to surprise her with the ring and my commitment she came to me and told me she was pregnant but the baby wasn't mine. She had all the dates down and I was in Europe when she conceived and knew well who the father was. I was blown away and she made all the rest of the decisions. She and the other guy never got married and she moved away. It just wasn't meant to be and my next season was proof as to how much the whole thing had screwed me up. After that I turned all my attention back into my riding and I guess I put up a wall around me as far as letting anybody too close." Mary was surprised by his story and didn't pursue more information but thought to herself what a catch this guy would be.

The next day, both Ellen and Steven went clean in their stadium rounds. Ellen was the first of the two to go since she was showing at a higher level. Steven noted to Mary that he could see Ellen's standings could have an effect on her stadium rides. When showing in reverse order the pressure just kept building. Being in first place she would be the last to go in her division. Once again she allowed herself to get a bit rushy and pulled a rail about three fences from the end. Her dressage score kept her in first place but Steven was concerned that it wouldn't be so easy as she continued to move up and the competition got tougher.

Ellen watched Steven's ride and was very impressed with how nicely his round went and how spectacular her horse looked. Steven finished in third place and knew it was the dressage phase that needed some more work if he was going to show him again. He was even approached back at the stable area by someone interested in buying Trick. "He's not mine but I'll tell you he is a nice horse. His owner is stabled right over here. She's helping to rinse the horse she rode but she should be back in a minute."

The stranger talked with Steven until Ellen returned with Stella and Mary. They wondered whom Steven was talking to as he stood there holding Trick. Steven introduced them to each other and then walked away after he handed Trick's lead to her. Mary grazed Stella for a bit and then put her away while she went and collected her shipping boots. Ellen talked for probably twenty minutes to the hopeful buyer and then he walked away. Mary then came and took Trick to rinse him off and started getting him ready to travel also.

Steven then approached Ellen. "Did you sell him? Was his offer pretty good?" he said half-heartedly. "Did you think I should sell him? Actually I'm mad that you sort of led him on that I might sell him. He's how I was able to get far enough with my riding to work with the likes of you."

Steven could tell he had touched a nerve that was having more effect on Ellen than he would have guessed.

"Hey! I'd be sick if you sold that horse. I enjoyed my ride today as much as I enjoyed riding Hawk and that's saying a lot. I really didn't mean to lead that guy on. I never said he was for sale. I just thought you might get a proud feeling talking to someone that was so taken by him that they wanted to buy him. They were throwing out some pretty good numbers to me." Steven then apologized to Ellen, who at least now was more understanding of the situation.

It was a pleasant ride back to the farm. Both horses had been successful and Ellen and Stella had convinced Steven with work she could easily go Advance level. They were all in a good mood and laughed and joked most of the way home. It was almost like a party atmosphere. They sang with the radio and Steven would occasionally turn the volume off to catch Ellen singing solo only to discover she had a really good voice.

They arrived late at night. They were tired but in good moods. Mary had fallen asleep for the last few miles but woke as they pulled in the driveway. Once again Jake and Sophie were there to greet them and help. Once the horses were unpacked and the essentials taken in they all headed into the house and after short conversations went to bed.

Chapter 12

MARY WAS NERVOUS as she wondered what the plan was going to call for next. She assumed that the show season was over and they would probably be heading back to upstate New York. Ellen and Steven had never discussed what was next. At least not that she knew of.

Mary went out to check the barn and to see if Jake needed any help. When she walked in she saw Jake in the stall of the horse they had rescued. Jake was brushing him and talking to him. He had put on weight and was starting to look like a horse again. Mary was complimenting him just as Ellen came in to collect them for breakfast. The three walked back to the house where Sophie had everything set out and Steven was on the phone in the family room.

Steven announced as they had breakfast that the trailer he had ordered was in and he could pick it up in another week. He was excited about it and looked forward to picking it up. "This one is a four horse and it has an enlarged tack room with custom cabinets and a built-in bathroom with a shower and facilities in between the horses and the tack room. Overall the size is bigger than a six-horse length yet smaller than an eight horse trailer. I'm really surprised they have it finished already. They originally said it wouldn't be ready for least another month. It's probably due to the poor economy and poor cash flow that they pushed it through so quickly."

Ellen was surprised by the description that Steven had just given them. "Why did you decide on a four horse trailer? Wasn't your other trailer just a three horse? I'm really surprised that you added the bathroom amenities. Is that something that you really wanted? It sounds wonderful I'm honestly just surprised about the extras."

Steven explained that he wanted the four stalls for the extra room for hay and supplies since he was planning on making longer trips especially out west in order to get back in the hunt someday for the Rolex and maybe some Canadian shows. He also knew before any of that could happen he'd need another horse. As far as the bathroom amenities he felt that it could be very handy especially if he started traveling west during the late fall or early spring for shows. He added the extra storage in the tack room would allow him to take more clothes and simple food supplies.

"Are you planning on sleeping in your new trailer?" Mary wondered. "Maybe on a rare occasion but I'm not giving up the good life of the hotels unless I really have to," Steven answered with a laugh.

Steven then changed the focus of the conversation as he inquired from Jake how the rescue horse was coming along. Jake told him he had put on weight and was looking a lot better. Mary added that she had seen him when Jake was brushing him this morning and he was looking like a totally different animal.

"How's his overall attitude been since he's eating regular and feeling better?" Jake told them that he was a sweet horse and got along with the other school horses really well. "We'll have to start riding him and see how he holds up. He seems to be OK but we don't know if he was lame before or not. We really don't know anything about him." Much to everyone's surprise Sophie spoke up. "He is a really a good boy. Jake has let me get on him when you have been gone and we have taken him for some longer walks. He listens really good," she added. Steven was blown away at Sophie's admission. Sophie was not thought to be a rider but she was comfortable with this horse and he was quiet enough for her. Steven suggested that she try to hack him more and that would help to get him in shape so they could find out just what he might be able to do. Sophie was very excited by Steven's approval.

They spent the day reorganizing everything and going through all the tack. Ellen had checked with Sue and found out things at the farm were all going well. Sue wanted to know when Ellen and Mary would be heading back. Ellen hadn't really given much thought to when they'd head back. Now as she thought about it she also realized how natural it felt being here at Steven's. Ellen worked at various chores the rest of the afternoon but her mind seemed to be elsewhere.

Steven was busy checking up on some billing and banking that were so necessary but also the least fun of anything that needed to be done. Once he was done he asked if Ellen wanted to take the horses for a hack. Ellen declined and so Steven went out and took Trick for a pleasant hack down the road.

At dinner they all seemed a little tired. No one had done anything that energy draining but the past few weeks were apparently taken a toll. Conversation was even at a low. Then Ellen started a conversation that needed to be had but all of them had put it deep in the back of their minds. "I talked with Sue today and everything at home has been good. It was good to hear all about things there but it also made me realize that I needed to get back there. It's hard to even think about the drive back, but at least Mary will be with me." Reality was setting in for Mary as she listened now and began to realize just how soon they would probably be leaving.

"When do you think you'll be leaving? I really haven't thought at all about you leaving. It seems so natural for you and Mary to be here. I hope you can stay a little longer," Steven said. Sophie and Jake also added their thoughts and hoped that the two could stay on a while longer. Mary had become very quiet but Ellen knew that she needed to make the decision as when to leave but she wasn't excited about making those plans now either.

Ellen shocked them all as she told them that she felt they should leave in the next two days. Weather in the northeast would be changing soon. Winter storms could happen as early as the next few weeks. "It's an unpredictable area," she explained and it would be risking hard travel if they waited much longer. "I am going to miss all of you so much and I really am sad to leave Stella and Steven's great lessons."

Everyone was quiet as Ellen finished talking. Mary was very sad about leaving but knew that this wasn't her option. Sophie seemed really down and Jake spoke to her in Spanish to try to settle her. Then Steven got up and came back to the table with a bottle of wine and a handful of wine glasses.

"We have had a wonderful and fulfilling experience. I speak for Jake and Sophie as well when I say that the two of you have made life very enjoyable. Ellen, you have helped me get back to this point. Without you I don't know where I might have been now." Steven then poured a glass of wine for all of them. "I want to make a toast. First, thank you all for helping me back and making it such a pleasant trip. May we be great friends always and spent great times together." They all clinked glasses and drank. Sophie and Mary were very touched and let it show as they both had a tear roll down their cheek.

Ellen wasn't saying anything and Steven realized that his little toast and thoughts hadn't answered one of Ellen's big questions. "Ellen I want to offer you a proposition. I would be happy if you'd like to take Stella home with you. I figure that you will be competing her next season. You should work with her and keep her going and your relationship growing." Ellen perked up as he told her his thoughts. She was pleased and excited about his idea. "But in fairness to me I was wondering if Trick could stay here. I'd like to compete him next year. I also figured it would ensure me a

An Event to Remember ~ 159

better chance of showing with you again next year." Steven said with a hopeful grin on his face.

There was silence for a moment as everyone waited for Ellen's answer. Ellen looked at Steven and then said. "I think it might be a good thing for Trick and it seems only fair if I am taking Stella with me. I definitely look forward to showing together next season. I'm hoping that I might be able to get you out over the winter to help me with Stella. We can work out the cost later." Steven answered her saying he was excited about working with Trick. He also made it clear that he would be happy to go out to help her but there would be no talk about payment.

Three days later Ellen, Mary and Stella started their ride home to Stamford, New York.

They had decided to try to do it in one shot as they had when they had come back. They felt confident they could do it including some good forty-five minute rest stops for Stella.

They were making good time as they crossed Ohio. Just as they were getting toward the border they had a blow out on the trailer. Mary had noticed a rest stop sign just moments before announcing it to be very close to their present location. After a fast stop to see the tire was ruined they decided to try to crawl at a slow speed hugging the shoulder in an attempt to get to reach the rest stop to change the tire. The mile or so they had to creep along to the rest stop seemed to take forever. Averaging 10 -15 mph made the short trip take a good half hour.

Once they parked they went about getting the 'trailer aid' and the tools they would need out. The tire was still warm even after the slow roll in. Ellen backed the trailer up on the 'trailer aid' and was proud how well she had done. Unfortunately they had forgot to loosen the lug nuts and had to pull it back down in order to start over. Seven of the lug nuts cooperated nicely but the last one made it known quickly that it wasn't going to give up without a fight. Both of the girls tried everything from WD40 to hitting the lug

160 ~ *Steve Farkos*

wrench with a hammer but it simply refused to relinquish its hold. No dice. They sat for a moment deciding if they would have to give in and call Triple A for help. Ellen was fighting the idea concerned that it would just add to the time the flat was costing them.

Now two burly looking men came from the truck parking area. "You ladies appear to be having some problems with that tire. Would you like some help? Mary was hesitant to respond when she saw the one carrying a three-foot pipe. Ellen didn't balk at it since she wanted only one thing, to get back on the road.

One of the men walked up and tried the lug wrench with no luck. His instant failure seemed to make the ladies a bit happier. He then asked the other guy to hand him the pipe. He slid the pipe over the end of the lug wrench giving him a huge advantage in the leverage department. With a few good grunts the last of the lug nuts surrendered. After they had the old tire off it took less than five minutes to have the spare on and the trailer back on the ground.

Ellen was very thankful and offered the guys twenty bucks for their help. The one refused it and then the other suggested that the ladies could buy them dinner at the truck stop just a few miles up the road. Ellen was fast to decline and that seemed to irritate the one guy. Mary then suggested that they needed to leave but would be happy to give them the money so they could have a great dinner. The two guys walked off and didn't take the money or say anything more.

"They did a great job and thank God for that but I don't think they were too happy about us not wanting dinner with them." Ellen said as she packed up the tools and the trailer aid. Mary said she was just happy that they had left and suggested now that they get going.

The rest of the trip was uneventful but long, very long. It was about 4:00 a.m. when they pulled into Ellen's place. They pulled up near the barn and unloaded Stella and Ellen asked Mary to walk her for a little while before they put her in her stall. While Mary walked Stella, Ellen took out some of the tack and put it away. As she entered the barn the other horses all greeted her and let them know they were happy she was back. As funny as it might sound to some, Ellen was always convinced that the horses knew her walk and voice quite well. Once they had Stella put away they grabbed two of their essential bags and went in the house. Sue was sound asleep with her boyfriend and so Mary and Ellen took the beds in the guest rooms.

It only took a couple of days to get back into the normal routines they had lived by for the past few years. The winter was approaching as the winds and storms drifted down over the Canadian border toward them. The changing weather would also mean that people would start looking again for indoor places to board, ride and get training. In less than a week they filled their empty stalls and had two new horses in training. Some of the return customers were surprised that Ellen had left Trick in Illinois. Ellen proudly told them about Stella and her successes and then once everyone saw her work Stella they accepted the change. She also convinced them that Trick was in extremely good hands while being worked by Steven Wilson.

Ellen and Steven would talk at least every other day or so. Most of the conversations seemed about the horses, their training and suggestions of exercises that might be helpful. Occasionally, Mary would talk with Sophie and they would share thoughts as friends but Sophie also talked about how nothing seemed the same since they had parted.

It was already the week of Thanksgiving and Steven called and asked if Ellen was ready for some of that good training he knew she was missing. They laughed about his assumption that Ellen was missing that training time but Ellen made it clear that they would be very excited to have him come in for Thanksgiving. Mary loved it when she saw Ellen on the phone with Steven because she almost always had a glow and happy smile during most of their conversations.

162 ~ *Steve Farkos*

After the phone call Ellen started planning the meal they would have. Steven booked a flight that would get him in on Tuesday night with a return flight for Saturday evening. Ellen let Steven know that she would pick him up from the airport. It was a little over an hour drive to the airport in light traffic. Based on his flight they should be behind all of the typical rush hour traffic and Ellen was happy for that.

Ellen started off to the airport about an hour and a half ahead of his arrival time. They had agreed that they would meet at the arrival pick up area and Ellen wouldn't have to park or come in to the airport. As Ellen arrived at the airport snow flurries had begun. If Steven's flight was on time it should have landed and he should be appearing at any moment she thought. The clock in the truck seemed to click louder every minute but still no Steven. Finally about thirty-five minutes after they had figured he showed up. "Our landing was put off for about twenty minutes it seemed they were having trouble with the brakes locking in the down position. You should have seen some of the faces when they announced that over the PA system. Sorry to make you wait so long." Ellen assured him that she was just happy that they were finally able to lock the brakes.

As they started back on the highway it seemed the snow was accumulating much faster now. The driving was going really slow as the road were becoming covered with snow. Ellen's cell phone rang and she asked Steven to answer it, as she was 100% focused on the road and surrounding traffic. Cars were sliding sideways and now there were a few collecting in the ditches along the side. Steven answered the phone it was Mary wondering if they were OK since she had figured them to be back already. "Steven, did you kidnap my boss? Are you two taking the long way home," she teased. Steven then explained the delay in his landing and proceeded to describe the current driving conditions. "How's the snow there?" he asked. Mary then admitted she hadn't been paying any attention but now she looked out the back patio door and saw the snow building up. "Wow. I didn't realize it was coming down so hard. Drive careful. Just how far are you away yet? We probably already have a good six inches and the wind is starting to blow it around pretty good." Mary's voice was beginning to sound concerned as she asked Steven to check with Ellen to get an idea how far they had to go. Ellen let Steven know to tell Mary that she couldn't see any mile markers but she felt that they were only about half way now. There was a tone of worry in Ellen's voice and as Steven relayed the information to Mary he sensed concern in her voice also.

For the next hour and a half Ellen drove with white knuckles as they passed more cars in the ditches or stranded. Steven offered several times to take over the driving but Ellen felt it would be too unsafe to stop and switch. It was onward and forward with a hope that they could keep going. Traffic had thinned out so that a lot of the time they couldn't see any tail lights ahead of them. That unfortunately also meant that it was near impossible to know where the lanes were and where the road shoulders were. As Ellen concentrated on the road Steven tried to keep talking to help her in any way her could. "I'm guessing that the fact the snow is covering most of the car tracks so fast is why there are so many cars going off the road. We don't see snow like this except about every twenty-five years or so where I come from." Ellen didn't even reply, she just kept carefully driving.

Eventually they reached the farm traveling the last ten miles very slowly in four-wheel drive. As they attempted to pull it the driveway they encountered a three-foot drift. The snow in general was at least a foot but the drifts were still growing. They weren't going any farther. "I'm afraid we'll have to hoof it from here. Do you have any other shoes in your bag? You should probably put them on. Anything you wear is going to get wet and probably full of snow. We'll get to the house and at daybreak I'll get the tractor with the bucket out to dig a path in for the truck. It's now almost

11:00 so I don't figure there will be much more traffic on this road tonight. The truck will be safe."

Steven then looked over at Ellen. "Look at you with your nice shoes on and nice pants too. You didn't even come with a winter coat just that cute jacket you love. You're going to be wet everywhere and damn cold in the wind." Ellen just looked at him and said they didn't have much choice if they hoped to get to the house and warm again.

Steven convinced Ellen that there was a little less snow on his side of the truck and the plan would be for her to get out on his side. Ellen took a second to call Mary and let her know that they were almost there but to be on the lookout for them as they were going to walk the last part in now that the truck was stuck.

Ellen put her cell phone away. Steven had pulled his barn boots out and grabbed his work gloves for his hands. Ellen didn't even have gloves. Steven exited the truck and waited for Ellen to crawl over the console. As she was about to slide out of the truck Steven grabbed her around the waist and tossed her up on his shoulder. "What are you doing? Ellen said in objection. Steven's reply was she going to keep him dry by being over his shoulder as he began the struggle through the snow.

Every drift presented a challenge as he could hardly lift his legs. He was walking almost heel to toe making the progress very slow. Mary had come to greet them at the front door and realized the door was stuck because a drift had blown up against it. She began to work at getting the door open as the two slowly covered ground to reach the door. Ellen would occasionally let out a giggle, as Steven would nearly lose her and then make some grab to stabilize his effort.

After almost twenty minutes the two made it to the door and Mary was able to get it open and even cleared a small area in front of it. Steven dropped Ellen just inside the door and then started to get some of the excess snow off before he stepped into the house.

"Good thing I finished the last of the shopping today. At least we know we'll have a good Thanksgiving dinner. Don't suppose too many people will be able to shop tomorrow. It's going to take some effort to clear these roads especially if the winds keep up," Mary said to them as Steven continued to brush snow off. Ellen had left already and was now returning with some kind of clothes in her arms.

"Steven get those pants off and put these sweat pants on. They're really big on me but they should fit although they'll probably be a bit short. Go to the powder room and change and give us your wet shoes and clothes so we can start drying them. There's also some sweat socks there too."

Steven returned in a few minutes and they all had a good laugh at the sight he was. Ellen was now in sweats and wooly slippers. Mary called them to the dining room where she made up a dinner from what it might have been earlier if they had made better time home. She poured three glasses of wine and they all relaxed and talked for a while. They were all tired and went to bed but Ellen was determined to get up at dawn to clear a path to the barn and to her new truck clear of the road.

Steven got up around 5:00 a.m. and fumbled around in the kitchen to get some plastic bags to use as insulators. He took one large bag and cut a slit for his head and arms and then took two smaller ones and put his feet in them before he pushed his feet into his still damp shoes. He figured that the plastic close to his skin would hold the heat in and keep the moisture out. He slipped on his jeans that were now dry and worked the sweats over them. He put his coat on and then found a stocking cap near the back door.

After the ordeal of dressing up he went out the front door and found the shovel that Mary had been using the night before. He started to dig a path to the barn that stood off in the distance probably a good football field length away from the house. The wind had died down to almost nothing and the snow was a light powdery consistency. The

166 ~ *Steve Farkos*

shoveling was going better that he assumed it would and his progress was going great.

He was nearly three quarters of the way to the barn when he heard a voice behind him. "Are you nuts? You sure look like you're nuts." It was Ellen who had come out to start a pathway to the barn. "If you just keep me going we'll be to the barn soon and we can get the tractor going. It's going to take a while to clear enough space to pull the truck in. One of us can use the tractor and the other can shovel where we need to."

Steven picked up the pace and made it to the barn in ten more minutes. He told Ellen to go in and start the tractor while he fed the horses. He suggested that she go in the tack room and warm up a bit since she hadn't been working yet and was probably getting cold. He was now sweating under the plastic now and needed to keep working to avoid getting cold.

Mary joined them in a while and the three of them worked for over three hours clearing snow and finally getting the truck into the yard. They were all exhausted and decided no one would work with the horses today. Mary would turn them out in the arena for some exercise and tomorrow they could get back out.

Wednesday was over before they knew it. It was now warming up again outside and there was water dripping from ice on every building and fence. "Mary, if you take care of feeding, I'll go get Steven up and we can start the turkey and stuffing for our dinner later," Ellen said.

Steven and Ellen prepared the bird and worked together chopping the makings for the stuffing. Before you knew it the kitchen smelled of Thanksgiving. It was always amazing as the stuffing got started how it would fill the room with early impressions of how the turkey would taste. Once Mary was in they made a breakfast and sat to eat it while their supper slowly cooked in the oven.

Shoes needed to be dried and reconditioned and clothes dried again. So it was a leisurely day they spent watching TV

An Event to Remember ~ 167

and discussing their favorite parts of each of the shows they had been to. It was a slow day and they all were winding down as the timer went off in the kitchen. All three jumped up, as they needed to fix some side dishes for the dinner. About a half hour later Steven was carving the turkey and the ladies finished setting the table. They enjoyed a feast that evening, one that they all had a hand in. Before they left the table Steven took a moment to tell them how very thankful that he was that they had found one another and become such good friends.

They spent the rest of Thanksgiving Day going through scrapbooks and old pictures. Mary offered some funny stories about mishaps and funny things that had happened to them over the years. It was a good afternoon and evening of bonding, laughs and of course recovery from their big snow day.

The next two days before they had to leave for the airport they worked horses. Ellen was amazed at what she could accomplish with Steven's guidance. For the amount of time that he had known both her and Stella he could see things and have answers so fast they could turn a rough movement around in minutes to a supple, floating dressage delight.

The roads back to the airport were clean and the skies were very bright as the sun reflected off the snow-covered fields. Ellen and Steven talked about the upcoming season and the shows they should try to do together. Then Steven added a question that Ellen wasn't expecting. "I would like to fly you and Mary in for at least a week at Christmas. We can get some rides in but I mainly would like to have both of you there as my very special guests and who I would like to share what I consider the most important and best holiday of the year. I hope that you can get Sue again to take care of things and I'd be more than happy to pay her. I really would like you there." Ellen didn't answer at first and then said she would love to but needed to check on several things before committing.

Steven's flight was on time and Ellen walked with him to the security gate. Just before he was about to pass through the gate he turned to her and gave her another hug and then he kissed her good-bye. This kiss wasn't the same as the few others that he had given her. It wasn't the kiss of a casual friend or a relative. They both came away from it a little numb with the good feelings they were having. The flight back was on schedule but seemed to go faster than his other flight. He spent a lot of time thinking about that kiss and why this one was felt so different. He knew he had feelings for Ellen and that he was grateful for her friendship, the opportunity to ride and show with her but he also realized there was more.

Ellen got back to her place and was greeted by Mary who instantly questioned the big smile and warm glow she was showing. Ellen didn't say very much and didn't offer too much information about their parting. Mary tried to get out of her what had her glowing but since Ellen didn't have an answer Mary offered her thoughts. "I think that someone has some big feelings for that guy she just dropped off. And I'm guessing that one of you actually acknowledged what you were feeling. Did he say that he loved you?" Ellen looked at her and said no nothing was said. "Maybe though I'm beginning to realize I do love him, but I'll not say a word first since I don't want to be forward or lose the friendship we've built so far." Mary just looked at her and said, "You're both holding back from what would make each other so happy. You're both afraid and yet you both long for it to be. Enough said by me. Let's go and get some horses worked and get your mind back to normal."

Ellen had said very little as Mary gave her thoughts and opinions. She knew that what she was saying was what she was feeling but was so afraid to acknowledge. Steven had come to mean so much to her in so many ways. Her mind was full of thoughts of Steven as she tried to get her rides in.

Chapter 13

STEVEN WAS HARD back at work and Trick was really coming along. Steven felt that the horse's lateral work, especially his half passes, were really coming along well. His balance had really improved and Steven loved the work ethic of the horse. He was a worker and wanted to please his rider. Trick was a great help in getting over the loss of Hawk. Trick would probably never be all that Hawk was, but no one would ever fault him for not trying.

Jake and Sophie often brought up both Ellen and Mary. They all got along so well and really missed their company, especially Sophie. Steven let Sophie continue to work with the rescue horse. Sophie's riding was starting to show her natural seat and good balance. She was enjoying it and hoped to show Ellen her improvement when she might come next. Sophie never missed getting any of her chores done but rarely missed a ride either. Steven was impressed by her efforts and began offering help and was encouraged by her efforts as a student. "I think you'll shock Ellen the next time she's here. Your riding is really coming along. You and that gelding are making great progress, both of you."

The next day as they sat eating dinner Sophie had an idea. "Mr. Steve I think you should ask Ellen and Mary to come here for Christmas. We could have a great time. We could even decorate the house and Trick's stall at least. I can make a great feast to celebrate Christmas together." Then Jake spoke. "If we're going to do that then you'll have to bake cookies and cakes like we knew when we were little. I'm game. I'll even buy some decorations so we can have a special tree this year." They both looked at Steven to see how he was reacting to their thoughts.

"OK. I'll call and see if they can come in. And I'll hope that she doesn't get snowed in if she does want to make the trip. Now if they are able to make it then Sophie you'll have to go get a fancy dress and Jake you might need some shoes other than your cowboy boots." Jake and Sophie looked at Steven trying to figure out where he was going with his thoughts. "So as soon as we know if they can come I will get tickets to the holiday ball they have every year at the Oak Brook Country Club. I understand they have a wonderful cocktail party, dinner and dancing. What do you think?"

Sophie was very excited about the possibility of going out all fancied up and dancing.

Jake was surprised by Steven's idea since he didn't normally think of outings like this. He was also excited about getting all cleaned up and dancing with the woman he loved. It was like a fantasy come true for Sophie and he was aware how excited she was already.

"Now we just have to make sure that our guests can make it in for the celebration we're so busily planning. And I guess if they can't the three of us will do it anyway." Steven announced. Jake was pleased with Steven's last statement after seeing Sophie so excited but she let her thoughts be known also. "It will be fun to go with the three of us but it won't be as much fun as if we all could go." None disagreed with that thought.

Steven called the next day and conveyed their Christmas plans and a week later Ellen and Mary were flying in. Everything worked out well and it came together like a fantasy. Steven and Jake had decorated outdoors and Sophie and Jake had put up a tree and decorated the entire house.

An Event to Remember ~ 171

When Mary and Ellen arrived and went in they felt like they were in a winter wonderland. The décor was impeccable and they felt already this would be a special Christmas for them.

The Christmas ball was the next night and that meant the next day would be the ladies' day for establishing the perfect look for the evening event. Jake and Steven worked outdoors most of the day. The horses had the day off spending most of the day outdoors grazing on the little nibbles of grass left in the small paddock. The men came in for lunch and teased the ladies about the lack of preparation that had taken place for their meal.

"I'm guessing that you gals are having a fun day if nothing else." Steven said as the ladies sat with towels around their damp hair while they painted one another's nails. They were a sight as they sat around as if they were at some fancy spa. As the guys were getting ready to go back out Jake announced that it was snowing outside. It had been predicted, but the ladies hoped that it might hold off until later in the evening. It was coming down pretty good at the moment so Steven wanted to get outside and bring the horses in so they wouldn't end up in wet blankets.

The snow had stopped after a while and left a light coating of white over everything. It was a pretty sight and yet had stopped before causing any problems. It was about 4:00 in the afternoon and the guys had fed a little earlier and now came in to clean up and dress for the evening's event. As Jake went to his room he realized that Sophie had abandoned the room and he had it all to himself. He actually had hoped they might be getting ready together because the day and the thought of the evening already had him in the mood.

Steven was the first to come out to the living room about 6:00, which was the time they had all agreed to leave. He waited a few minutes and then yelled out the time as if he were a town crier. Moments later Jake joined him. The two men noticed how good each other looked but didn't make mention of it because they were typical men. Now the bedroom door opened and down the hall came a parade of angels. Sophie was first and she had a girlish look on her face as she waited to hear something from Jake. Jake's mouth had opened but no sounds were coming out.

Sophie was in a long white dress with a simple red ribbon around her waist. Her Hispanic caramel colored skin tone was beautiful against the snow-white dress. Jake was very taken but it was Steven that uttered the "Wow!" Both men's eyes were like those of a young boy's in a candy store. Immediately behind Sophie was Mary in a short black dress with a lacey cape over her shoulders and high heels that seemed to accentuate her muscular legs. Steven was quick to comment. "Mary, you look great. I never saw your legs before. They're very good." They all laughed at his comment as Ellen now appeared in the hallway. Steven at first seemed speechless but then rambled on as she approached. "My God, you are beautiful. You look stunning and it's all just perfect." Ellen's reply seemed silly based on Steven's reaction. "So you really like it?" She said as she did a little turn around.

Ellen was a knock out in her long red dress. It was form fitting and showed her strong shoulders in a very feminine way. Her dark hair was the perfect accent against the red of the dress. Steven was starting to look like a deer in the headlights as he continued to take it all in. "So what do you think?" Mary asked as she made a hand motion toward Ellen. "I think she looks much taller!" Steven said in a mindless response that generated laughter from all. Ellen looked at him and pushed a leg forward exhibiting the high heels she was wearing." You all look incredible and I feel very honored to be going to the ball with you all. Everyone looks so different all dressed up. I am more than impressed," Steven said and then Mary offered her opinion as she noted how outstanding he looked in a suit and tie.

They went to the ball and Steven and Jake felt they were entering with the beauty pageant winners. The cocktail portion was nice and a few people recognized Steven and

Jake and they both proudly introduced the ladies. Steven even referred to Ellen as a very special friend and put his arm around her waist as he introduced her to a good looking guy who had a reputation of being a player.

Dinner was good and they had a table to themselves. The ladies all left at one time to go powder their noses and Steven and Jake noticed that many men and women in the crowd were watching the three women cross the open dance floor. "I guess we take a lot for granted." Jake said as they watched the ladies returning. Steven then admitted that he really never thought of them as beautiful model-like women, but more like nice looking riders.

After dinner a band started to play and people started dancing. The guys didn't make an effort to get the ladies out on the dance floor; in fact it was Sophie who got things going. "Come on Jake, it's been years since we've had the opportunity. In fact the last time we danced all dressed up was our wedding." Moments later the two were dancing and made a wonderful picture. Steven then got Ellen to join him and the two of them started to dance. They were seen to laugh often as they danced and later it came out that they were laughing at Ellen's efforts to lead.

When they returned to the table Mary was gone and Ellen was instantly concerned about her. Steven pointed to the bar where Mary was amongst three good looking gentlemen and before you knew it she was dancing up a storm with one of them. "That Mary sure can move. She looks like a dancer," Jake commented. Sophie gave him a playful punch on his arm and then hugged him to let him know she was still at his side.

They all enjoyed the dancing and danced for the next few hours. As they were leaving they had to retrieve Mary, who was being closely kept by her new friend. Mary and her new friend, Paul, exchanged numbers and then they were all off and headed home. The car ride home was a buzz of happy conversation reliving all the high points of the night. They were all a bit tired but they were all very happy.

When they got home they all were going to head off to bed as the dancing and the dinner had done them all in. Mary got Steven and Ellen into a conversation near the hall and then she reached over their two heads and called their attention to the mistletoe she held above them. Steven took Ellen into his arms and kissed her passionately as Mary and Sophie applauded and cheered. Ellen didn't resist in the least in fact there was little doubt how happy she was.

They all headed off to bed as they had put in a long day and they needed to start early in the morning to catch up with the horses. Ellen and Mary talked in their bedroom for another hour before dropping off to sleep. Ellen was feeling like a princess who had just been swept totally off her feet. Mary kept trying to talk about Paul but Ellen always managed to get the conversation back around to how wonderful Steven was.

The next day they worked with the horses and Steven did a lesson with Ellen on Trick. Ellen was impressed at how well Trick was going. He seemed very attentive to even the softest aids and that kept Ellen very conscious of every movement her body made. For the next two days they worked the horses and enjoyed each other's company more each day. Mary had received a call from Paul and spent an afternoon with him.

It was their last night as the return flight was scheduled for around noon the next day. Dinner had a quieter air about it that night, as they all were not looking forward to the morning. Steven and Ellen drank wine that night and discussed the probable show plans for the year. The thought of showing together was exciting to both of them. It was about 1:30 in the morning and all the others had already turned in. "I really need to get some sleep." Ellen said in a sad voice. But before Steven could comment or protest she reached up and took Steven's face softly into her hands and then kissed him tenderly. They remained there for a time and kissed often neither of them ever thinking they could feel this way.

An Event to Remember ~ 175

Steven dropped them at the airport the next morning and kissed both of the women goodbye. Ellen held her hug and kiss longer and she was really sad that they needed to leave.

Once they got back to Ellen's they realized that they needed to put the holidays behind and get things going as far as conditioning the horses and taking care of the two that had come in for training. It felt good to get back to work but every night either Steven would call or Ellen would. They were surprised at how long they talked and couldn't always remember what they had discussed so long.

It was now mid-February and the winter had been tough on the New York area, with several rough winter storms bringing excessive snowfall and freezing temperature. Steven had hoped to come in but one of his client's horses in for training had come in from the paddock with a deep wound on its leg and had to be carefully cared for daily if there was any chance they the horse could compete again. Ellen was tired of the weather and now realized how much she missed Steven. Even Mary felt sequestered since Paul had called several times a week and had offered to have her come in for a visit, but it just wasn't possible.

March was coming on and the training and conditioning was intensifying. Ellen really wished that Steven could help with Stella as she felt things just weren't all they could be or had been but it seemed the more she tried the worst things were getting. Ellen sat down after dinner and called Steven to ask for his help.

"Hi, Ellen. I was just about to call you. I wanted to ask you something special." Ellen was quiet and let him go on before asking him her question. "I honestly think we need one another, Ellen. And we are planning on showing together all this year so I think and I would like you and Mary to come and live here. You could rent or even sell your place if you wanted." Ellen didn't say anything for a moment but then asked. "Are you like asking me to move in with you? Like we were dating and you're asking me to move in? You really think that I would consider renting or selling my place to move in with you without more of a commitment from you? Honestly, I have realized that I love you but I'm not stupid either. You have never expressed your feelings in words, or made any commitment, but you want me to give up everything I worked for so I can move in with you. I don't think so."

Now both ends of the phone line went quiet. Ellen was wound up and maybe a little upset by the whole thought. Steven on the other hand thought he was offering a great situation to someone he had feelings for and figured he was offering something she would think was special. After a rather long pause and uncomfortable moment Ellen said good night and said she would talk to him soon. Steven offered an apology but wasn't even sure if she had listened to his words.

Once they were off the phone they both went to their corners and looked for encouragement and help. Ellen talked into the night with Mary and Steven actually woke Jake and Sophie looking for their thoughts and help.

Neither called the other for the next day two days. It was the next morning as Ellen was walking out to start working the horses that a taxicab pulled into the driveway. That was a very unusual sight for this countryside of New York. She stopped in her tracks assuming the driver was looking for directions. The snow was still piled high everywhere. The cab started to make a three point turn so it could exit. Now it stopped as Ellen went towards the driver's door. As she neared the stopped cab the back door opened and the trunk popped open. Ellen stopped in her tracks again only to see Steven getting out of the cab and the driver pulling his suitcase from the trunk.

"What are you doing here? Ellen asked as he exited the cab. "I needed to see you. I felt we needed to talk about a few things. I think maybe I messed things up without even trying. Can we go inside and talk for a while before you go out to the barn?" Ellen hadn't said anything else but turned and headed back into the house. She wasn't upset, more surprised and cautious. She was happy to see him but unhappy that she hadn't heard from him after the awkward last phone call.

As they entered the house they Mary greeted both of them, as she was getting ready to go out to help Ellen. "Hi, Steven. I didn't know you were coming in. It's good to see you." Ellen gave her a slight head movement to tell Mary that she should still head out. Mary excused herself and then went out.

Steven then told Ellen how much he had missed her and how much she had come to mean to him. He apologized for his surprise of showing up but he felt he had no choice but to come. Ellen still had said very little but admitted she was happy to see him. She wanted to be with him but was unsettled by the conversation that they had shared days before. "Can I get you a cup of coffee? It should still be pretty warm and if not there's always the microwave," She offered. Steven agreed and then took a seat at the table as Ellen got the coffee.

"I have to tell you I haven't been able to accomplish much since we talked the other day. I realized my approach was awful and thoughtless and I also have realized how much you mean to me and how much I have missed you and feel that I need you. I have never been more excited to see or be with someone as I have been with you." Ellen then admitted that she had many of the same feelings and she even apologized for the way she came off on the phone the other day. "I guess I was being a little protective since I had been burned once before. I had moved in with a guy who I thought was pretty special. I was young and of course there was no commitment and after the fun and games he took a walk and had taken most of the savings I had managed to put together by then. I think that fueled my feelings. The thought of living with you has crossed my mind but never with any thought that it would ever happen." Steven acknowledged her thoughts and then asked her to sit down with him.

"Ellen I have to ask you something. I 'm not sure I know the right or exact words to say but I was wondering if you might spend the rest of your life with me? "As he said it he pulled a small box out of his pocket and opened its top. It was a diamond engagement ring. "I know now that I love you and I am ready to make that commitment."

Ellen took the ring out of the box and was taken by its size and brightness. "Now where did you come up with this in the past two days? Don't get me wrong--it's beautiful-- but I don't know how you could come up with it so fast." Steven laughed and told her that Jake's father was a jeweler and he spent an afternoon with him to come up with the design and it didn't hurt that I promised him a big tip if you really liked it. I had to guess the size so I only hope that it fits.

Ellen slowly slid it on her finger and admired it in the sunlight that poured through the window. "It is beautiful and it actually fits. I never thought that it might happen like this to be honest," she told him. Steven then looked at her and told her he was a little unsure if she had ever said yes or no. "Steven, it's exciting and I am honored but it comes somewhat as a shock since we've never even talked about it. I know that I have strong feelings for you, but I need to know that I'm ready for it too." Steven was a little shocked but respected her answer. "Can I keep it at least tonight and give you the answer before you leave?" Steven agreed but felt numb that she hadn't committed.

Ellen walked over and gave him a very tender and loving kiss. Then she suggested that they have a normal day without making it a big discussion. He agreed as long as she promised that the two of them could go to dinner that night.

They worked horses and Ellen and Stella were both happy to have him there for help. It was a productive afternoon and the two of them got along as good as ever. Ellen chose not to say anything to Mary but she did say that just she and Steven were going to dinner.

They had a romantic dinner and Steven felt it was everything that he could ever want. He also knew that Ellen was what he wanted more than anything now in his life. There was no discussion about the morning, the ring or a commitment. It was just a fantastic night because they were together. Ellen curled up next to him in the truck on the way back to the ranch. Steven put his arm around her and felt a sensation assuring him that he had something wonderful and special at hand. Once they were in the house she took him in her arms and kissed him like they had never kissed before. He was excited and hugged her as if he never would let her go and kissed her passionately and then tenderly kissed her on her neck. She broke the long passionate silence when she bid him good night and told him she would take him to the airport for his flight in the morning.

Steven went to bed and lay there wondering why she didn't give him the pleasure of knowing after such an incredible evening. He was tired from the very long day and his very early morning flight. Just as he was drifting off the bedroom door opened. It was Ellen and she came in and over to the bed. As she stood there Steven started to get up but she gently pushed his shoulder back and then unwrapped her robe and let it drop to the floor. Steven pulled the covers back inviting her now naked body to join him in bed. She was even more beautiful than he had imagined. As her skin pressed against his, he realized how soft her skin was over her very fit body. She didn't say anything but began to kiss him where they had left off before saying good night. Steven kissed her and allowed his kisses and now his hands to freely roam over her body. Neither chose to wait longer as they joined and made passionate love. Neither had experienced such a feeling ever before, even with those they thought were the 'right' ones.

They then lay side by side and enjoyed their closeness to each other. They shared their thoughts of love with each other and commented on the sharing experience they just had. Then Ellen took her left hand and made a fist and pushed gently down on Steven's chest as she dragged her hand down. Steven felt the drag of what he assumed was the ring and at that same moment Ellen flashed the engagement ring on her finger at him. "Just in case you missed my answer a minute ago this should make it clear. Yes. I will marry you and be with you forever."

They hugged and kissed and then agreed they would discuss timing on the way to the airport in the morning. Then Ellen giggled as she tried to imitate what Mary's reaction would be when she realized they had slept together and, even more surprising, that they were engaged.

Mary was more than a little shocked but very happy. She had a million questions but Ellen promised answers to things when she returned from the airport. On the way to the airport Ellen and Steven agreed to a fall wedding. Both wanted to compete together and have plenty of time after the season to maybe travel and have fun while the horses could all have a break. They hoped to come up with a plan for Ellen and Mary to come to live in Illinois in the next month or so. Before they knew it Steven had to board and they were forced to say good-bye for the moment

Chapter 12

STEVEN AND ELLEN realized in that first week they were apart that they missed one another as they never had before. They were working the horses planning the event schedule and planning and looking forward to a marriage date. Mary was also pushing to make the move to Illinois.

Because time toward the season was flying forward, Ellen decided that for now she would lease the house and barn. After the season and over the next winter they could decide the farm's final direction.

Ellen started the long drive to Steven's taking Stella and one of the better school horses. She had contacted the owners who she had been working horses for and let them know of her location change. One owner was excited for her and the other had picked up their horse just days after the phone call. Ellen had packed up most of all her clothes and all of her show stuff and planned on driving all the way through with stops as needed by her or the horses. Mary was packing stuff to put in storage and then made a shipment of other items to Steven's that she and Ellen might need.

Once Ellen finally arrived at Steven's they unpacked, put the horses into their new homes and then took the night off. They were happy to be together and Sophie and Jake were excited to have her there. "When will the rest of your stuff arrive? Do you know when Mary will be coming in?" Sophie wondered. Ellen explained that the people that had signed the lease would be moving in at the end of the month. All the paperwork had been left with a lawyer that Ellen had known most of her life and he would meet with them and turn over the keys once the first month's fee and the security deposit was paid. Everything was going according to plan and now Steven and Ellen needed to focus on conditioning the horses and themselves.

Training was going well for both of them and they once again proved valuable to each other, coaching from the ground. As instructors and clinicians they were firm believers in not teaching from the back of a horse. "Since neither of us are qualified or ready for the Rolex at the end of April I think we should do the dressage show at Lamplight, one of the most prestigious show grounds in the Midwest, as a good test of where we stand in our efforts so far. I also think it will be a great warm up to our first event in May. The best part is that we could just trailer in since we're less than fifteen miles from there." Steven agreed and they filled out the paper work that evening.

They had both done dressage only shows before but never on the two horses that they were showing today. They were also showing together and even against each other in one class. Warm ups were going well for both and they were just minutes out from their scheduled times. Steven was scheduled in the ring first and after they both had their bits checked so he headed to the ring as Ellen found a place from where she could watch. Ellen hoped to see as much of his test as possible. There was only one rider scheduled between them. Ellen watched as Steven and Trick went through the movements. She was excited to watch the horse she had competed the last few years now being shown by the man she loved.

Ellen walked toward the arena entrance as Steven was exiting after his test. "You guys looked really great. How did he feel for you?" Ellen said with a huge smile on her face. Now the rider between them was finishing her ride and Ellen had the right to begin her final warm up around the arena. As she was circling around the arena a young girl passing had the balloon she was carrying suddenly explode. The girl was a good thirty feet away but several horses spooked and started to act up including Stella. Ellen was shocked as Stella spun and then went up on her hind legs. Ellen tried to settle her, as Steven looked on with concern. Ellen's whistle for her ride sounded and she hoped to get Stella's full attention with one final trip around the outside of the arena. Stella seemed settled as they approached 'A' for their entrance. Down the centerline and Ellen asked for the halt and began to salute the judge when Stella decided to wheel around in a 360-degree circle. As soon as she was facing the judge's box she started her test and tried to forget about what had just happened.

The rest of the test showed a sense of tension instead of the relaxed teamwork they had showed in the fall. Ellen was unhappy with her ride and Steven did his best to console her. They both had only a short while until they were scheduled for their next test. Steven was riding first level test four for the second time but Ellen had signed up for second level test one. Steven's test rode even better than his first had gone he felt and now it was time to walk over and watch Ellen's test in the other ring. Ellen's test wasn't much like the work they had been doing at home. They were more supple than before but the tempo changed as Stella seemed unsure of what she was being asked to do.

After they had cleaned up the horses and had them ready and on the trailer they walked back to the scoreboard to see what their scores were. There was a small crowd waiting for results around the board. One of the women from the scoring office was posting now the last class that Ellen had recently finished. They were able to see the results from their first test. Steven had taken a second with Trick with a score of 65.7 Ellen's score was 58.2 and she hadn't made the ribbon cut. As the crowd thinned and the woman with the master sheet left they were able to find Steven's second test, a 68.4 for second place again. Ellen had found her score and pointed to it with a defeated look on her face. The score of 55.6 was a huge disappointment even if it was a higher-level test than her first one she had ridden.

Steven had picked up his two second place ribbons and they were walking back to the trailer. "You really did a good job today. Trick looked stunning and I think he has put on some good muscle. He looks bigger than I even remember," Ellen said in a very proud tone. She was happy for Steven and very proud of Trick.

"I know that you're disappointed, and I was a bit surprised by Stella's reaction to the balloon. She's always been so unshakable it seems. You handled the situation well I thought. It was a good outing to see where we're at. We need to get her back to where she was at the end of the season. Remember the eventing dressage test that you'll be doing will be a good step down from what you were doing now. Honestly, I still think that the true dressage judges score a bit tougher than most at the events. As we plan on moving up, the dressage gets tougher and we need to be better prepared. I'm going to call one of the clinicians I know and see if we can get someone in to work with both of us," Steven told her as they prepared to leave the show grounds.

Ellen knew that Steven was trying to ease her disappointment. She was concerned though since she had finished so strong a year ago and she had been working well she thought. In the next few days they needed to fill out their entries for their first event in Kentucky at the end of May. After discussing it they decided to both enter at the prelim level.

Steven was lucky enough to secure a couple of lessons from Otto Gualt, who had ridden and trained in Europe throughout his life and was now considered one of the best clinicians in the United States. The help made a difference

An Event to Remember ~ 185

for both of them and with each other's help they were able to keep things correctly on track.

They arrived in Kentucky on a Wednesday and they were scheduled to compete Friday, Saturday and Sunday. They used Thursday as a warm up day and let the horses graze in their rented paddock that afternoon. Friday would be their dressage day and they were scheduled as early morning rides. They figured they would arrive at 5:30 in the morning and they could help with things as Mary braided.

The morning came fast and they got to the farm on time. Steven fed and Ellen watered as Mary got ready to braid Trick. Trick was the first to ride and his time was at 8:04, as the fifth horse to go. Ellen's ride was scheduled for 8:46 but she wanted to make sure she could watch Steven's ride. The open division, they were both in as professionals, was larger than normal. Steven was pleased with the competition and the amount of entries. Ellen was a bit nervous as she reviewed the entries in the division before she mounted to warm up.

Steven's ride seemed flawless as she watched from the corner of the warm up area. He was pleased with his ride as he came over to see Ellen during her final moments of warm up. "You really looked good from here," Ellen said. "I'll be happy to get a ride of that caliber when I go in. Stella feels good now, as long as I can hold it together we'll be fine, I'm sure." Steven agreed with her and then dismounted. Mary had come back up and he handed Trick over to her to take him back to the stalls. Steven watched nervously as Ellen rode her test. He was hoping that she would have one of her great tests and regain the little bit of confidence she may have lost at the dressage show.

"Ellen, you were great. My score won't stand a chance against the test you just rode. I'm really proud of the two of you. Good job!" Ellen dismounted and happily gave her husband-to-be a rewarding hug for his nice words. Toward the end of the day after they had fed the horses for the

186 ~ *Steve Farkos*

evening and walked their cross-country course another time they went to check the scoreboard.

"I told you that you had a damn good test. Look at your score and then look at poor me," Steven said teasing Ellen a bit. Ellen was surprised as she saw her posting. She and Stella were in second place with a score of 30.6, and Steven and Trick were in sixth place with a score of 35.5. Ellen was truly surprised but also pointed out that the first-place horse was at 26.4, less than a rail apart. Then she pointed out and that there was just a little more than a rail between her second position and Steven's sixth place. "Those top ten places are all very close and then the remaining ten are really spread out. Let's remember that we've only just started, "Steven said in his reality based voice.

They had early cross-country times and they were close enough time wise that they would warm up together. It was an early morning scramble for the three of them as they worked to get ready. Mary was amazing and like a machine as she worked to get the two horses and riders ready. Steven helped her getting the studs on Trick, as he was a bit antsy and obviously ready to do his job today.

Steven was first of the two to get out of the start box. Ellen wouldn't be leaving for another four minutes so Mary and she waited and listened for any words they might hear coming in from fence judge's walkie-talkies. Just after Steven started she clearly heard "Number 6 has cleared fences one, two and three and is going well." Then she didn't hear anything until she heard that he had cleared number six. She knew the water complex was next and they both thought it was a tough line after coming down the steep incline. "Whoa! That was a scary ride for number six as he ended up on the horse's neck as they entered the water. My god, they made it over the duck jump, but how I'll never know. I'm not sure how that rider stayed on, but he did. He's fixed his position and is now on his way with obvious intentions of making up any time he may have lost." Ellen had heard the gasp of the crowd and the loud

An Event to Remember ~ 187

applause over the P.A. system as the announcer described Steven's trip through the water.

Ellen now heard the starter calling her number again with a 15 second countdown started. As she entered the box the starter finished her countdown, "three, two, one go ... and have a good ride." With that Ellen and Stella were off and galloping to the first fence.

Steven came into the finish line with less of a horse than he had started with. Trick was lathered and breathing hard but Steven had made it in on time and clean, even though parts were scary. Mary started to untack Trick and was loading the tack into their golf cart as she and Steven tried to listen for information on Ellen's round.

Shortly they saw Ellen coming into the finish line and watched her as she checked and turned off her watch. As she approached Steven and Mary she made a face and told them that she had gone over time. "I'll have time penalties. I went clean but I kept messing too much with her as we came down the hill and into the water. I almost didn't have enough horse under me for the duck. Stella clearly saved me at the duck."

After they wrapped things up for the day they left to clean up and grab an early dinner. After dinner they came back to the stables to check water and to give the horses another couple flakes of hay. Before leaving they went to the scoreboard to see where the day's events would have them placed now. Steven had moved into third place. Ellen along with another rider had time penalties, while another had two refusals also. Ellen with her time penalties had fallen to fifth place. Steven was still about nine points out of first but only a point behind the second-place rider.

That night Ellen was down on herself as she felt she had taken away her placing by over-thinking the water complex after listening to Steven's go. Steven told her several times again how important it was to ride her plan and not to focus on what may happen to another rider. "Too many times I've heard a rider blame a fence for a refusal only to find out the rider listening to the story had the same problem when they went out," he explained to Ellen.

Stadium went well for both and it was apparent that Ellen had worked on her rhythm since she had such a beautiful ride. Stella breezed over every fence with plenty of clearance and as round as the most expensive hunter you'll ever see. Steven finished in third and Ellen took fifth. Both rode proudly in the victory gallop and enjoyed, for the first time, a lap of honor together.

As they drove back home they discussed what they would need to work on before the next event in two weeks. The next event was local but would have some really good competition even though their division might be smaller than Kentucky. They also discussed wedding plans and what they hoped to accomplish by the end of the season. Mary was half asleep in the back seat but teased the two about their conversation shifting from wedding plans then back to their secondary love, their horses. Mary wanted to rest, though, because she had a date for the evening with Paul who had been calling since she had got in from New York.

Chapter 15

THE NEXT EVENT they went to was within 30 miles of home. They had worked on what they felt would be necessary to keep them in the top six at the event. Steven loved the old cowboy saying he had once seen on a poster, "Make dust, don't eat it." He felt strongly that it was smartest to develop the whole package as carefully as you could. It was best to try to be in first place after dressage and to fight to stay there. It always irritated him when riders were content to be in the upper half of the pack after dressage knowing that they could probably finish in the ribbons. They believed it was because of their horse's God-given talents instead of what they had worked to make happen. He always had a great respect for the person who had a horse that showed potential talent but who had to work to develop it. He felt any good rider had to live through that experience and be driven by desire in order to be truly rewarded for their work. He could always pick out the rider who bought that special developed horse but didn't know how the talent had been developed.

The event went well although there were fewer entries at their level. Their scores were excellent and both were able to finish on their dressage scores, having had double clear rounds on cross-country and in stadium. The effort that they were putting into their training was very obvious and people were starting to notice both them and their horses. Ellen had never had such recognition but was enjoying as people consistently talked with her and Steven encouraging and applauding them.

190 ~ *Steve Farkos*

When they pulled into the farm they saw Sophie jumping the rescued horse. The two were really looking good and Steven was excited about how far they had come along. Even before they had the horses unloaded Steven and Ellen walked over to watch Sophie as she went through a gymnastic that Mary had set up for her before they left. "She's really looking good. We should keep encouraging her," Steven said. Then Jake walked up and hoped that Steven didn't mind that they were taking a mid-afternoon break from chores so Sophie could ride and he could watch. Steven again was very happy with what he was seeing and made sure both Sophie and Jake knew it.

There was a two-week break between events and they went back to making slight adjustments and conditioning work. They jumped but worked mainly over simple grids and at lower heights. They both spent some time working with Sophie who was amazing as a rookie. She had what it takes to feel the ride and also the guts to try new things.

The next event was uneventful and both Steven and Ellen finished in the ribbons and this time Steven led the victory gallop. Ellen was so very impressed at what Steven was doing with Trick. He had already made a difference and it was enjoyable to watch them whether they were training or competing. It was nearly a month before they were back on the road. This event would be in northwest Wisconsin and would be about a seven hour ride up. Mary and Paul were getting along rather well and Mary asked if they could drive separately since Paul was coming to watch and help at this event. Ellen and Steven agreed as it would give them some additional time to discuss the wedding without feeling they might be boring Mary.

This event Steven was moving Trick up to advanced for the first time in their partnership. He felt that he was ready and they had also moved Ellen and Stella up to Intermediate. The terrain had more hills that what they had done with these horses and there were many more technical situations on the course. Before they would actually go out of the start box they would each have walked their courses a half dozen times each.

Steven was able to start his weekend in fourth place after his dressage test. Ellen was very excited and proud of the showing they had made. Then Ellen rode and as she went through her test as her smile became bigger and brighter as she knew how good her ride was going. At the end of the day she was in first place and six points ahead of the horse in second place.

Steven's division was small but at a higher level and he had his cross-country first. Because of tight timing though it would be impossible for Ellen to see any of his go.
"How did it go Steven?" Ellen asked as she was headed to the warm up area and saw him returning from his cross-country go. "It went really well. He's showing a lot of courage but the hills really got to him. He's been heaving since we finished and is just now slowing down. According to my watch we were only two seconds off time and clear at all of the fences." Ellen was so very proud of the two of them, but now she needed to get warmed up since she was less than twenty minutes out from her scheduled cross country time.

Ellen left the start box feeling really good. She couldn't have asked for a better warm up. She was ready and they looked great as they galloped off after the first fence. The ride was going just as planned. They were starting their approach to number ten. It was a very narrow bank up loaded with foliage on either side followed by a very tight left turn. She steadied Stella and the bank up rode great and she responded well as she demanded the sharp left turn. Fence eleven was eight strides away if you had a normal pace but Stella was a bit too fast. The fence itself presented a huge optical illusion for both the horse and rider. The fence was a window effect that they would jump through with a wide open space over the horizontal log that joined the two sides. The space underneath was enough to distract them both but it was the illusion presented through the window that would provide a mental challenge to many. The land on the backside was a huge downhill slope that seemed to go for miles. It looked as if they would be airborne for the afternoon once they took off.

Ellen felt that Stella had just too much steam and started fighting with her, as they were three strides out. The mare fought and then took over catapulting the two off them over the fence before Ellen had wanted. Ellen came out of position and landed heavily in her left stirrup disrupting both Stella's and her balance. The mare took a harsh stumble step but recovered herself but that wasn't the case for Ellen. She came falling off and rolled for about twenty feet. It took Stella about thirty yards till she could stop and then she patiently waited for Ellen.

Ellen wasn't hurt bad, but she knew she'd be sore in the morning. The biggest hurt was losing her first place as her fall had eliminated her now. Ellen got back in the saddle with the help of the fence judge and then started her long walk back.

Steven, Mary and Paul were all waiting at the finish line and quickly realized something had happened as the three horses that started behind Ellen were coming through the finish line in their normal sequence. Finally they saw Ellen walking in and knew she had trouble. As she came closer Mary announced, "She must have fallen. She's grass stained everywhere. It looks like she fell several times with all the dirt she's wearing. I just hope she's OK." With that said Steven jogged out to meet her and to find out what had happened.

Ellen had a tear of disappointment in her eye as Steven reached her. She felt that she had let them down but Steven made it clear that wasn't any issue at all. After Ellen had given her recap of what happened Steven looked at her and was ready to say something but Ellen spoke first. "I know it was me. I was unsure of my pace and braced and got into a fight with her. I hope someday I can learn to use what I

An Event to Remember ~ 193

know and not let my emotions and subconscious take control."

Steven had a good stadium round and even with his time penalty was able to finish in fourth place. It was a huge victory for Steven, as he knew now he was on his way back. Kansas was next on the list and that was a mere two weeks away. Ellen was sore the first week but continued to work towards the event. Ellen was really enjoying working with Sophie and was so proud of what she was accomplishing in her riding. Ellen was so excited about her efforts she went and bought Sophie a really good pair of riding breeches to encourage her efforts even more.

They left for Kansas and Mary and Paul drove separately again and it had become obvious that this was going beyond any relationship that Ellen had ever seen Mary in. Steven and Ellen were getting more excited about their wedding, which they had now planned for Thanksgiving weekend. They were sure that their season would be complete by then. Ellen dropped down to prelim for the event as she felt that she wanted a good confidence building go before moving up again. Steven would compete again at advanced and was getting more excited about each event that he and Trick entered.

Paul was getting the hang of things and was actually a welcome set of hands in setting up or breaking down the stabling areas. He was also becoming more confident as he occasionally helped with the horses. He and Mary would often take the horses for long walks so they could enjoy each other and where they were. Steven and Ellen would also take advantage of those moments for extra course walks or just taking in the love that was growing stronger all the time between them.

The first day of the event went very well. Steven was in second after his dressage and kept his position after his double clear cross-country round. Ellen pulled out all the stops and nailed her dressage test and sat in first place with a lead of six points. She rode her cross-country with a look of control and confidence and finished with a double clear also.

That night Steven found a great old fashioned steak house in the old side of town, where they used to ship out all the cattle for the East coast. The meal was incredible and the four of them had a great time. Paul was an interesting guy and came up with some fun mind opening games at the table. He started by asking what animal each would want to be if they were to come back as an animal. Then they had to explain why that animal. From there it went to body parts and beliefs. Before they realized it they were starting to know more about each other and certainly understanding each other even better. The four sat at the restaurant long enough that they were holding up closing the place. As they drove back to the hotel they laughed now about some of the answers that were given but laughed with each other and not at one another.

The next day stadium went very well for Ellen as she had a beautiful clean round and led the lap of honor with a huge smile. Steven wasn't as lucky. As he did his turn back from the Swedish oxer Trick slipped a bit with his inside hind leg and didn't get back to the proper pace. As he entered the triple line the first fence went well but the oxer in the middle was a stretch to clear and the last fence came down like a bundle of kindling wood exploding. Steven's destruction of that third element cost him two places, but he was still happy with the final result.

As they started home Steven surprised Ellen when he said, "I think I'll pull Trick from the event in Missouri. I want to give him a break and be sure that the slip didn't twist or pull anything in that back leg. Ellen was a bit surprised since she had missed the slip and thought that Trick seemed fine as they walked him out and got him ready for the trip home.

Mary and Paul went ahead and reached the farm a good half hour ahead of Ellen and Steven. Ellen was happy to have the extra time with Steven. She enjoyed his company so very much and the ride home was like a bonus after her strong finish. She decided to withdraw also from Missouri and use the time to tie up any loose ends for the wedding plans.

Once they pulled into the farm they were greeted by Mary, Paul, Jake and Sophie in the new breeches with damp hair, showing again that she was working hard at her riding every chance she got. They all pitched in and unloaded the horses, cleaned the trailer and put everything in its place. While they were working Ellen let them know that they were canceling out of the Missouri event. They then decided to get cleaned up and go to town for some pizza and a chance to relax. Sophie was especially happy with the idea since she hadn't started anything for dinner. She hadn't received a call letting her know when they might return.

Once Ellen told Mary that she was going to bow out of the Missouri event, Mary asked if she could take a vacation over that weekend and the following week. Ellen agreed but was surprised since she couldn't remember the last time Mary had taken personal time off.

That night at supper Steven came up with a fun idea that surprised them all. Sophie had made such progress and the rescued horse trusted her as if they had been together forever. Steven was excited as he explained his idea. "I think since we aren't going to Missouri I'd like to take Sophie and her newfound prince up to Silverwood to compete in her first-ever event. We'll have the time and she's worked so hard with that horse I feel she deserves it. I'm even volunteering myself and Ellen as your personal grooms and trainers." Sophie looked shocked and excited at the same time. She had dreamed about showing but assumed it would always just be a dream.

Jake then offered her encouragement and asked if he would be able to go also. Of course you can come," Steven said but then was interrupted by Ellen. "I just gave Mary an OK to vacation that week since we weren't going to Missouri." Jake looked down and Sophie saw his reaction.

"I probably shouldn't plan on going. I don't really have any of my own clothes or equipment. I think it was a great idea and I appreciate your thought, I know Mary is looking to her special time also.

Steven put his hands up indicating stop. "Sophie's going and so is Jake. Mary can still take her vacation and Ellen you'll take them up to the event. School her, walk the cross-country course with her and I'll feed in the morning and leave early to be there by her show times. It's only about an hour and a half away on a normal day." It was a great solution and everyone was pleased.

They entered Sophie the next morning. They entered the rescue horse as "Her Prince", which was the name Sophie now used ever since the dinner when Steven had told her she could work with him. Ellen took Sophie shopping and bought her all the equipment that she might need. Everyone was excited about the event.

Trick had taken a few stiff steps after the event but now showed no signs of anything being wrong but Steven decided to give him an extra week off to be safe. He rode one of the school horses and spent more of his time working with Ellen and Stella. He made it part of the daily schedule to do a lesson with Sophie and Her Prince. On some days he and Ellen would take two of the school horses out and just go for long relaxing hack together. Their time together was more enjoyable and special that they had ever felt with any other persons.

The weekend of the event came and Sophie was nervous and excited. Both Ellen and Steven felt that she was ready and believed she was going to do well. Several hours before they would leave for the event they saw Mary and Paul depart for the vacation they had planned. Mary was as excited as Sophie was on her end. Mary and Paul left full of chatter and lots of smiles heading west, toward Las Vegas.

Sophie was born to be a rider. She looked amazing as she rode her first dressage test. Her nervousness might have been apparent to them as they saw her ride into the ring but

An Event to Remember ~ 197

no other person could have possibly been aware of just how shaky she was. Sophie and Her Prince delivered a nearly impeccable test and Steven was convinced that she had to be in the ribbons.

Her stadium ride went well but she ended up with a refusal on the cross-country course. When it was all done and over with she had still finished in the ribbons in sixth place. The green ribbon that they handed her might as well been made of gold as Sophie held it high for Jake to see and then clutched against her chest. Everyone shared in her success and both Ellen and Steven continued praising her for what she had just accomplished. Once at home Steven took them all out to celebrate the start of a new equestrian career.

The following weekend Mary and Paul returned to the farm. Mary skipped out of the car and to Ellen like lamb in the spring. She had such a bounce in her step Ellen couldn't figure what had put her in such a state. Once Mary reached Ellen she gave her hug and swung her around. Mary was beaming like Ellen had never seen before. "What has gotten into you, girl? Did you win the lotto while you were away? What's going on?" Ellen stared into Mary's happy eyes and suddenly was given the answer she had been looking for. Mary simply held her hands up showing a sparkling ring on her left hand. "You got engaged?" Ellen yelled but Mary shook her head negatively as she announced the fact that she and Paul had gotten married in Las Vegas. It was all crazy wonderful as they found all the others to break the news. As they reached the house, Paul and Steven were already preparing a bottle of wine for the celebration.

Both Sophie's and Mary's weekend had charged up Ellen's emotions and desires. She wanted to get back out there and finish the season moving back up to intermediate and even more she wanted to get married. Her feelings for Steven had grown so much even from when Steven had proposed. They had agreed to wait but Mary's surprise had now ignited her desire to do it now. She talked with Steven

198 ~ *Steve Farkos*

that night in bed and explained how much she wanted it to be a fact and not just a dream. Steven appreciated her evaluation but after they had talked she was again in agreement they were right to wait and the reality was it would only be another two months at most.

The remaining season played out as well as any could. Ellen's last show for the season was down in Georgia. The ride down seemed so long and yet it was exciting since it would be another intermediate with Stella. Steven and Trick were enjoying the improvements that kept coming throughout the season. They both finished in the ribbons at the show and Steven had amassed enough points during the year at Intermediate that he felt Trick now had a chance of placing in the USEA Area IV Horse of the Year awards. Ellen was excited about the possibility as much as Steven.

On the trip home they talked about the season and relived the up and down moments. Ellen had conquered many a fence and even similar situations that had found her on the ground in Wisconsin. It was a tough way to learn a lesson but it was one that stuck and made her an even better rider. Steven suggested that they give the horses a good vacation for a month or so. It would be easy to plan it around the wedding, making it a guilt-free plan. They spent the rest of the drive home talking about the wedding and nailing down the details of the honeymoon they were planning.

Weeks later it was time for the big event. Since neither Ellen nor Steven had family alive they had planned a smaller wedding. Even though it would be a smaller wedding it would have all the detail and wonderfulness as if they were a royal couple.

Paul and Sophie led the procession down the aisle of the church. They were followed down the aisle by Mary, the maid of honor, and Jake as the best man. As Ellen came up the aisle all the heads in the church focused upon her. She was a stunning bride in her form fitting dress with the flowing train behind it. The top of the dress was without

An Event to Remember ~ 199

straps or sleeves and showed her well-toned shoulders. She had long gloves on while she held a bouquet of white roses and daisies and just enough greens to offset it against her dress.

Ellen had cut her hair shorter than usual, which surprised Steven as she neared the altar. She wore only a simple headpiece with no veil attached.

"You are so beautiful. I love you and this is the best day of my life." Ellen smiled and gave Steven an acknowledging look for his comments. The ceremony was short enough but Steven was fidgeting as he looked forward to the moment he would be allowed to kiss his beautiful bride. As the priest pronounced them as Mr. and Mrs. Steven Wilson they both had the happiest smile that anyone had ever seen. There were probably less than two dozen people at the function but every person there could sense the love that existed between the two of them.

Steven had planned the reception at an exclusive restaurant not far from the farm. It was a beautiful setting but the room they had was actually pretty small compared to the overall size of the place. Of course the size or the place didn't matter because every moment before dinner, dinner, and all of the toasting were fit for a royal couple.

The bride and groom were so pleased and happy it seemed that nothing could spoil the moment. They had a small band that played light classical music as they ate and visited. Ellen was so excited and pleased she leaned over to kiss and hug her husband as the most insane level of noise now started up in the next room. The divider between the rooms had been presented as nearly sound proof. That wasn't the case at all. The noise level hit the divider as if it was a series of tidal waves. Ellen was becoming upset as it became harder and harder to even talk with Steven, who sat next to her.

Jake leaned over and asked Steven if he should go to the management. "No. I'm going to go. I'm paying a lot and we were having the moment of a lifetime and now this." He

200 ~ *Steve Farkos*

threw his hands up and stood up to go. "Should I go with you maybe?" Ellen asked. Steven felt he would handle it better on his own.

Steven went down the long hall toward the manager's office. He was tempted to just go into the room to see if he could make it change but then thought better to go on to the Manager's office. After he explained what was going on the manager walked back with him to the noisy room. Next door Sophie and Mary were comforting Ellen who was starting to feel that everything was coming apart on her special day.

As Steven and the manager walked into the noisy room the noise level dropped quickly. Steven marched alongside the manager as he headed to the microphone and DJ. Steven was feeling a bit angry as he walked in but something seemed strange now. There were faces that suddenly seemed familiar yet Steven was sure he didn't know them. As the restaurant manager took up the microphone and asked for everyone's attention the divider between the rooms started to move. The motorized divider made odd noises as it opened now alerting the bridal party. "What is going on now? This is turning into a bad story," Ellen said as her eyes welled up with a tear or two.

Before anyone could say anything to Ellen the microphone in the other room let out a loud feedback squelch as the manager handed the microphone to Patrick. "I apologize for the recent moments of craziness. At this moment I would like to present the bride and groom, Mr. and Mrs. Steven Wilson." Steven and Ellen were a room apart as Steven asked the manager what was going on. Patrick used the mic now and encouraged people to mingle and get the bride and groom together again. The crowd now had spilled into the other room and people started to approach Steven and Ellen at different ends of the enlarged hall and slowly drove the couple together.

Ellen saw Mary now introducing people to Jake and Sophie. Then it dawned on Steven and Ellen at almost the

An Event to Remember ~ 201

same moment. This unruly crowd were people they had known and competed against and knew but rarely saw in street clothes let alone all dressed up. These were their peers and competition friends. Many faces now were obvious. Some of the better acquaintances had hidden more toward the background as to not blow the surprise.

Mary and Sophie had contacted many of the eventers they knew and then invited others who had been competing against the two all season long. Mary knew it would be a small wedding but she knew there were many supporters that would love to be there as well wishers. The whole place was alive and there was a happy buzz everywhere.

Ralph, an eventer who had competed probably four times during the season took up the microphone and began to speak. "First, I want to toast the bride and groom. We all wish you the best of lives together and a wonderful career as a team." With that all raised their glasses and you could hear clinks of crystal through the room. Then a cheer for the two sounded through the room. Ralph now continued. "Thanks to Mary and Sophie for reaching all of us. We have seen you compete together and help one another this season. I speak for most of us when I say we think that you are the event couple and team of the decade. From what we've seen you belong together. We wish you great success, sound horses, clear rounds and all the happiness anyone can have. Just remember to leave a few awards behind for the rest of us." The crowd laughed at Ralph's last comment while other unsolicited toasts were thrown out from around the room. Patrick was still at the microphone and raised his beer and toasted the newlyweds. As he finished his simple toast he added, "I could have told you all this would happen." Then Patrick jumped from the stage and found his way to the couple and embraced them with happiness.

Ellen and Steven were happy with the way things had now gone. It was a wonderful surprise. Everyone danced and enjoyed this non-equestrian moment. It was fun to be together and not competing against each other. It also worked to bring this community of riders closer together as the good people they are. Steven and Ellen really enjoyed their time and conversations and the night drifted away with no regrets of the unusual change of plans that had come about.

As the winter months came on Ellen and Mary felt the season was much milder than what they had been used to in New York. Steven and Ellen went back to check on things at Ellen's farm and actually did get caught in blizzard conditions again and acted as a good reminder of the harsh winters Ellen had lived with for years. The people leasing Ellen's farm were nice and the place was being well kept. The people were quite pleased with the deal they had and their upkeep was proof of that.

Married life suited them well and Mary and Paul who lived in town were truly a happily married couple. Now it came to February and it was time to get back to some serious conditioning. It was a slow start up with long sessions of collected walk and varied trot work. Mary occasionally would show up late for work but interestingly Sophie was always there to help. Sophie's desire to ride and work with the horses was very apparent. She had learned so much in the past six months--she was like a sponge absorbing all the new knowledge.

Their conditioning was going well and even Steven did some personal conditioning since married life seemed to change his figure over the winter a little too. Steven was focused though and it took very little time for him to get back to his competing condition. As April approached they decided to go back to Wisconsin to compete instead of going to watch the Rolex. Steven was convinced that if this season went as well as he planned, they would both be competing in the Rolex next year.

Chapter 16

THE EVENT UP in Wisconsin went well for both Steven and Ellen. Both were riding at the advanced level and once again found they were competing against each other. The window jump, with the optical illusion of jumping off the face of the earth, was now set higher for the Advanced level they were riding. "Remember this fence?" Steven teased Ellen as they walked the course on Friday. Ellen laughed it off and teased back that she would gladly meet him at the finish line mounted. Saturday Ellen rode the fence with no problems. It seemed apparent that her competitive spirit could be a good tool to help push her through some worrisome situations. Sunday was stadium and Ellen pulled a rail again and fell from second in the division to fifth place. Steven and Trick placed first with two points ahead of the next competitor.

Both Mary and Sophie had come along to groom and help. Paul had offered to stay and help Jake so that Sophie could go. Sophie had been bitten by the bug the year before and wanted to event again.

The trip home was fun and Steven used the time to tease Ellen about her loss of second place by pulling a rail again. Steven had worried about this aspect of Ellen and Stella's competition. Too often he felt that it had come up to hurt Ellen's final placing. At first he felt it was Ellen's mental relaxing that was causing it. He felt that she would mentally finish her ride before it was all done and wasn't riding the last fence. They had spent a lot of time working at it and now Steven couldn't help but wonder how much of the problem was actually Stella's let down. Either way he wanted to find a solution to the problem.

The next event for them would be the Indy event. They were excited since it was only a few weeks away now. Once again Sophie asked if she could come along to help. Steven didn't mind as long as it didn't hold Jake back from getting all the chores done. Once again it all fell in place and both Mary and Sophie came along. The four were having a lot of fun and it seemed no matter where they went now that there was an outpouring of friendship as they continually ran into people who had come to the wedding or at least heard about it.

The event went well but there were only six riders that were competing at the Advanced level. Steven and Ellen rode well and Ellen didn't have any rails in stadium. Steven and Trick were not as fluid looking during their dressage test as usual and that proved to be the difference in the end. Ellen and Stella took the blue ribbon and Steven and Trick finished with the red ribbon. Their finish at the event made them even more popular as they became known as the "Eventing Couple."

As a surprise, Steven had entered Sophie into the Barrington event with Jake's approval. Sophie was so excited and it was like a dream come true. The event was very close to home and Sophie knew that some of her friends could come and watch. Jake was pleased with the idea since he'd also be able to be there to support his wife in her new found love. Even Paul planned to be there to watch and help. It was as if they were all a part of a family.

As they pulled out for the event Sophie was so very excited it made it special for everyone. Once they arrived they all looked like a well-oiled machine as they cared for the horses and set up the tack room. "I'll pick up your packet for you, Steven." Ellen called out. "I'm going to take Sophie up with me and make sure that her entry is correct. They had e-mailed her at my e-mail account saying she owed money but there was some other question also."

Steven gave her a wave as they walked off and he started to bathe Trick.

At the office the additional charge was demanded as a novice level competitor. The show secretary said it was for her USEA membership that was required at the novice level and above. "But I am riding beginner novice not novice." Sophie stated. The show secretary reached into the book of entries and pulled Sophie's out. She then flipped it around so it was facing Ellen and Sophie. There it was. It clearly stated Novice Division. Steven had made a mistake while filling out his well-intended surprise.

"Isn't there any way we can get her into the Beginner Novice Division?" Ellen asked as she watched Sophie start to get nervous. The secretary wouldn't bend. Sophie had two choices. One was to ride in the Novice Division and the second option was to not ride. Ellen encouraged her to ride and was doing everything to convince her that she could handle it and do well.

When they walked back and told Steven he was very apologetic and at the same time started immediately to reinforce all that Ellen had been telling her. Sophie was nervous but Ellen guaranteed her she would feel much more confident after they walked her course.

Steven and Ellen went out and walked their cross-country course. It hadn't really changed much from Steven's go last year but Ellen hadn't ridden it before. The plus that Ellen felt as they walked the course was that they were sharing some of the fences she had ridden at the prelim level last year. Both felt very confident as they came back.

"Sophie, are you ready to go walk your course now?" Ellen asked as Sophie sat learning the different dressage test she would be riding now. Sophie agreed in a moment and she, Ellen and Mary went off to walk Sophie's cross country course. Sophie seemed to be more relaxed as they walked the course. Then Ellen could see that Sophie was nervous about the drop and the water jump since she had never done those type of obstacles before. "That horse trusts you

206 ~ *Steve Farkos*

so much all you have to do is believe in him and trust him," Mary stated and Ellen quickly agreed.

After they all had competed the next morning Steven was in first in their division and again Ellen was in second. Sophie surprised them all as she rode the new test and in a division of twenty riders she was sitting in fourth place.

Mary, Jake and Paul all helped get Trick and Stella ready for cross-country. As they went out everyone listed to the distant voices as they called in the fences as riders cleared them. Steven finished his round and gave a thumb up as he crossed the finish line indicating his clear round. Four riders later, Ellen was on course. All was going well and then at the fourteenth combination the announcer put a scare into Steven and the group as they listened. The combination started with a steeplechase fence with good height followed two strides later by three stairs downward. The last step fell off to a steep downhill with a coup on the way down. Steven and Ellen had noticed as they walked the course that the hoof prints clearly read a fast arrival at the coup and a very far out landing after the coup. It was the landing after the coup that unseated Ellen as they flew down the hill in the woods. The path was very narrow and Ellen was caught forward and for most part out of the saddle hanging on to Stella's neck as the trees on either side guided her down the path. Once the land leveled and a clearing was there Ellen worked to get back in the saddle. Stella slowed down and let her regain her seat. In the meantime the announcer had no idea what was happening and had now started calling out the fences of the next two riders.

Steven and the others started to assume at this point that Ellen had fallen or been disqualified and was probably doing an embarrassed walk back. "We haven't heard anything for a while so I'm guessing she may be doing the 'walk of shame'. We should just hang out here and wait for her." Just as Steven finished his thought they heard pounding hooves as the next horse was now coming into the finish line. "Look. It's Ellen and Stella. They're still going but that next rider is very close behind her." Mary said with excitement. Ellen finished and recounted her ride to everyone. Her biggest concern was her time. How badly would she be penalized?

At the end of the day they went to look at the scoreboard where Steven was pleased to see he had maintained his first place standing. Steven then ran his finger down the board and pointed to Ellen's score. She was marked as clean but had been assessed six points for time penalties. As Ellen looked at it she was a little surprised since she felt she had recovered from the whole situation in really short amount of time. At this point she was out of the ribbons and could only hope that another rider or two might be unfortunate enough tomorrow to pull a rail or two.

Sophie left the start box and Jake was obviously the nervous husband as he watched her take the first two fences on course. She looked great but now was out of his sight. Sophie as many riders do rode the fence she was concerned about best. The water jump that she had never done before, she rode strong to and her horse never skipped a beat as he dove in and cantered nicely out. As she approached the drop she took on the same attitude in her ride but now she was riding too strong. Steven and Ellen had walked out to watch and now saw Sophie coming to the drop. "Oh shit! I hope she has a strong half halt planned she's coming too fast. Sit back." Ellen was saying as Sophie and her horse launched themselves from a spot really far back. The gelding banged his back legs on the edge of the drop and tightened on the landing followed by a few funky steps as he felt the sting of the hit. The sudden slow down on the landing and skip steps that followed had sent Sophie forward and she now hung unto the gelding's neck. Steven and Ellen were sure she was going to fall but somehow she managed to get back in the saddle. "She'll end up with some time penalties. She really slowed down almost to a walk to regain her position." Ellen noted but she tapped Steven as she was speaking and pointed toward where Sophie had finished righting herself. "I'm not too sure, look at her go. If she can maintain that for the last three fences to the finish line I bet she doesn't get any time penalties."

The next day they wrapped up the event. Steven finished first; Ellen's time penalties dropped her to seventh place while Sophie miraculously finished in fourth, where she had started. They were all excited and they filled the conversation with the replays of their accomplishments at dinner that night.

The next event that they had scheduled was all the way out in Colorado. Steven, Ellen and Mary would make the trip. They were gone for ten days but they were really pleased with the results. The Event at Otter Creek up in Wisconsin made them better prepared than they could have guessed. They actually felt that the fences on the hill at Otter Creek were actually more technical than those they faced in Colorado. They finished in second and third place, this time with Ellen on top. Both of them had two double clear rounds and Steven was really getting confident about what the two of them could accomplish.

Ellen and Steven went to the Area IV championships that were held in Heritage, Kansas that year. Steven was disappointed in his dressage test and knew it would affect his final placing. Steven again had two double clear rounds and finished in fifth place. Ellen on the other hand had one of her best dressage tests and was sitting in second place after that phase of the event. The cross–country rode great and she produced a double clear. Stadium was a disappointment as she pulled a rail on the last fence of stadium and dropped to fourth place.

As they were driving home Steven surprised Ellen. "I think we should pull out of that last event we planned in Georgia. I think we have pushed these horses pretty hard this season. I think the rest would be good for them I guess." Ellen responded, "Well I do agree we've had a crazy

An Event to Remember ~ 209

year and we've done well but I want us to make that trip to Georgia. We're entered in the two star there and I think it will be a great test for the end of the season but also to see if the horses can handle it." They talked about it several times on the trip home. By the time they had reached the farm they agreed that they would do the event. They had another three weeks and they would rest the horses the first week, back to some lighter conditioning the second week and then they would ramp up their efforts for a half-week and then travel to the event. Things went as planned and before they knew it time had come to leave.

On the way down they made an overnight layup in Lexington. Steven and Ellen enjoyed a private dinner out while Mary stayed at the hotel and enjoyed a cocktail and a movie on the tube. As they drove the next day Mary started a conversation that led to a discussion about how much travel they had done. Mary was suggesting that possibly in the next years they might consider rotating Sophie and herself as grooms. "Mary, I'm surprised. I wouldn't have guessed that you'd ever want to give up going to the events. We've always had so much fun." Mary turned to Ellen and said, "I have always had a great time. Even now. But the truth is 'We' now means you and Steven and not so much you and me. And I'm married, too. I miss Paul and he can't always come with us even though he wishes he could." Steven thought it was a good plan. He saw it as a possibility for Sophie to get more involved in the sport she had fallen in love with. "Maybe we could work it that you and Paul could care for the farm when we were gone and we could let Jake travel with Sophie. You and Paul could both travel together also whenever his work would allow him the time." They all agreed that it was a good idea and would see how the others felt when they got back.

It would be the last event of the year. They were both excited and wanted to do this two star as their stepping stone to next year's plans and hopes. After they pulled into the event they quickly set up their stalls and tack room as usual. Once they had the horses out of their shipping wraps and picked up their numbers they planned to take the horses for a walk and to let them graze.

"There's a big open area over that way that I saw as we pulled in. It will be a nice walk and it looked like a nice place to graze the horses. The three walked with the horses and each carried a nice cold beer for the walk. They had plenty of daylight and felt after they cared for the horses they could walk the cross-country course. The three walked along telling stories of different years and having a few good laughs when they thought how far they had come and some of the funny and sometimes embarrassing things that happened along the way.

Once they reached the large clearing they let slack out on the lead lines and let the horses graze. There was a group of rocks that a farmer had probably put together as he cleared the land and planted. These were very large rocks and obviously stacked and left there by man and probably not by nature. The bottom boulders sunk into the ground and had been there for some time. Mary looked at the pile and thought it was a great place to catch some sun. Mary sat there and talked with Ellen and Steven as they grazed the horses. Ellen had finished the beer she had brought and walked toward Mary on the rocks to hand her the empty bottle. Less than six feet from Mary, Ellen called to her and then flipped the bottle for her to catch.

Mary missed the bottle and it bounced off the large rock at the base and slapped the ground as it landed. Ellen began to walk over to pick it up just as a snake came slithering out from the rocks toward her and Stella. Ellen jumped and screamed and they weren't sure if was Ellen or the snake that then spooked Stella. Stella yanked the lead from Ellen's hand as she reared and fell backwards. She then scrambled to her feet and tore off at a gallop. As Stella went off Trick became worked up and jerked at the leadrope as Steven attempted to settle him. "Whoa! Easy! Whoa, Trick, we'll get her back." Trick continued to try to rip away from

An Event to Remember ~ 211

Steven in an effort to join Stella on her fun run. Both Ellen and Mary had run off after Stella and finally Steven had Trick walking and prancing alongside of him as he headed back to the stable area.

Once Steven reached the stable area, Trick was back to normal and very obedient. Mary and Ellen were fussing over one of Stella's back legs as Steven got close enough to ask what they were checking. "Once we caught up with her she was walking off. We've checked her and saw no injuries but when we tried to trot her off she was lame. God, Steven are you OK? You have blood all over your hand and pants." Steven looked at his hand. He had felt the lead rope burning his hand as Trick tried to yank it out but he hadn't realized that it had put several cuts across the palm of his hand.

"Mary, please take Trick to his stall and bring me a rag or something to wrap around this hand of mine. I want to check out Stella now." After Mary left with Trick Steven proceeded to check Stella's leg. As he pulsed along her suspensory tendon she flinched. Steven then asked Ellen to trot her off so he could watch her. She was definitely off and wouldn't be competing this weekend. "Let's get her wrapped and I'll give her some bute. Maybe we should just head back in the morning." Ellen wasn't going to stand for that. "You and Trick deserve to go. Let's get Stella taken care of and then we'll walk your course."

It felt strange to Ellen to have to be on the sidelines and watch the one she loved compete while she was just a spectator. Ever since she had been with Steven, even at the Rolex, she was always a fellow competitor and never a sideline spectator. Also, unlike at the Rolex, when she had watched Steven compete with Hawk she would be watching the person she loved on the horse she had practically raised. The emotional aspect certainly had an effect on the way one felt. She was surprised as she felt some concern and fear of danger as they walked this cross-country course. As they walked Ellen was sure to not express any negative thoughts she might have since she knew that was one thing that really would get Steven mad. He was a strong believer in positive mental reinforcement. You never discussed the negative possibilities you thought about an obstacle. You were to turn your thoughts positive and imagine just how good you would ride that obstacle. Jane Savoie had written several books promoting the theories of positive mental riding and Steven was a believer. Ellen had learned to discuss the technical quirks about a fence or a combination without ever mentioning what disaster you might be imagining. The positive worked and she had also become a fan and promoter of it. But it also seemed to work differently depending if you were a rider or a spectator.

Once Steven went off to warm up for dressage, he was all business and Ellen felt she knew how he must have been all those years before they showed together and so nicely supported and helped one another. As Steven headed out he was focused, confident and yet relaxed in his position. He was an example of supple and not of tension. Not walking along side of him on a horse was totally different as far as the conversation. As a teammate on a horse Steven had ears for your thoughts. As a walk along Ellen wasn't sure that he was hearing everything she was saying.

Once again Steven and Trick had a fantastic weekend. Out of a field of eleven riders they took second, only a fraction of a point out of first and two full rails ahead of the third-place finisher. Other than a slight stutter step at the head of the water jump, Trick had performed flawlessly. Trick trusted Steven and obviously wanted to please him. They had become a partnership that many dream about but few ever really reach.

Steven talked all the way home about how great of a horse and partner Trick had become. He was really proud of him and Ellen was so happy that she had been able to give Steven the opportunity to compete him. What could have been a better gift to the one you loved especially after knowing how much he had cared for and trusted his beloved Hawk.

An Event to Remember ~ 213

Once they reached home they settled in and let the horses have the time off. They tried to wait for Stella's leg to improve with stall rest but after two days they wrapped her well and let her out. "I can't believe how upset that mare is about the others being out without her. I thought she was going to tear that damn stall down. Now look at her out there. She's not running or being crazy she's just grazing and happy enough to be out near the others." Steven said, "Thinking about it I'm not sure that since we have had her she's ever been confined and away from the others. Even when you were in the hospital and I had put her at the stable in Lafayette, the guy put her out right away even though I had asked him not to," Ellen added.

Winter and the holidays were upon them before they knew it. Ellen got a call from the New York renters who wanted to purchase her farm there. She and Steven talked about it and came up with a figure they felt was acceptable. The renters were offering less than they had figured but within the month they all came to an agreement on the price. It was just before Christmas when the closing would be. Steven, Ellen, Mary and Sophie all flew back for the closing, and to go through everything and pack up whatever was necessary.

The closing went smoothly and the packing was less involved than expected. They were able to wrap everything up within a week. Steven surprised the ladies with a wonderful dinner in downtown New York and a night at the Plaza Hotel the night before their scheduled flight out. As they enjoyed dinner that night Steven had still another surprise for Ellen. "Sophie, you and Mary will take the scheduled flight out. Ellen and I will make sure the movers have picked up everything we packed and then we'll fly out. Ellen and I will be gone then for the next few days also." Ellen looked at Steven with a totally surprised look on her face.

"I'm going to take Ellen on a trip out to the vineyards in northern California. I've booked a bed and breakfast for a change of pace. I figured it would be good for us to get away and not have to worry about the horses or the farm." Ellen was very surprised and told Steven he should have let her know so she could have packed differently. Steven laughed a little and then said. "I'll buy you all new stuff-- after all you are the love of my life."

Before they knew it the ladies were back at the farm and Steven and Ellen were in a rented car driving up the coast. The bed and breakfast offered them a very romantic setting and the tours they took during the days made the time fly and the two wishing they had booked a longer stay.

The love between them was at a new high after the stay at the vineyard. They talked about so many special things that had happened to them since they had met. As they now drove back they enjoyed all the amazing scenery they were seeing. The rolling hills covered in vineyards and orchards. As the drove along the ocean coastline would appear and show the grandeur and size of the ocean and then disappear as the road moved away from the shoreline and a hill would cut off their view.

They were still about an hour away from the airport when Ellen spotted a small herd of horses up on a ridge grazing. They were too far away to get an idea of what type of horses they might be. "Steven we're actually ahead of schedule. Let's take another side trip and look for the farm that those horses belong to. It will be fun. What do you think?" she asked. Steven agreed and they turned up the next roadway.

It only took a few minutes it seemed before they spotted the farm they believed the horses were from. As they pulled up to the gateway they spotted a sign that told them they must be at the right place. "'Wineway Stud Farm. Breeders of quality sporthorses and the home of Rahman one of eventing's leading sires.' I really would like to go in there." Ellen said. "I've never heard of this place or the stud. But I want to go in also." Steven said as he leaned out and hit the

An Event to Remember ~ 215

call button by the gate. A voice came through the speaker. The voice sounded like an older man with a German accent. The gates opened and they drove up the very long driveway. As they drove they saw single horses in huge paddocks and guessed those were the stallions of the farm. They reached the stable area and were greeted by a younger woman and an older man. The woman introduced herself as Yvonne and her father as Otto. Steven then introduced Ellen as his wife and himself. "We're eventers from the Midwest and we were on a short holiday and spotted some of your horses as we drove down the highway. They pulled us here like they were magnets." They all laughed at his analogy.

"Have you ever gone to the Rolex? I've gone as a spectator several times and I think it is one of the greatest sporting events in the world," Yvonne said in an excited tone. Ellen then chimed in. "We've both actually ridden at the Rolex and Steven finished in the ribbons," she said with great pride." "What did you say your last name was? Did you compete there recently?" Yvonne asked. Ellen looked at Steven assuming he was going to answer her but then she realized it had stirred something inside him so she then answered. "Steven Wilson and he finished in the ribbons a couple a years ago on his first ever attempt there." Yvonne had a shocked expression on her face.

Yvonne then asked them to sit on the lawn chairs that were nearby. She then explained that she had been at that Rolex. She and her friend had stayed an extra two nights in Lexington, since it was their first time there. "We heard all about your tragedy and the fact that you had lost your horse." She couldn't believe that she was talking with the same person now. "You've been competing again, right?" She said in her accent. "I think you are incredible. Where did you find a horse so fast that you could connect with?" Steven then started talking and explained how Ellen had come into his life and how grateful he was for letting him compete her horse. Conversations went on long enough

216 ~ *Steve Farkos*

that they would now miss their scheduled flight. Yvonne and her father then offered them the guest room for the night. It really didn't take much to convince them.

That night Steven changed their flights and Ellen contacted the farm and let them know they would be coming back a day later. They had a wonderful dinner and they all took part in its preparation. The conversations and stories went long into the night. Yvonne was really excited to show them around and promised them a full tour in the morning.

As they toured around the farm in the morning Steven and Ellen were impressed by all the really good looking and quality horses they were seeing. It was fun walking from field to field and being able to walk amongst the animals. The field with many of the yearlings and two year olds was the most fun as their curiosity brought them as a herd to see them. "I love the young ones. They are so brave and curious that they will approach almost anything and left alone they try eating it, too. I once knew a breeder in Kentucky who left his truck parked in a huge field where he was working on a well. After he had been working for a couple of hours he looked over and saw some two year olds tearing apart his truck. There were scratches from their teeth, the rear view mirror was hanging by the control wire and a lot of the surface had saliva all over it. They really can get pretty destructive," Ellen told them with a little laugh.

They were enjoying their walk around this wonderful piece of property. The day was developing into an award winner even for California. The skies were bluer than Ellen had even seen before she thought. Her thoughts of the day and property came to an end as her eyes caught sight of a horse racing toward them. Several others followed the beautiful animal but he was clearly the leader of this group. "Here come our three year olds and one four year old mare that we keep with them," Yvonne said, as the lead horse now was less than twenty feet away. Both Ellen and Steven were quiet as they approached and now stood in front of

An Event to Remember ~ 217

them. "What a collection of young horse flesh. They are absolutely gorgeous," Ellen said as the young curious horses surrounded them.

Steven had not said a word as he had approached the lead horse. The horse stood about seventeen hands tall and as good looking as any young horse Steven had ever seen. The horse was curious but balked away from Steven several times but made no attempt to run off. Finally he was able to stroke the horse on his neck and the horse allowed his kind eyes to let him know that he was acceptable as a friend.

Yvonne poked Ellen and pointed to Steven and the young gelding. "Looks like your husband has found a friend. That gelding isn't normally that quiet. Steven must have a good way with the animals." Ellen told her that he was amazing in the way he handled horses and she wasn't surprised at how the young horse had approved of him.

"We need to start back or we'll have to schedule still another flight," Ellen said. Steven acknowledged Ellen's comment and started back toward the two women. The young gelding followed Steven like a puppy. "We didn't buy him a seat on the flight. He'll have to stay behind," Ellen said.

Steven turned and flung his arms up and let out a war hoop. The big gelding wheeled and took off after the others who had already started up the hillside. His stride was breathtaking as he caught the others in seconds it seemed. Steven was quiet as they walked back toward the house. Ellen and Yvonne talked and seemed to be making plans to get together again possibly meeting up at an event. Steven remained silent until they had reached the house.

Steven and Ellen thanked both Yvonne and her father Otto for their hospitality and company. They needed to get going as they would be late to check into their flight if traffic was even a little heavy. As they drove down the highway Ellen talked about the wonderful farm they had come upon. She felt that she had made a new friend in

Yvonne and was hoping that they could possibly get together in the future.

Ellen realized now that she was the only one talking. It seemed that Steven's thoughts were off somewhere else. "Steven. You've hardly said a word since we were in that last field. Are you all right? You're not sick are you? This was such a fun trip I hope that you're OK."

Steven reassured her that he was fine. He said that he was a little down at the moment. "That gelding was so like Hawk as a youngster. Those eyes were haunting me and brought back so many memories of him. Then as I watched him cover the ground with his huge stride to catch up to the others I truly thought I was watching my Hawk again." Ellen knew now why he had been so quiet. As she thought about it more she even thought the gelding looked somewhat like Hawk but she decided not to mention that to Steven now.

Chapter 17

DURING THE NEXT year there were many changes. Ellen had taken a fall at a clinic and broken an arm. Her recovery went well but her time off put her behind for the competition season. For the first event of the season Mary and Ellen groomed for Steven and Sophie.

Sophie's riding had come so far and it was exciting to watch her. She competed in Kentucky at the Novice level and placed second in her division. Steven was still on a strong roll. Steven and Trick were known now in the eventing community and had gained the respect of many. Ellen was always proud as she watched them compete.

After Kentucky the three of them would compete at Barrington. It was near home and they could have good helping hands from Mary, Jake and Paul. It was more fun than ever to be able to go out as a full team but Steven realized that they needed to go out east, where the highest concentration of strong competition would be. Steven felt now that he was up for testing himself and Trick.

They had entered an event in Virginia and another in North Carolina. Steven planned to stay out east until they had completed both the competitions. The events were two weeks apart and Steven had made arrangements to stay at a stable of a fellow eventer while they were out there. Everything seemed to be set up perfectly but then they were hit with a surprise when Mary explained she was three months pregnant and there were some concerns after her doctor's visit the other day about her stressing herself. After her checkup the doctor had grounded her from travel any long distances and lifting anything heavy. Ellen was excited for her but was disappointed that she wouldn't be with them. "I'd like to go and groom for you," Sophie offered. Jake was a little surprised since it would mean she would be gone for almost a month total.

After looking at all the issues they all agreed that it would be great for her to come along and Paul could help in the evenings so Jake wouldn't have to shoulder all the responsibilities at home.

The first event was in Virginia and all the divisions were full of named riders. The course was tough and had some good technical questions. The fun was they were amidst many of the country's better riders and some who had been at the wedding party. They hung out each night and reviewed the day's efforts and told stories of their eventing through the years. Sophie and Ellen really enjoyed listening to the stories and also felt closer to many of them as they heard of their trials. Ellen also heard stories and things about Steven and his efforts to get to his first Rolex. As Ellen listened she began to feel a drive in herself to find a way to get Steven back there again. She knew listening how bad Steven hoped to get there. Ellen wondered if Trick could do it. It was now several years since she had competed Trick at the Rolex. They had completed the course but over these years Steven had brought him to a new level. Trick was well muscled and conditioned for the events he had been doing. She felt that Steven had Trick going incredibly well and together they seemed awesome, but was it enough? The question on her mind was the extra years Trick now had on him.

The event went really well. Trick's dressage was really good but they had finished that phase in fourth place. Cross-country went clear but saw Steven pick up some time

An Event to Remember ~ 221

penalties, something they were not used to. After their time penalties were assessed they had fallen to seventh place and Steven was definitely disappointed at that point. Stadium ran during an absolute downpour. Many riders had rails or time faults but Steven and Trick showed their talent with a double clear. They finished the event in fifth place after the other rider's faults were calculated.

Ellen's dressage was one of her best and she again sat in first place after all in her division had gone. Her cross-country round wasn't as good however. Stella took the number three fence, the steeplechase fence, absolutely huge. Her gigantic spot jolted Ellen out of position and she lost her stirrups as Stella raced to fence four. Fence four rode big as Stella twisted her hindquarters to ensure her clearance. Ellen finally got her to come back a little but then realized that the mare wasn't feeling quite right. They went to the next fence but after it Ellen was even more convinced that the mare wasn't 100%. Ellen brought her down to a walk and told the fence judges that she was withdrawing.

Sophie waited for Ellen's return at the finish line and realized something was wrong as she saw riders scheduled after Ellen now finishing. Finally Ellen and Stella came to the finish with Ellen leading her on foot. "What happened? Are you OK?" Sophie inquired. Ellen assured her that it didn't seem like anything too serious but she didn't want to take any chances.

Steven found out about a woman who was set up at the event to massage horses. When they got up to her she was taking down her area and getting ready to leave. Steven told he would pay extra if necessary but felt that she might be able to identify what was going on. The woman appeared to hardly be touching the mare but the mare responded as she slowly went over her. When she got to the left hip she looked at Steven and Ellen and said "Oh there's the problem. Easy, girl. We need to work on this a bit and will get you back to normal." Ellen was very impressed as she watched the woman work. The woman then asked Ellen and Steven to feel the deep knot she was working on. It was very obvious once they were able to feel it.

Ellen was glad she had pulled her and agreed to pull her from the next event, as it was a little too close to risk knotting that muscle again. If it was a lower level go she might have been OK but not at the higher level they were signed up to ride. After two days of rest Ellen hacked Stella and was pleased to find that she felt herself again. Ellen knew that a little time spent on light work would make things right again for the mare.

They traveled to North Carolina after a week and Steven and Trick would compete and Sophie and Ellen would care for Stella and groom for Steven. The Event showed Trick at his best. Steven again captured first after dressage and then two double clear rounds. Steven was on a real high after his first-place finish. Steven was feeling that he had a horse now that could compete at the big events.

After they arrived home and unpacked they had dinner and then decided to make it an early night since they were all exhausted. As they settled in bed the phone rang. "Who do you suppose that is at this time of night?" Steven inquired. Ellen grabbed the phone and then started grinning even before she answered. "Steven, it's Patrick! We haven't heard from him since the wedding!" Ellen said as she handed the phone to Stephen.

Patrick and Steven talked for fifteen minutes or so with Patrick seeming to do most of the talking. Then Steven handed the phone to Ellen so she could say hello. Patrick again did most of the talking as he told Ellen he had gone to the event's web site to see how Steven might have finished. After seeing he finished first against some good riders and horses, Patrick wanted to congratulate Steven and encourage him to go for another Rolex attempt.

Ellen could sense Steven's excitement about the encouragement Patrick had given him. They fell asleep as they discussed the possibility of doing the Rolex again.

An Event to Remember ~ 223

Before the year was over Steven now planned to get to the Radnor Event in Pennsylvania and the famous Ledyard Event in Massachusetts. Everything seemed to be going according to plan. Ellen noticed how focused Steven was. She was finding it as exciting to watch him and being there to help him. He was amazing and definitely back in the groove.

Steven and Ellen did another event in Colorado and would finish the season in Kentucky. As they sat at dinner one night Steven surprised Ellen with a question she had never considered before. "Ellen you have been really doing well with Stella. Are you enjoying taking her out at the higher levels? She really seems to know her job and she appears to enjoy jumping, especially those steeplechase fences." They both laughed a little about that comment since Stella always seemed to fly over and through that type of fence. Ellen couldn't say enough good things about Stella but she also sensed that Steven had something else in mind with his questions. "I think she has a great trust in you. How do you think she'd do with me?" Ellen thought that Stella would do all right, but she still wasn't sure what Steven was going for.

"I don't want you to feel that I'm cutting you out of an event, but I was wondering if you'd let me show Stella in Kentucky too." Steven asked with hope in his vote. Ellen was surprised by his request and asked why he wanted to do that and did he mean he wanted to show them both? "I want to show both of them. I want to know where I lack in endurance, reactions and raw instincts. I want to know what I have to work on the most during the upcoming winter because I want to go back to the Rolex next spring." Steven said with a lot of conviction.

Ellen was little shocked by his request but knew at the same time that this had been a dream and a goal since the day he had completed his first ever Rolex. He had been doing so well and she wouldn't have been surprised if he had announced that he wanted to take Trick in the spring

224 ~ *Steve Farkos*

but she never expected he'd want to take Stella now as a test.

They talked it over during the night and Ellen had finally agreed. It wasn't till the morning though that Steven felt that he really had Ellen's full approval. They both stayed in bed for a while longer that morning and finished their time together by telling him in the most sincere and loving manner that she would be proud to have him show Stella also and looked forward to being there for him.

It was the end of October when they would leave for Kentucky. Both Sophie and Jake would go along. It wasn't the Rolex but it was almost important because it would prove to be the doorway to the Rolex in the spring if Steve could prove to himself that he could do it again. For the next few weeks they changed how they trained. It was important to ride both of them and they would switch off so Ellen could be his eyes from the side.

Training sessions went longer and Steven was adjusting to jumping Stella which he had done very little of previously. There were some shaky moments as Steven took some awkward spots at fences, but by the end of two weeks it was going smoothly on both horses. Ellen had never really seen Steven this focused before. He was up earlier in the morning and he would run and work out on his Bowflex before breakfast. Ellen could tell what this meant to him and she supported him in every way she could. She was also enjoying the change as his physique was showing his extra effort and even Mary and Sophie made comments about her hot man.

They made it to Kentucky on a Wednesday afternoon and set up for the weekend. When they picked up the packets and reviewed the program they were surprised at how small Steven's division was. There were just nine horses and he and another would be riding two horses. The timing in between his rides would be much closer than he had hoped for. Steven was acting a little concerned about the timing and Ellen was picking up on it. She and Sophie

An Event to Remember ~ 225

both made it their job to convince him that they would be there and the horses would be ready for him at each phase. Warm ups would have to start earlier and be well planned to make it work out.

Thursday Steven hacked the horses and probably worked them in their dressage for only about twenty minutes each. Stella was being really sticky on her one shoulder in and had not maintained her counter canter to the left as long as she should have. Steven had fixed both of those problems when Ellen was first riding Stella but the shoe was on the other foot now. Steven was getting frustrated and Ellen called him over to the rail. She reminded him what he had taught her. Moments later they were doing it correctly and both Sophie and Ellen gave him a cheer.

Friday morning at eight o'clock Steven had his first ride on Trick and then he would ride Stella nineteen minutes later. Trick was wound up as they circled the arena waiting for their whistle. Steven did a series of lead changes around the arena adding a couple of halts to get Trick's full attention. Then he heard his whistle and entered at 'A'. The test went quite nicely the ladies felt as they watched and held Stella at their side. With Steven's halt and salute the crowd around the arena broke into a loud applause and hoopla that spooked Stella a bit.

No sooner did Steven walk out of the arena than he swung down out of the saddle and jogged Trick over toward the ladies. Ellen held Stella as he mounted her and Sophie walked Trick around to let him cool. Moments later it seemed Steven was circling the arena waiting now for Stella's whistle. Her test went well with just a little show of anticipation on her left lead counter canter. As they halted there was a nice round of applause making Steven feel that he had done a pretty good job with her also.

Both cross-country rounds were clean and only Stella had a few time penalties. Steven was tired after the fast paced morning. But he had held up well and he felt he had presented both horses well. They walked and then bathed the two horses. After they had grazed a while they poulticed their legs and wrapped them for the night. Sophie had the stalls all cleaned and put fresh water in for them. They tossed some hay for them and then went off to get some lunch. After lunch they decided to check scores for the first time.

As they looked at the scoreboard they were excited to see that Trick after dressage was in second place and that Stella was fourth. After their cross-country rounds Trick was still in second but Stella's time penalties had pushed her down to sixth place.

Sunday morning it was chilly as there was a good wind and it was overcast. It had rained overnight and the stadium arena had a few puddles sitting in it. Sophie fed and started grooming while Steven and Ellen went to walk the stadium course one more time.

The warm up seemed to be going well and so Steven decided to go much easier than what he normally would have done. Stadium would be run in reverse order so Stella would go before Trick with her sixth place. The rounds would average about two minutes each so between Stella's round and Trick's there would be hardly six minutes for him to remount and be ready to ride. The first couple of horses pulled rails and one had a refusal. Stella's round went beautifully but Steven misjudged his pace a little and ended up with a time penalty. It was only a point and he felt it shouldn't drop her in the placings. Trick was fussy as Steven tried to quickly mount him, as he wanted to get one more warm-up fence before his round. The third place horse was now leaving the arena after pulling two rails and having a refusal. His horse had seemed tired and didn't seem to like the mud he kicked up as he went around.

Steven entered the arena and even before his whistle Trick was wound up and bounced as if he wanted to rear and go. Steven disciplined him and softened repeatedly trying to get him to settle. The whistle then sounded his need to start the round. Trick was more than ready to go. It seemed that he was mad having to watch Stella go before him. The first fence rode as a steeplechase fence on cross-country. The second fence, a big oxer, backed him off a little bit but it was apparent to Ellen that Trick thought that it was his job to set the pace. The round looked reckless and way too fast but somehow Steven was still on and Trick was still clean as the headed to the triple line. The big horse somehow made it through the combination and only pulled the last rail as he exited. The combo seemed to slow him down a little as he finished over the last two fences. The announcer made a comment as they exited the arena saying he was certain that they had just witnessed the fastest stadium round ever. Steven was embarrassed some but stayed mounted as he watched the last round and waited to hear the placings.

Moments after the first place finished his round the announcer called out the placings. When he was done Trick had fallen to third place and Stella had moved up to fourth place. Steven rode Trick during the pinning ceremony and Ellen jogged Stella in to collect her ribbon.

They were all proud of the job the horses had done even though Steven admitted several times he was very surprised by Trick's antics during his stadium. Steven assured Ellen he would never go that light on his warm-up ever again.

It was a happy and very encouraging event and Steven announced that with more work over the winter and during the spring that he would enter Trick in the Rolex. Ellen and Sophie were excited at his announcement and Sophie called ahead to let the others know the results and the decision about next year's Rolex. Ellen was so proud of the horse she had started and the man she admired.

When they got home Mary, Paul and Jake were waiting. They all gave a hand in unpacking and putting the horses up. Once they got to the house Mary had set up a surprise celebration. Champagne and happiness flowed freely through the night.

During the next few months the horses were given some time off and then worked a little easier with a lot of leisurely hacks. Ellen and Steven would even go trail riding just for a good change of pace for the horses. That winter also brought Ellen and Steven even closer in the way they felt about one another. Their love and marriage were all and more than either of them imagined that it could be and their happiness showed to all.

It was a happy house and the winter allowed a good break in the action and also a time for a bouncing baby girl to be born for Mary and Paul. She looked so very much like Mary with huge blue eyes and light colored hair. They named her Margaret and called her Maggie although it seemed that Paul thought her given name was 'princess'. They asked Steven and Ellen to be the Godparents, which they proudly accepted.

Chapter 18

THE WINTER SEEMED to drag on and the sky seemed overcast almost every day. Steven didn't waste any time though as he added some additional lockable storage in the new trailer. All of the tack was reviewed and made ready for the show season even though it was months away. Ellen and Steven went to an expo in Wisconsin and saw some great demonstrations and bought some new tack and sheets. Steven had found a new dressage saddle and also a new running martingale that he wanted for jumping.

While the training was in a lighter mode Steven and Ellen took time to make short trips around the Midwest. It was a great way to just get away and enjoy one another. Shopping seemed a priority as every trip netted something for someone. If they weren't buying horse stuff they were buying something for baby Maggie. Ellen found some needed items for Sophie as she continued to ride and showed a strong desire to show more. Steven had fun buying things for Ellen and enjoyed watching her try on different stuff sometimes just for fun and laughs. Their little escapades brought them closer together and turned out to be more relaxing that watching TV or reading during the winter.

Once February arrived training would be all business. Ellen rode Stella and worked the same conditioning schedule as Steven was riding with Trick. Although they might talk during walk segments in the regime there was no conversation during other times unless it was a training suggestion. They trained six days a week and in that first month the horses were already showing a difference and it seemed they knew that show season was coming.

As March rolled in so did a lot of weather. Early in the month they were hit with one of the biggest snowstorms they had seen in probably ten years. The snow was deep enough and icy enough as it started to melt down and freeze overnight that they were confined to working in the arena for the first two weeks. Once the snows were gone and the roads were open they would use the country roads to condition since the ground was still too messy and possibly unsafe. They were able to work one day out on some of the cross-country fences on the property but that was it. For the next week and a half it seemed to rain every minute. In his frustration and the horses becoming barn sour, Steven would put on all his rain gear and condition on the roads. The good thing was the rains brought some interesting flooding and that offered some fun challenges with the horses.

Before March ended opening day to enter the Rolex had arrived. Steven had everything ready and was excited as he filled out the forms. He thought he had everything he needed. Steven realized as he was stuffing the envelope that Trick's coggins test wasn't dated to cover the event. Ellen was able to reach the vet who was still out on calls. The vet promised to be to the farm within the hour to pull blood for the coggins.

Steven was apologetic as he held Trick for the vet. "Sorry about the last minute call. I was entering an event and realized I didn't have the coggins I would need. Do you think that you can pull the test on all of the horses since you're here?" The vet said he had another call yet and was going to have to pull a miracle off to get the blood to the lab today. "OK doc, but you have to pull Stella's too so we have back up here if we need her." The doctor agreed and raced out of the driveway as soon as he had pulled blood from Stella.

An Event to Remember ~ 231

Late the next day Ellen was able to pick up the coggins test directly from the lab with the vet's approval and so Steven was able to complete the show entries and take the envelope directly to the post office. Steven couldn't believe it yet. He was going back to the Rolex. He remembered his time in the hospital and the months after that it hurt just to walk. He really hadn't been sure that he would ever make it back again but he was ready now.

His thoughts about his first Rolex and all that changed in his life after the success he had experienced also made him sad. He couldn't think of anything but Hawk at the moment. Hawk was everything to him after he had lost his parents and sister. He had trained him from an overgrown clown to a contender at the Rolex, the most prestigious event in the USA. He remembered as he packed up that day that thoughts of competing in Europe had danced in his head. He remembered how much he believed in Hawk and now once again felt the sorrow of his loss again.

Ellen came in and saw Steven looking down. "Hey didn't you just send out your entry, mister? What's with the long face? I'd guess that you'd be on top of the world right now." Ellen was surprised to see him just sitting in the den at the desk at this time. Then Ellen realized he was holding a picture of Hawk in his hand. Steven looked up to Ellen and said. "I really don't know what I would have done without you. I love you. You came into my life and kept me going forward when there's a good chance I might have just shut down. You are so incredible and I don't know if I've ever shown you how much you mean to me." Steven was standing now and wrapped his arms around Ellen and pulled her tight to himself. He kissed her and repeated several times how grateful he was for her and how much he loved her.

Steven then sat down again as did Ellen and he talked about what he had just been reflecting on. He was so grateful for Trick and believed that they had a chance to do something at the Rolex. "I don't have the same connection with Trick as I did with my Hawk but I appreciate his talent and enjoy him all the time. There's just a difference when you bring one on totally by yourself. It's a stronger connection I guess. You had done so much with Trick before I ever rode him. I hope you're as proud of him as I am."

Ellen assured him that she was proud of him and even more now of the job Steven had done with him.

"I couldn't have done what you have with him. You have a special way in your training and your ability to connect with them and it shows with any horse you ride."

They took the afternoon off and looked at some old pictures. It was then that they both realized that Steven didn't have any pictures of Hawk and himself from their Rolex appearance. Once they had realized it and talked about how it was overlooked while everything else was happening. "I will guarantee you Steven I will find the pictures you should have. I'm sure I can find the photographers that were taking pictures back then. Hopefully they will still have some in their archives and I will get you some. I promise you." With that said Ellen went to the Internet to find the individuals that might help her.

Training continued through mid-April and Steven was able to go to a couple of really good clinics. Ellen went on Stella but the focus for the moment was really all on Steven. The dressage clinic really paid off as Trick was very wound up the first day and the clinician showed Steven a few different ways to regain Trick's full attention. At the jumping clinic they attended Trick and Steven were nothing short of super stars. The two handled all the gymnastics as if they practiced them every day.

Mary and her new family were doing well. It became apparent that Mary was a little sad that Sophie would be grooming for the big event. She had been with Steven and Ellen at every event since their last Rolex. She had been there at the crash and saw how all their lives had changed and now grown together.

An Event to Remember ~ 233

It was the weekend and Steven and Ellen had just finished their workout when Mary pulled up to the barn and walked in with Maggie in her arm. Sophie was starting to take care of the horses and Ellen was handling Stella herself. Sophie was talking about how exciting it was getting ready for the Rolex. She told Mary that she had never been before and couldn't even imagine how great it was going to be. "Well I came to let you know that I'll be there too. I think you said that Jake was going also. I know you had planned on me being here to help but I've talked Paul into taking care of the farm if I take Maggie with me. I'll drive up on Friday and I booked a room at the hotel next to you. I can't miss this. I won't miss this. I'm here for you guys 100%." Everyone was excited especially Ellen, who knew how Mary was feeling.

It was the week that they would be heading to Kentucky. They would be leaving on Monday morning and Steven must have checked the trailer and supplies both Saturday and Sunday at least a dozen times. Sophie watched and made sure that she was aware of everything and also knew where Steven had packed stuff in the new sections he had added. Jake helped to load the hay they would take since they had plenty of room in the trailer since Trick would be the only one riding in it.

Steven was up at 4:30 on Monday morning packing some extra clothes for the trip. Ellen woke at about 5:15 as she heard Steven leaving the bedroom. Once she made her way to the kitchen Sophie already had breakfast on the table and all three of them sat there already anxious to get going. "We thought you might be sleeping in today," Steven teased her since she was the only one still in her robe. "I thought you said that we were leaving at 10:00. I think you all got going a little earlier than needed. At least we know that one of us will be awake at least till this evening," Ellen teased them as she sat down to have her breakfast.

At 10:00 on schedule they were able to pull out of the farm. It was the first time that Jake would be making a trip with them. Sophie on the other hand was used to making the trip with them and today was ready and excited for anything it seemed. They stopped for fuel and a snack on the way down but Steven didn't want to take any longer breaks as they normally might have. He wanted to get Trick to the park and have the rest of the day to settle him. The trip was smooth and seemed to go much faster than usual. Once they arrived at the park they were able to get set up quickly with just the one horse. Steven had rented a paddock and once they had unwrapped Trick and gave him the opportunity to have a drink they put him out in the paddock to graze and stretch his legs.

Ellen and Sophie set up the tack stall so that everything that would be used was in the order and purpose it would be needed. Jake organized the feed and cleaning supplies and then cleaned out the trailer from their trip. Steven check on everything they were doing and walked back and forth checking on Trick every ten minutes or so. Ellen had never seen him so obviously nervous or wound up.

For the next two days Steven would work Trick and continued to fine-tune his dressage. It was all going quite well and Steven had a really good feeling about the results he was getting. Each day it seemed that he would run into a fellow competitor that knew of his last Rolex or that Mary had got to come to their wedding dance. Steven felt welcomed and a lot of people, both riders and grooms, sincerely wished him a great weekend. On two of the evenings the competitor parties were a great way to see others that they may have missed. The announcer at one of the parties made a public welcome to Steven and applauded him for the recovery and comeback that now brought him back.

It was all touching and Ellen was very touched and also extremely proud of the man she had married. As they mingled amongst the people Ellen's pride was very obvious. Sophie and Jake had never been around so many of these people who knew and respected Steven. It gave them a

An Event to Remember ~ 235

special feeling knowing that he was the one they worked for and the one who had cared for them so much.

Trick had passed the first horse inspection prior to the dressage test. He was a bit jumpy at first but settled nicely Steven felt that Trick was sensing the importance of this show. Steven was ready and Ellen fussed with his stock tie a little while Sophie gave Trick and his tack one more once over. "Steven, I just want you to know how very proud I am of you. You'll do great I'm sure, but no matter the final outcome remember you did it. You came back. You showed your strength as a person and as a competitor. I'm so proud of you. Now go show them how good you are." Steven gave her a hug and then mounted and headed to the warm up ring without saying anything.

Their warm up went well and there were a lot of well-wishers as they exited the warm up area. Steven pulled up Trick and waited for his bit check before going on. Once they had reached the final staging area, Sophie and Ellen were like little maids doing a final inspection and brushing of any dirt that may have snuck onto Steven or Trick.

As the rider before him saluted and started his loose rein walk from the arena Steven cued Trick and began his final warm up and preparation around the arena waiting for his bell. Trick was feeling really good as Steven could feel his suspension unfold underneath him. Steven gently moved Trick's neck from side to side as they trotted and then cantered around the edge of the arena. Trick was as soft and supple as he had ever been. Steven was definitely ready and so was Trick.

The judge at 'C' rang the bell and in a few steps Steven brought Trick to a halt and reached up with both hands and patted him on the neck as most riders might at the end of their test. Steven then took the reins back up and cued him into a collected canter as they headed to the entrance at 'A'.

Steven entered the arena and you could hear a pin drop. There was absolute silence around the arena as he went through his test. It was going great and Steven looked like a statue in the saddle and more focused than ever. On his first trot lengthening Trick broke to the canter at one point but came back immediately. On the right-lead canter Trick picked it up a bit early and maybe with too much enthusiasm Ellen thought. Steven then came down centerline and nailed his halt. Steven took his top hat off and saluted the judges as the spectators around the arena gave him a great round of applause.

Steven exited the arena and quickly dismounted. Sophie ran the stirrups up and loosened the girth. Sophie walked ahead with Trick as Ellen and Steven verbally replayed his test. They were in agreement with the couple of glitches they felt had occurred. "Well I was pretty happy overall and we'll see what the judges felt when we pick up the test later." Steven said.

By the end of the day they had everything ready for tomorrow and cross-country. Before they left the park they stopped in at the office and picked up Steven's dressage test. It read very much like they had guessed, but the marks overall were really good. Steven was really proud of the 9s Trick had received for gaits and submission. They walked out to the scoreboard to see where they had placed with their dressage score. With a score of 35.8 Steven and Trick were sitting in fifth place and Steven was more than a little shocked at his placing. There was a long list of very good competitors on that board and many were behind him. Steven believed that Trick could jump anything and couldn't believe how well he was placed and what two clear rounds could mean.

The next morning they all came very early and fussed over Trick as never before. They had him shining as they went for the vet inspection. Again there was no problem at the vet's box as they both passed him and admired him. Once back at the stable they got Trick ready for the roads and track phase. They put his studs in and went to the start box. Steven and Trick finish in good time in the roads and track phase and passed the vet inspection in great shape.

His recovery time was good and Ellen thought he was one of the best conditioned horses as she watched other horses go through the inspection.

They all huddled around the start box as Steven waited on the final countdown. As the starter was saying five in his countdown Steven reached forward and started his watch. Then they were off and all Ellen and Sophie could see was the first fence. As soon as he had cleared it Sophie and Ellen ran to the roadway where Jake was waiting to pick them up with the rented golf cart so they could get across the park to where the finish flags were. As they made their way across the park they realized that they were missing any announcements about Steven's progress. Jake stopped for a moment near to where they could see one of the jumbotron screens. As they watched a few horses go through the sunken road Sophie called their attention to the screen as it now was focused on Steven as he rode through the water complex. He looked brilliant and now Ellen wanted to get to the finish line to be there for him.

The three waited at the finish line for Steven and Trick to appear. Jake caught a glimpse of Steven up on the ridge and let the ladies know. Jake wanted a picture of them as they came through the window jump just before the finish. Jake went to ensure himself a good angle for his shot and Sophie and Ellen just waited. In the final strides before the finish Steven was forward and patting Trick on the neck and then reached his watch and stopped it as they went through the finish line. Steven was happy enough that even a blind man would have noticed.

Steven went over to the inspection area. Trick again showed great recovery in a short time and they were excused to go on. Sophie and Ellen were quick to help Steven with Trick and the tack as they stripped the lathered horse down. Ellen wanted to know how they had done and pushed Steven for answers.

"Trick was brilliant and he was a joy to ride. When I hit the half way mark I realized that I was running behind on

238 ~ *Steve Farkos*

time. I tried to make up the time but I was destroying the great rhythm we had been cruising along with. In my attempt to pick up the time I caused a bad approach at the 'sawmill' complex. After that we had the water complex and the sunken road so I decided to maintain the pace we were doing so well at instead of trying so hard to make up the time. So I'm guessing I have time penalties and a refusal at the 'skinny' after the 'sunken road.' But I'm really happy. We did it and Trick was all that I thought he could be."

That evening they checked the scoreboard as they walked to the competitor's party. Steven had received a half dozen time penalties and was assessed twenty points on the refusal. The twenty-six additional points had dropped him from fourth place down to tenth place. It wasn't enough though to dampen Steven's spirits and they were all very proud of what Trick had accomplished. Steven felt the skinny was his fault because of a bad approach.

The next morning after the jog for soundness, the vets asked Steven to jog Trick a second time. Ellen had not seen anything and now worried that the vets were seeing something she had missed. After the second jog the vets put Trick through with an OK to compete. Ellen and Sophie both asked Steven what the vets had thought or saw but Steven told them they never had said a thing.

Stadium presented a lot of problems to horse and riders. It was obvious watching that the cross-country and weather had taken a toll on a lot of them. Trick looked great and as he entered looking full of life and really ready to go. As the bell rang Steven started his round. Steven was focused on the triple line because of what had happened at the last event. The round went beautifully and the triple rode perfectly as Steven now headed to the last fence. Steven took the last fence and as he did he realized that he hadn't truly ridden it, resulting in a pulled top rail. He knew the rail would cost him another four points and a further drop in the placings.

An Event to Remember ~ 239

Steven was disappointed in his mistake but was still proud of having completed another Rolex and that was something he hadn't been sure would ever happen again. They waited around for the awards ceremony. The four points for the rail down dropped Steven down to fifteenth place but would allow him again to ride in the victory gallop. After they had finished the victory gallop Steven was asked to wait before leaving the area. Trick was honored as the best conditioned horse and Steven was very proud as they went out and picked up the award. Ellen was hugging Steven and asking Jake for a picture of the three of them as the loud speaker now called for Sophie. They all looked at one another and they heard the request again for Sophie to come forward. Sophie had won the award for the best-groomed horse. She was shaking as she received the brand new saddle being presented to her by the CEO of Stüben Saddles. What a day this had been.

They all walked back to the stable area talking, laughing and full of wonderful feelings of success. As they reached the stall area there were several people waiting to congratulate Steven and Sophie. There was even a reporter from the Lexington paper who hoped for an interview. The reporter told Steven that it would be an honor for him as he was the reporter who had written the story about the crash years before. Steven was on such a good feeling high. As he talked and answered questions his eyes kept scanning all the activity that was around him. As he did he now saw Yvonne from California as she approached him with glasses and a bottle of champagne being carried by Patrick who had come to witness his friend's comeback. "Wow. Hi. When did you get here?" Steven fumbled with his words at the surprise of seeing both Yvonne and Patrick there. Yvonne told him she had been delivering a horse and realized the Rolex was this weekend and then decided to make it here after realizing Steven would be competing. Steven felt very honored that she had made the effort. "This is Trick and he just helped me do what I wasn't sure I'd be able to do ever again. Now

I'm ready and I know that I'll be back for more," he said with a huge smile on his face. Patrick was smiling ear to ear as he hugged Ellen and Steven and made it known to all that there was never a doubt that Steven would be back, especially with Ellen at his side.

As they all enjoyed the moment they also all knew how much hard work had been required and the mental baggage that Steven had to overcome to achieve what he had. Then Yvonne excused herself and said she needed to leave. Steven thanked her for coming and then Ellen offered to walk a ways with her. It was about a half hour later when Jake started asking where Ellen had gone. Steven assumed that they were carried away talking and wasn't worried about her return. Sophie never said a word but seemed to keep looking down the way as if she knew Ellen would be returning from that direction at any moment.

Then Sophie spotted what she had been watching for. Ellen and Yvonne both were walking back from the other end of the aisle. They were leading a horse. Steven thought that they were bringing the horse that Yvonne had talked about delivering just for him to take a look at him. It would be like Ellen to get Yvonne to bring the horse back for Steven to see if it was a nice piece of horseflesh. There was a security guard walking with them also since the stable area was a secured area during the competition. Now they were about twelve feet away. Jake noticed a huge smile on Sophie's face, as if she knew something the rest didn't, but he also saw her put a finger to her lips asking for no questions just yet.

"That's the gelding we saw in California. He's grown and matured over the winter, I knew he'd sell soon. He's going to be a great horse for someone, mark my words," Steven was saying to Yvonne as they came closer. "I believe you're right especially if he falls into the right hands," Yvonne said as she handed the lead rope to Steven. "He's yours now and I believe you will have a great career with him." Steven was in shock and stumbled for some words to say. Then Yvonne told Steven that it was Ellen who had made it all possible. "Ellen called me over the winter months and had me do a full vet check on him and when he passed with flying colors she bought him for the man she loves."

Ellen was overwhelmed with joy as a tear ran down her cheek as she watched Steven glow with pleasure while he stumbled for the words he wanted to say. "I wanted to do this from the very beginning when I had to tell you about Hawk. I never thought that I would be able to afford what you deserved knowing the quality and character of what you had lost. The sale of my farm and seeing the instant connection that occurred between you and this gelding made it possible, and in my eyes, the right thing to do."

Steven was still searching for the words to convey all he was feeling. "I can't begin to tell you what you mean to me. You were my angel as I recovered in the hospital. You offered me the horse that I could trust enough to pursue getting back to the Rolex again. You have stayed by my side and in every way given me all I needed to succeed. It's me who should be giving to you for all you are for me. Instead you've tried to set goals for my recovery, help me regain my abilities and courage to make it back to the Rolex and now you are replacing what I had lost. You've certainly made this an event to remember."

For the next few hours they shared happiness and conversation with all who came by to see them. Steven found himself packing slowly and reliving his first Rolex. It was like starting all over. Steven had suffered a great loss back then, especially Hawk. Now he stopped and hugged Ellen as he realized that he had everything that he could ever need for a good life. He had a great wife, supportive friends, nice horses and a seemingly endless stream of well wishers in the sport he cared so much about. It was a great ride home as they planned for the future and were thankful for all they had especially one another.

Glossary

Eventing: Thought of as the equestrian triathlon, horse and rider must complete three different riding tests in order to obtain a final score.

Phase 1. Dressage. A series of compulsorily figures to prove the suppleness and obedience of the horse and his partnership with the rider.

Phase 2. Cross Country. A series of immovable obstacles set out in the countryside that the rider must negotiate in a set time limit. This phase is to prove the courage, athleticism and heart of the horse.

Phase 3. Stadium Jumping. Jumping over a series of obstacles made to fall if rubbed or hit by the horse. Tests the ability of horse to jump in a more controlled manner with tighter turns and combinations of fences.

Event. A name given to the type of show that tests horse and rider in three different disciplines of English riding. The highest level, most famous and prestigious event in the United States is the Rolex Kentucky Three-Day Event, held in Lexington.

Levels of Eventing. The lowest level offered is Starter or Elementary, then Beginner Novice, Novice, Training, Preliminary, Intermediate, and Advanced. Advanced is then structured as a 1 Star, 2 Star, 3 Star and 4 Star. The Rolex Event is the only 4 Star in the United States.

****

Bit. The metal part of the bridle that goes in the horse's mouth for control and steering. There are dozens of types of bits varying in their severity.

An Event to Remember ~ 243

Bute. An anti-inflammatory agent given to horses to help control swelling or pain.

Coffin Fence. A combination of three fences on cross-country with the middle element being an open ditch.

Cooler. A wool or polyester blanket used on a horse to help wick up moisture from the horse's coat.

Dressage Letters. The dressage arena is marked by letters of the alphabet to indicate where test movements should be performed.

Equitation. The correct posture and position shown by the rider.

Gaits. The movements of a horse: walk, trot, and canter.

Gelding. A neutered male horse.

Half Halt. A means of communication between the horse and rider.

Lap of Honor *(Victory gallop)* A parade of the horses and riders who have placed in the competition that is part of the award ceremony.

Lengthened Trot. An animated trot with great suspension and ground covering ability.

Mare. A female horse

Oxer. A type of fence most commonly seen in stadium jumping having two rails parallel on the top to develop the fence's width.

Pinney. An apron type device worn over the riders shoulder exhibiting their number for their cross-country phase in a large format, visible both on their chest and back.

Probiotics. Used to help digestion especially in stressful situations.

Reverse Order-of-go. The order that riders will ride Stadium with the person currently in last going first and the first place rider going last in the order.

Sitting Bones. The two most lateral pelvic points that a rider can feel as he sits the trot.

Stirrups. The metal footrest part on the saddle for the rider. They are used by the rider to aid in position and balance.

Stallion or Stud. A male horse capable of breeding.

Start Box. The start area for the cross-country phase, where the rider gets a countdown to start and recorded time begins.

Studs Small metal shapes of different length and design that can be screwed unto the bottom of the horse shoe to provide extra traction for the horse.

Transition. Going from one gait to another or to a halt.

Two Point. The position used by the rider when galloping or approaching a fence.

About the Author

After a tour in the corporate world for several decades and a lifetime of participating in contact sports, Steve discovered a special passion that had been inside since his childhood. Horses had become an obsession in his drawings and hopeful experiences as he traveled through his younger years.

It wasn't until later with a shared love of horses with his young wife that horsemanship became a reality. As they learned more of the aspects of horse care and riding, the family's horse desires grew. Steve's observation of his first ever equestrian 3-day event hooked him and he went from obsessed to possessed. His first competitive years were infiltrated with mistakes, mishaps and learning experiences. It was a partnership with a gray horse, named Petoskey, which provided him with the memories that he would cherish forever. During a decade of competitive riding, Steve placed consistently in the ribbons and was fortunate enough to place four different times in Regional Championships with three of the horses he'd trained. His love of the sport led him to start instructing others so that they could experience the sport he had come to adore. Steve and his family bought and developed a farm. They all made it 'event friendly' and a good place for training. Today he has an event team that competes throughout the Midwest and his farm holds mini-events for newcomers to test their skills.

To this day Steve believes in the philosophy once stated by Dr. Reimer Klimke (who won six Olympic Gold Medals in Dressage and one as a member of the German Eventing Team), "Eventing is the ultimate equestrian sport for the most complete development of both the horse and rider." It is on this belief that Steve trains his horses and students.